LAST
NIGHT
OF
THE
WORLD

LAST NIGHT OF THE WORLD

JOYCE WAYNE

Library and Archives Canada Cataloguing in Publication

Wayne, Joyce, 1951-, author
 Last night of the world / Joyce Wayne.

Issued in print and electronic formats.
ISBN 978-1-77161-301-9 (softcover).--ISBN 978-1-77161-302-6 (EPUB).--
ISBN 978-1-77161-304-0 (Kindle)

 I. Title.

PS8645.A92L37 2018   C813'.6   C2017-906801-6
                                             C2017-906802-4

This is a work of fiction. Names, characters, organizations, and incidents are products of the author's imagination or are used fictitiously. Any resemblance to actual events, places, organizations, or persons, living or dead, is entirely coincidental.

Published by Mosaic Press, Oakville, Ontario, Canada, 2018.
MOSAIC PRESS, Publishers
Copyright © Joyce Wayne 2018
Cover design by PolyStudio / Interior design by Courtney Blok
Printed and Bound in Canada

ONTARIO ARTS COUNCIL
CONSEIL DES ARTS DE L'ONTARIO
an Ontario government agency
un organisme du gouvernement de l'Ontario

We acknowledge the Ontario Arts Council
for their support of our publishing program
We acknowledge the Ontario Media Development Corporation
for their support of our publishing program

Funded by the   Financé par le
Government   gouvernement
of Canada   du Canada

MOSAIC PRESS
1252 Speers Road, Units 1 & 2
Oakville, Ontario L6L 5N9
phone: (905) 825-2130

info@mosaic-press.com

In memory of my mother and father

"Resistance can take the shape of insisting on making a choice, even when the choice is framed as one between unacceptable options."

—Masha Gessen

Chernobyl journal
1988

We live together, as feral animals do, a small group of survivors hiding in the forest beside the smouldering Reactor Number Four at Chernobyl. No one could have imagined that I would remain near Pripyat after the nuclear disaster, not after circulating with the beau monde as I once did. Yet I stayed on. I had nowhere else to go. The isolation suited me after what I'd witnessed and what I'd done. The Chernobyl forest is my refuge. If anyone cares to search for me, a former lover, let's say, he would never consider looking here, where the atmosphere shimmers with radiation.

It's been two years since the explosion. Forty-three years since the war ended and Igor Gouzenko betrayed us—Fred Rose, Sybil Romanescu, Harry Vine and me. Or that's what we believed at first; that the cipher clerk acted alone when he handed over more than two hundred pages of Soviet crypto-grams fingering us as atomic spies. As as it turned out, Gouzenko's defection was only a small part of the fallout from the war ending, but it was the spark that ignited the new conflict—the Cold War. A conflict that, like the oozing radiation from Reactor Number Four, would continue to expand, spread-ing its deadly contents across the globe. Some might say we were duped by Moscow or that the wars turned us into willing participants in the Kremlin's plans. I'm not so sure we didn't long to follow orders, as did so many others, once the lines were drawn between the fledgling Soviet Union and the West.

Today I kneel down to fill my pots with water from the radiated river. I'm able to carry one earthen pot at a time, and I've calculated that by making seven trips we'll have enough water to drink, to wash with and to boil our homegrown vegetables for one day. It's my responsibility to tend to the garden, to weed and water it, to rip the onions, radishes and carrots from the ground, to collect the potatoes, garlic and cabbages in the wide pockets of my apron. I must admit to enjoying my work. When my hands are digging in the dirt behind our shack, I think back to early days, to my home in Nesvicz or to my years in Canada before we were betrayed.

Chernobyl projects its own special beauty. On clear nights, I believe I can see the air glowing with nuclear particles. They are everywhere, these particles: overhead in the starry heavens and beneath my feet in the glistening wet weeds growing around our cabin.

PART ONE

Chapter One

1945
Ottawa

The troubles that would cause the nuclear meltdown at Chernobyl in 1986 began for me in 1945. I couldn't have known then that my life would change forever and that I would never be free of the detritus of these events.

During the summer of 1945, I was living in Ottawa and feeling as if the ground beneath my feet were shifting. My companions and I had made it through alive when everyone else we knew in Eastern Europe, if the rumours were true, had been murdered. Or displaced. How could I ever forget the day when my lover told me Moscow was recalling the unlucky cipher clerk, Igor Gouzenko, back to Russia?

The sky was a luminescent blue, as it could be in the northern capital of the country, and I was imagining that it ought to turn to rose pink and then to a throbbing purple. Back then, I often thought about the sky changing colours. It was one of the ways in which my mind was playing tricks on me, trying to prepare me for who I was destined to become.

Ottawa was a city I never wished to leave, although as long as I lived there I experienced the overriding feeling that it was temporary and that I would need to leave. No matter how diligent I was, how hard I tried to please my bosses and the Party, it would never be enough. Somewhere deep inside me, I understood that my years in this capital city were only a reprieve from what had befallen the others who had remained in Europe.

Whenever I could, I tried to enjoy the city. Ottawa was splendidly calm;

a northern outpost far away from the chaos and horror, with a landscape much like my home inside the Russian Pale, where the Jews were ordered to settle by the czar. On days like this one, I imagined I was back home in the old country, and that it, like Canada, hadn't changed since the war.

I should have guessed that when Nikolai Zabotin followed me on my walk that day, he'd tracked me down for a reason—it wasn't simply that it was too gorgeous to remain indoors.

At first I hadn't noticed him. My mind was on other things; mainly, how to dodge the Labour Day celebration at the Soviet Embassy. Since arriving in Canada more than twenty years ago, I'd become attached to the Communist Party and I had no idea how to disentangle myself from all that it meant, or even if I truly wished to be alone without friends or protectors.

During my early days in Canada, I was the comrades' pet, the orphaned Russian girl with the heart-shaped face and only the young rebel Harry Vine to watch out for me. Then the honours student, obedient but sagacious. Later the irresistibly exotic operative, the one who coaxed men to whisper their cloaked secrets in her ear. Secrets laden with information that Moscow savoured.

That day, I had wanted nothing more than to avoid another Party function. No one of any stature at the Soviet Embassy, other than Zabotin, would care if I spent a night alone reading on the fire escape beside my flat. But Zabotin never forgave any of my indiscretions or weaknesses, nor did my old friend Harry Vine. Vine had rescued me from Europe long before the war and, to his mind, I was to be forever grateful to him for saving me.

Later, when we were all implicated in the little cipher clerk Gouzenko's accusations, and after the Mounties began rounding up members of our circle into custody, Zabotin reminded me of that glorious afternoon in Ottawa.

I had been sitting in the bright afternoon sun, beseeching my old-country God, who I'd ignored since I'd left the shtetl. If I don't attend the embassy's soiree on Monday night, will you still lead me to Mama and Papa? My sister and brother?

By the middle of 1945, I'd run out of rational solutions. My family was missing in the tumult of the war, and I was desperate to find them now that the conflict had ended. I'd tried all the official channels, Jewish social services, the Red Cross, but it was too early, they told me; or too late. How I was dreading another dreary night with the same drab comrades, repeating the same nonsensical slogans about the surety of history. History had failed me, and everyone I loved. Then I felt his presence.

"Who are you seducing now?" Zabotin whispered.

I turned around to see him standing behind me. "If you really want to know, I am talking to my God; to Hashem himself."

Zabotin smiled his broad inviting grin. "I see. Bargaining with God."

He hadn't managed to frighten me as much as he'd intended, although he was my superior and I was expected to acquiesce to his every command.

Zabotin, dressed in civilian clothes, moved closer and stood before me. As the rezident in charge of Soviet military intelligence at the embassy, he answered to the Director of the GRU in Moscow. It was Zabotin's job to supply the secret police with information about the Canadian government; to be its eyes and ears in this foreign land perched so close to the United States. The Director's instructions to Zabotin were to find out how to reproduce the atomic bomb the Americans had tested at Los Alamos. Not much else mattered to the Director or to Stalin, now that the war was over.

In public spaces Zabotin was expected to wear his military uniform, but today he wore an expensive civilian's suit expertly cut from taupe linen, his white shirt unbuttoned at the starched collar. In his good hand he held a Panama boater with a fine silver band. Zabotin's blond curls glowed under the late afternoon northern sun as he caught me up, brushing my waist with his gloved hand. His right hand was fingerless, shot out by a German soldier at point blank during the first World War. That afternoon in late August, he was confident that no one was watching us. Not even the GRU could find us in the secluded parkland along the Rideau Canal.

Years later he admitted to me that he wasn't even carrying his silver revolver that day; the one he placed on the night table beside his good arm when we were making love.

"Nikolai, how did you find me?"

"It is not difficult to anticipate your next move," he said. Zabotin's eyes were as sharp and blue as the afternoon sky.

Colonel Nikolai Zabotin was a powerful man, in his own way; a blond

Cossack entirely certain of his undeniable desirability. Descended from a distinguished Russian military family, canny and charming, he'd fought courageously for the Bolsheviks at St. Petersburg and was decorated while in the Red Cavalry during the Revolution.

Even today, so many years later as I draw water from the flowing Dnieper River near the desiccated nuclear reactor at Chernobyl, I have no precise idea what Zabotin believes in, other than himself and his family's name. After so many of his misadventures with the Soviet regime and after so many betrayals, I can never be certain of what he'll do next. In that way, we're a perfect match.

He, too, was a survivor. He had made it through the 1917 revolution and outwitted the punishing arm of Stalin's Great Terror during the 1930s. His posting as rezident to Ottawa demonstrated that he remained useful to Moscow. His lack of ruthlessness when it came to traitors meant Lavrentiy Beria did not want him close at hand, but the chief of the NKVD still found a role for him. Zabotin's aristocratic bearing was of considerable advantage in Ottawa, where certain carefully compromised bureaucrats and scientists provided the information that Moscow needed to compete with Washington. Zabotin would work for the GRU, military intelligence. If he disappointed, it would be on the GRU's watch and not the NKVD's.

I must admit that, although I feared Zabotin, I also admired him. Sometimes I even loved him. Speaking French or English with a fluency and intonation not common among Soviets abroad, he brought important people under his influence while making it all appear so effortless.

The way he ran his circle of agents seemed effortless, too. Harry Vine, Fred Rose, Sybil Romanescu and the fourteen other spies whose lives would be destroyed by the Gouzenko defection hung on his every word. I, too, was a member of his spy ring.

"I don't know how you manage to look eternally young," Zabotin said, still smiling down at me. He looked at me that way when he wanted me to undress before him.

At certain times, I loathed him for believing I could be so easily manipulated. I'd done everything he'd ever asked. I'd lured too many men to count into my bed until I finally caught the big fish that Moscow needed. If

Zabotin cared about me as he claimed he did, surely he would have put an stop to my endless deceptions with men who should have known better, but he never did.

Despite his casualness with me, Zabotin was on edge. It was only days since the Americans had dropped two bombs, Fat Man and Little Boy, on the Japanese. I'd seen the photos in LIFE, the first ones of the destruction of Hiroshima and Nagasaki. I'd purchased a copy at the newsstand on the corner of Elgin and Somerset and carried it with me to the nearby bus stop. I couldn't stop turning the pages as I waited, and when the bus arrived, my feet would not move. My hands were shaking as I stood alone watching the others climb the bus steps and drop their coins in the fare receptacle next to the driver. They couldn't have been aware of the carnage. They must not have known. How could they and just continue as if this were a normal day like any other? The bus rumbled up Elgin toward the Parliament Buildings, leaving a trail of exhaust fumes behind it. I breathed them in and for a moment I believed I would never move. When I did force myself to cross the road, I was unsteady on my feet. I never again regained the equilibrium I'd clung to before seeing the pictures of what an atomic bomb could do.

The war was ending in a manner I never could have imagined. This was not the way it was supposed to go. Not the way the comrades promised it would go. Immediately I realized that our Ottawa cell was linked to the horrible images on the page. It was why we were here. Stalin wanted the formula for the atomic bomb and, with our help, he would get it. If Soviet intelligence and our friends in the US failed, Zabotin would be recalled to Moscow and my work would be done. I had no idea where the Party would send me next. Or if they would even need me. I was already thirty-eight, and Zabotin alluding to my age only made me more anxious. I didn't want to have anything to do with the bomb, but like most of my work on behalf of the Party, I was in no position to question or object.

I asked him again. "How did you find me?"

"Marxist philosophical materialism holds that the world and all its laws are fully knowable… there is nothing in the world that is not knowable. Not even you, my darling Freda," he declared, quoting Comrade Stalin.

"Yes, but even Stalin cannot decipher the inner workings of a woman's mind," I shot back at him. I knew Zabotin admired me for my sharp tongue and my abilities with men. When he murmured in my ear, he often praised me for my delicate waist, my height, which he claimed was tall for a Jewess, and particularly my legs, which he insisted in dressing in sheer silk stockings sent from the newly established Soviet Embassy in Paris.

"What I would give to have my beloved parents see how beautiful and clever you are. Equal parts beauty and brains," Zabotin said.

His elderly parents, now dead, had then been counting out their days in the family's dacha in the Ukraine, the very one where in which we would hide after the nuclear disaster in Chernobyl. They'd wondered how the world had gone so terribly wrong. How quickly the count, a czarist military officer, and Countess Zabotin would dismiss me, a Jewess. The shape of my nose would give me away immediately. My nose was long and crooked, as though someone had broken the bone.

I turned away from Zabotin, itching to ask him if he'd seen the photographs in LIFE and if he believed Comrade Stalin would use the bomb in the same way as the Americans had, but I remained silent.

Zabotin stood so close to me I could smell his musky cologne. "You are unhappy today?" he asked in his kind voice.

"No more than usual."

"*Taska*, then?" he inquired, using the Russian word in all its complexity.

"Yes, *taska*. Melancholic."

"You look anxious." He offered me a cigarette and lit it with the end of his burning one.

I couldn't reveal my fears to him about my future with the Party, and the inescapable dread about how the politburo might use an atomic bomb if it got its hands on the formula. If I were to tell Zabotin about my misgivings, he would pat my backside and tell me I was being foolish. Or worse, in his official capacity, he could punish me. Trusting Zabotin was not an option, not then. So, I lied.

"No, more nostalgic than anxious. How can this blue sky not remind me of my sky above Nesvicz?" I was quite certain Zabotin considered the Nesvicz sky as his and his family's alone, but I said, "Excuse me, Comrade Zabotin. The people's sky."

It was true, Zabotin and I were both born in tiny Nesvicz, a mud-soaked village that undulated along the Soviet–Polish border. Of course, though, we had not associated as children, he being the son of the Cossack count, the golden family of the medieval castle who ruled the village, and me a Jew. Soon after the revolutionary war, it would fall expressly within Soviet territory. It was Zabotin's good luck that he'd taken a chance in 1917 and sided with the Reds, betting that the Bolsheviks would come out on top. When we had met again years later in Ottawa, Zabotin swore that he had immediately recognized me. He said he remembered me from the day Harry Vine and I escaped the last pogrom of Nesvicz, when the Red Army captured our village and made it their own until the Nazis arrived. When we met again all those years later in Canada, he never mentioned his role in the ransacking of our shtetl.

Before the war, more than four thousand Jews resided in Nesvicz. Now the Jews had disappeared from our shtetl. We knew the Red Army managed to push back into Nazi-occupied territory in the Pale of Settlement, but that was all we were told. No one actually knew then how many Jews remained in our dark corner of Eastern Europe or the extent of the damage. In my mind, I could visualize Nesvicz as it had once been. A sleepy place hidden from the world by its quaint traditions, its own petty feuds, its own minuscule victories. Perhaps my family was among the survivors and I would be able to find them and bring them back to Canada with me.

From time to time, because of our shared homeland and because we understood each other's disenchantment with the Revolution, Zabotin and I dared to partake in little jokes at the Bolsheviks' expense. Secretly, to each other, after moments of passion, when I spread my black hair across his broad chest, we spoke in whispered tones of the appalling mess Stalin had made of the people's regime. How could Lenin's brilliant plan have gone so horribly wrong?

Zabotin could read my mind. "You wish to return to Europe, you silly woman."

"I do," I admitted. "However small the chance is to find my family, it's worth the gamble."

"Aren't you finished with gambling?" he asked me.

"I'd hoped to be, to stay right here in Ottawa. But I can't. It is my duty to find them, no matter the chances anyone is alive."

Zabotin understood. He'd tried to save his own parents during the German invasion and failed." After Stalin and the Allies divide Europe, perhaps I could arrange it, a trip for you. Party business. I suppose you deserve it, after everything you've done for us."

He'd admitted it, I thought to myself. After everything I'd done for the Party.

Now that the war was ending, I was down to a just few men: One high-placed director at the Wartime Information Bureau, a gentleman who didn't resist. A few journalists covering the bickering in Parliament were still eager to accompany me to the Château Laurier or a dreary hotel room on the other side of the Ottawa River, in Hull. My work was slowing down. Zabotin could afford to send me back to Russia for a few months, perhaps for a year. It would take that long to find them, my family.

Instead of talking, he and I strolled along the canal and crossed the iron lift-bridge until we came upon a plain wooden bench in the little park at Kent Street. We sat together, drenched in the declining orange sun. A handsome couple, I suspect, if anyone cared to admire us.

Well-nourished boys in ball caps played catch. Young mothers wheeled their infants in canvas-quilted prams. We didn't need to say a word. We were both thinking the same thing: the war had hardly touched these people.

Chapter Two

It was easily the loveliest day of the year. Surrounded by a million colours of green, only the tips of the tallest trees swayed in the rush of a gentle breeze. Birds were chirping, some insistent, others lackadaisical. A beam of light shone on the wide trunk of a white birch as if the hand of an angel was preparing the tree for the autumn certain to come. I broke off a perfectly shaped leaf from the ash tree beside us and pressed the caressing swatch of green against my cheek. A tiny bird with a blue breast and grey markings hopped before me. Grey squirrels romped from high branch to branch. How daring these little creatures were.

I wanted to be like the Canadians, and so did Zabotin: to be free of the demons of Nesvicz. Slowly, news was trickling out about what had happened when the Nazis invaded. Young mothers and their children, like the ones who shared the park with us, were hauled out of their homes and shot.

"You won't find them," Zabotin said, breaking the silence, sensing what I was thinking. "Nobody will, not even you. There are mass graves across Russia and Poland. What are you going to do? Dig them up?"

I might have accepted his brutal truth, but I couldn't allow myself to give up before I even started. "There are records. Even the Soviets keep records of the dead."

"You believe so?" Zabotin shook his head. "Nesvicz will end up on the Polish side of the border. No one remains to record the names of the dead."

"Yes, but Poland will be Poland in name only, no matter how much the Poles wish to remain free," I said. "There will be records of who died and where. Even if I must go to Germany to find the reports. No matter where Poland ends up, with us or the West, I'll search for them."

"Always one step ahead," Zabotin said. "But this time you might be out-smarting yourself."

How he knew me, this man, this Cossack count from my village. How utterly strange that we would end up sitting on a park bench in the capital of Canada, discussing the chances of discovering my lost family, or of finding the dead.

"Stay here with me, no?" he implored. "It's safer. Don't take so many chances. It's not worth it. Not now."

If I could love this man from minute to minute, day in and day out, not just when he held me in his arms, would my life be enveloped in happiness, just as we were encased by the glowing orange sun?

Zabotin stretched his long legs and raised the hem of his pants. "The sun. I love the sun. It makes me feel decadent."

"I love it most in winter," I said. "When the ground is white, frozen like thick glass, and the sun is as cold as the glistening moon."

"Canada, it's hardly a country, this place," he said. "More a huge ice rink, where no one ever falls down. Not like at home."

"I heard the prime minister speaks to his dead mother through a spiritu-alist," I giggled. "Perhaps I could pose as Madame Blavatsky and entice him to tell me his secrets."

For a moment, Zabotin thought I was serious. "What secrets?" he asked, but I remained silent. Then he said, "I wonder what the commissars would think if they could see us now? Beria, what would he do to us?" He clasped my hand in his good one, as I began to imagine out loud what Beria's reac-tion would be.

"I bet he would think that you are doing your duty as the rezident at the embassy, diligently pumping me for information from my distinguished sources," I told Zabotin. "He would think that you are feeding my vanity as a woman and my avarice as a Jew, fanning the flames with Swiss chocolates and French perfume now that the war is over. Molotov probably wonders if that bachelor Mackenzie King is a homosexual or if it's worth trying to get me into 21 Sussex Drive, disguised as a palm reader."

"Enough, Zabotin said. "Shame on you, Freda."

"Beria would also wonder how you decide what trinkets to give me and which to present to your lovely wife," I couldn't resist adding.

Zabotin did not smile. Everyone at the embassy knew how entirely unhappy the couple were. At night the servants overheard Lydia, his wife, throwing figurines at him. Apparently one evening, she broke a statue of Lenin over Zabotin's head.

"Don't be smug," he reminded me. "The world is a dangerous place for the likes of you and me. For months your feckless comrades haven't brought me a single useful piece of information about the formula for the atomic bomb. Klaus Fuchs is giving us much more at Los Alamos than Nunn May is at Chalk River, even though security in New Mexico is ten times what it is here. If Harry Vine doesn't come up with new equations very, very soon, I shall be re-called to Moscow. Where will you be then, my darling Freda?"

How could I answer? By putting Zabotin's good hand between my legs or sticking my sweet tongue deep inside his mouth? Where would I be without him?

"Without you, Nikolai, I would be a withered leaf buffeted in a blustery winter storm. I would be nowhere," I said.

For the last six years, along with doing my duty for the Party and the worldwide cause of socialism, I'd been working as a correspondent for TASS, the Soviet news agency. The other Russian journalists knew who I really belonged to: the GRU, as a Soviet military intelligence operative run by Nikolai Zabotin. It was acceptable behaviour in our little newsroom. Everyone was doing his or her duty to defeat the Nazis and fortify the motherland. Even the Canadian newsmen I drank beer with at the Press Club suspected me, but Russia had won the war on the Eastern Front. Canada and the Soviet Union would carry their hard-fought victory into this new post-war world. We would be the best of friends.

The TASS office was in the same building on Slater Street as the War-time Information Bureau, a grey concrete structure not unlike the apartment buildings Stalin built in Moscow before the war. My post was to stay close to John Grierson, the director and top man at the bureau, to ensure that his documentaries in support of the Soviet Union were revered by the Centre.

As I looked over at Zabotin's fine profile, I knew how quickly I could be betrayed by a twist of his wrist. Although a naturalized Canadian, it would take little effort to deport me to Eastern Europe within days. Without a Canadian passport, I would be sent to a displaced person's camp or back to my village. But who would be there to meet me in Nesvicz? Ghosts.

"I want you to attend the party at Gouzenko's on Monday night," Zabotin said in his official voice.

How I'd wished to keep it informal between us that early evening under the simmering orange sun. "Must we talk about that grubby little cipher clerk Gouzenko and this Labour Day affair for the Party faithful?"

During embassy soirees in winter, the Soviets kept expenses down by ordering that the heat in the public rooms stay so low that we needed to wear our coats during the coldest months. But not Gouzenko. He was always sweating. On a typical day, Igor Gouzenko wore a tightly cut, permanently wrinkled, shiny suit. And when he removed his shoes to dance the kazotskys, there were holes in his yellowed socks.

"Why is it at the Gouzenkos' stuffy little apartment on Somerset? It's such a dreary place," I said. "Why there and not at the embassy?"

"Igor is an amusing fellow," said Zabotin. "I don't wish to host a celebration in the embassy. Too many eyes on us. Why not enjoy ourselves for once?"

"Are you hoping to catch Gouzenko out? Has he broken the rules and displeased you?" I asked. There was always a possibility with Zabotin, always a motive or a directive from the GRU in Moscow that prompted his behaviour. Besides, I'd never liked Gouzenko. His ingratiating manner was fraudulent. If Zabotin had already decided to turn on Gouzenko, I wouldn't be the one to stop him.

"Lydia's in bed with a migraine. The drapes have been drawn for days," he informed me. "She longs to return to Moscow."

"How sad for Lydia. And for you." My lover was tall, more than six feet, and I often felt that he towered over me like the Zabotin castle had haunted me during my childhood in Nesvicz. "Must we deceive ourselves so, Nikolai?

Why do you never talk about the past? About the village?"

"We have no past, my dear. Only the present," he replied and looked away.

Zabotin checked his watch and scanned the little park where we sat. The orange sun was beginning its slow descent in the sky and a cooling breeze was coming off the resplendent Ottawa River, only a few kilometres to the north. Soon it would be autumn. At night there was a chill in the air. I'd covered myself with a woollen blanket the night before last, rather than the crocheted throw I'd kept on my bed all summer. By October, the city would be sprinkled with sparkling white snow, the children dressed in plaid wool coats and brown leather galoshes, ready to play. For me it would soon be the same ethereal smell of the cold, the same snow-light in the air from the blue snow squeaking underfoot. If I made it to the winter, I must buy myself a pair of flat-soled boots to guard against slipping on the ice.

"Yesterday the GRU ordered me to send Gouzenko home. Wednesday, a week from today, is his last day in the cipher room. Thursday morning he and his wife and their child will be on a plane to Moscow," Zabotin said, turning toward me again. He'd been calculating whether to tell me about Gouzenko's misfortune or allow me to find out on my own.

"What has he done? Why so quickly?"

"Exactly. You tell me why so quickly? Last time the Director asked for him back, I persuaded Moscow to allow me to keep him here. I enjoy the little fellow. He's jolly. A quick study too, as the Americans say."

"I've never liked him. To me, he is nothing," I replied. "If he didn't flatter you, you'd have complied with the Centre's orders earlier. You should send Gouzenko back immediately." I was worried for Zabotin. He was above the law in his own mind, playing tricks with the Director and his henchmen back home, enjoying himself to the fullest in Ottawa. I was terrified that he would pay for his insouciance.

"So harsh, my darling." But I could tell that Zabotin was concerned. We knew each other that well, knew the face of trouble. If it came to pass that Zabotin was recalled to Moscow, as he never tired of reminding me, I'd be at the mercy of his replacement at the embassy. "I've also been cabled from Moscow to organize materials on the bomb," he said. "The Director wants the technical process, drawings and calculations for making an atomic bomb. He wants an actual sample of plutonium. He won't wait any longer, now that the Americans have used it. That's why I'm sending your Harry Vine to Chalk River. Perhaps the Canadian scientists might finally have come up with the equation or at least copied enough of it from the Americans for our physicists to make sense of it in Moscow. This time Alan Nunn May must deliver the goods. No more stalling. Only a one gram sample of plutonium will satisfy Moscow."

The few boys loafing about in the park in the encroaching twilight were nonchalantly rolling cigarettes.

"Will you still ask Gouzenko to encrypt the messages you transmit about Nunn May's findings? Are you certain you can trust him? Who takes the sample back to Moscow, Gouzenko or Vine?" I didn't want Vine involved, any more than I wished Zabotin to be in trouble with the Centre. Although the two men disliked each other, I believed then, as I do now in Chernobyl, that my feelings for them held us together and protected us. We needed each other.

"Why do you insist on asking about Nunn May and his plutonium if you don't wish to be in harm's way? I've already told you more than you need to know." Zabotin was fidgeting. "These scientists are prima donnas. Unreliable. Fussy. Nunn May is working for us, and it makes him edgy. He's English, he has no scruples and is unlike Klaus Fuchs at Los Alamos. Fuchs saw first hand what the Nazis did to Germany, to his own parents. His father was tortured and his mother committed suicide. The German is more reliable."

I was surprised that Zabotin would speak so openly about Klaus Fuchs. He was the GRU's main source at Los Alamos. In June, on Zabotin's orders, Vine had travelled to New Mexico to meet with Fuchs outside the confines of the Manhattan Project's grounds. After he returned, Vine informed me that the formula was complete; the Americans were prepared to drop the bomb on the Japanese, on twelve more cities, if that's what it took to make them surrender unconditionally. Fuchs sent drawings of how to build the bomb with Vine who handed it over to Zabotin upon his return to Ottawa. Now Zabotin was claiming he needed more—a sample of plutonium and exact instructions about how to ignite it. Only then would the package satisfy

Moscow. Finally the Soviets would be able to make their own bomb.

Although I should have paid more attention to Zabotin's words—he was cursing Nunn May and the British for their elusive ways—my mind began to wander. I couldn't face thinking about how close the Soviets were to making the bomb and what they might do with it once they had it. I didn't want to recall the pictures of the destruction in Hiroshima. If Moscow acted without hesitation, as the US had, there would be no end to the destruction.

I forced myself to consider lighter subjects. That is what I did to try to remain sane.

I had yet to meet Nunn May, but I liked British men, their fine manners and well-cut suits. The ones I knew had attended Oxford or Cambridge. They could recite Wordsworth and the war poet Wilfred Owen, and when they did, their defenses came down. It was easier and more pleasant seducing an Englishman than it was a White Russian, although I'd known plenty of both. The English were lazy lovers, they took their time, unlike my Russians, the ones who I knew in my bones. Always in a hurry, the Russians.

Zabotin sat, not talking, reviewing his options. If he failed to gather the intelligence on the bomb that the Director wanted, he was certain to be recalled to Moscow, imprisoned in the Lubyanka for failing to deliver the formula for the A-bomb.

When Zabotin noticed that I wasn't paying attention to him, he shook his gloved hand in the air as much to remind himself as me that it was best to stop talking about highly classified operations. Quickly he brought my fingers to his mouth once again and kissed them.

The temperature was dropping.

I pulled away. I was suddenly chilled and my spine tingled. "If only there was a safe place for ghosts to congregate."

Zabotin placed his gloved hand on my breast.

"You are delicious. How do the red-blooded Yankees say it? All the fellas are crazy about you, even when you talk nonsense."

I brushed his arm away, careful not to hurt his wounded hand. Zabotin was obsessed with Americans and their suggestive phrases. Their languorous ways, lingering around the bar at the Château Laurier, where international spies and foreign diplomats congregated in Ottawa after dark. That was what he enjoyed most about his posting.

And if I was being truthful, it's what I found best about being in Ottawa during the war. It wasn't the safety, although I celebrated that. It was being caught in the drama of how the war would end. I savoured the feeling that I was a part of the battle in the greatest confrontation of history. It made me feel important and less helpless. I didn't want it to end in humiliation or failure, with our circle of operatives disbanded, or worse, punished for our crimes. If Stalin dropped an atomic bomb on innocent civilians, it was only a matter of time before we, the Soviet operatives and illegals, would be blamed.

I'd never intended it to go so far. I don't think any of my Canadian comrades did. Vine and I became involved with the Party because we believed we were on the right side of history. After Nesvicz, after Vine and I arrived in Canada, we wanted more, we no longer wished to be the little people of the Pale. Life in Canada showed me that our shtetl had been untouched by modern times. There were dybbuks and evil spirits that haunted the corners of our crookedly constructed rooms back home. When I became a Canadian, I stopped believing in devils. Or at least, I thought I had outrun their evil eye until the war was over and I learned of the extermination camps, of the mass graves.

"I don't wish to leave Ottawa for good," I said. Our thighs were touching now, sitting on the bench in the Kent Street Park. "It will only be for a short time. To find my family. Then I will come back to you."

Zabotin rose to his full height. Gingerly, he placed the Panama boater on his head and pointed the brow downward. How dashing he was, how irresistible! Once, not that long ago, it had all appeared so straightforward. The Soviets and the Allies were the best of friends. The Fascists their common enemy. But it was all so fleeting. Now a new phase had started. The Russians and Americans were jockeying for territory on the bloodied European continent.

Zabotin put his hand on my head and ruffled my hair. "As an officer, I want you to know how much I respect what you are doing for the Soviet Socialist Republic, for Communism, for our people. Without you, I couldn't go on. Moscow needs you."

I remained silent.

"After midnight tomorrow let us meet to spend the entire night together," he cajoled. "I won't leave until dawn. The house on the canal is empty."

The Soviet safe house was on the west side of the Rideau Canal, not far from the government's experimental farm on Dow's Lake. In summer it was a lush, green place with placid water for swimming. I'd secured the house from a Canadian career diplomat now serving his government in Buenos Aires. The ambassador, mild-mannered with a healthy apple-cheeked face, was remarkably easy to turn when we walked together along the water's edge under a full moon.

Grierson, my contact at the Wartime Information Bureau, assured me he would be. Always willing to do his bit for Moscow, was the enthusiastic diplomat. Now Zabotin advised me that the ambassador didn't expect payment from the Soviet Embassy for the use of his lavishly appointed home. It was a gift to the people.

Recently, the ambassador had reported to Zabotin that Nazis were pouring into Argentina and the Americans were helping them to escape. Many were scientists and engineers who'd worked on the bomb in Germany during the war. A few had already been collected from Buenos Aires and deposited at Los Alamos where they were busy inventing a bigger atomic bomb than the two dropped on the Japanese.

"The old Nazis prefer the warm, dry climate of New Mexico. Chalk River is too cold, which leaves me with exactly nothing to give the Centre," Zabotin murmured more to himself than to me. "All the action is at Los Alamos."

Perhaps it was not the war's end, but the bomb that was changing everything and making it so complicated and so deadly. If I had to choose sides at that very moment, I couldn't say who I would choose. I was accustomed to the Russians, as was Zabotin, and I hated the Americans for aiding the old Nazis and sickened by how readily they'd annihilated two Japanese cities. But now the stakes were different.

Soon I would be required to choose once again, to try to be on the right side of history. As chickens do before an earthquake, I felt the earth stirring.

Upon returning to my flat, I still wondered if Zabotin would help me to re-unite with my family, my parents and my sister and brother, or if he was humouring me. With all the talk about atomic secrets, my first duty was to my family. I'd neglected them long ago when I left Nesvicz and I couldn't allow myself to make the same mistake twice and live with the shame of abandoning them. Harry Vine had forced me to leave them during the revolutionary war in Russia. This time I'd accept whoever would help me find them. I was certain I couldn't do it on my own.

In fact, for twenty-four years, I'd remained amazed that Harry Vine had forced me to abandon my family. True, I'd set my sights on him, even though he was older than me. He was handsome in a pointed fashion, with intense hazel eyes that met my own without trepidation and red hair, as bright as a sprouting poppy, combed straight back under his yarmulke. When he knocked on my door back home in Nesvicz, he was pulling himself up, as tall as he could, holding a bouquet of purple and white wildflowers. He was my first and only crush. I've never entertained another, having learned how dangerous a girlish crush can be.

I'd mustered up the courage to invite Vine to my sister Masha's piano recital. She was playing Chopin. Girls did not encourage boys in my shtetl— we waited for them to approach us. I was different, and I realized he was, too. Different from the other young men who would remain in Nesvicz and eventually die there, never straying from the ancient traditions of our kind. From the very beginning, I realized that Vine was not warmhearted. No, it was the totality of his reverence for God, his seriousness, or so I thought, that won me over just as I was starting to question my own girlish devotion. My mother was a supplicant to God, so free of doubt as I watched her reciting the blessing over the candles the night before the recital, while I wondered if her lack of curiosity was a flaw, like a blot of ink spilled on a white tablecloth.

On the particular Saturday afternoon we disappeared from Nesvicz, the afternoon of the ransacking of our village by the Red Cavalry, we found ourselves walking all the way to Danzig in our best Shabbos shoes. At the Baltic Sea, me, fourteen years old, speaking only Russian or Yiddish, and not a single word of English, Vine and I boarded the ship to the New World. It was Vine's decision, and I complied. What choice did I have but to leave my parents behind, even if I was to be eternally punished for my disloyalty?

LAST NIGHT OF THE WORLD

I could never have foreseen what would happen to the settlements within the Pale and how they would be decimated, no worse than that, erased by the invading Nazi army. As our ship bound for Canada sailed out of the harbour, I was more frightened for myself than for my family. I told myself that a life obsessed with tradition and strict devotion to Talmudic law would continue for them as it always had in Nesvicz. The invading Cossacks would disappear after a few days of plunder, as they had before. All the Jews in Nesvicz could recount tales of the centuries of pogroms. I imagined the rabbi saying, "The Red Cavalry are not the first, and they won't be the last." Vine, on the other hand, pulling me behind him, as we fled our village, promised to protect me and give me a different life in the New World, not one where we sat waiting for the next pogrom. I didn't know how to question him or to think for myself.

When he came down with typhus on the ship, I held him close in my arms and beseeched God to save him. During the darkest moments of Vine's illness, I recited the little Hebrew I'd memorized from singing the blessing over the candles with Mama. "Lord, our God, King of the universe ... " improvising as I went. "I implore you to give Vine the strength to survive," I sang, tilting my face upward toward the sea-grey sky. Without him I would float up to the heavens above the cold Atlantic. Surely I would surrender my ties to the earth.

Chapter Three

1921
Nesvicz

Everything in Nesvicz was lopsided. The baker's shop was missing the top step leading to the store, and so you had to enter from the window. The tailor was forced to board up the windows at the front of his shop after the last pogrom, so the only way to enter was through the kitchen at the back. Even the three *Talmud Torahs,* and the eight synagogues, were worn crooked by the biting cold, the layers of snow breaking through their roofs each winter.

The houses of Nesvicz were one or two storeys and made of wood, painted blue and yellow and even crimson. Wooden shutters framed the small windows, where lace curtains hung askew. Some houses were surrounded by uneven peg fences. Most families kept a cow and a donkey in a rickety stable. Behind the barn, the outhouse was hidden. In summer, the mamas cooked in lopsided lean-tos covered by green canvas awnings, remains of the last Great War. The insects were the only creatures that were big. I recall the homes, the shops, the animals, even the people being small. Nesvicz was a village of the little, and of the unassuming.

My house, however, was different from all the rest. It was three storeys tall, constructed of red brick, with a cement basement. In the cold room, Mama stored the burlap satchels of apples, potatoes, carrots and cabbages; the bottles of cherry and strawberry jams; the salamis and pickled meats and a variety of preserved dills and peppers that fed our family. On the main floor, the kitchen walls were adorned with white porcelain tile, and grey flag-stone covered the floors, not wood or dirt as in the other homes. My papa had installed running water. And off the scullery, we kept a huge enamel tub placed near the cast-iron stove. It operated on coal rather than wood.

An orphan girl came in from Sunday noon to Friday sunset to do the heavy cleaning and help Mama prepare our hearty meals. The laundress, a young, slender widow with three tiny ragamuffins, picked up the baskets of soiled clothes and linen every Monday morning and deposited them, neatly ironed and folded by Tuesday evening, weather permitting. In spring and summer, the sweet-smelling sheets were still warm when my bed was made. Mama often placed a sprig of lavender under my pillow, for good luck. "Pu, pu, pu," she would say, spitting on the knuckle of her index finger. "May your dreams always be free of demons."

We were as happy a family as most. Papa was strict, but not unkind. My little brother Simcha was Papa's main concern. Simcha was unlike me or my sister, Masha, who obeyed his every word. When Papa arrived home, I would run to pull the boots from his feet while Masha brought his fur-lined slippers. He'd pat our heads, like the little yapping dogs we were, and we adored him for his attention. Simcha was different. He often hid when Papa returned from work or from playing chess in the village square. Too often, my brother was in trouble with the rabbi at cheder and he'd come home from school with a disciplinary note.

Why must Simcha question the Lord's edicts? Why did he disagree with the rabbi's interpretations of the Torah? Why doesn't he acquiesce to the rabbi, as the other boys do?

When these letters would arrive, Papa removed the belt from his trousers to beat Simcha. Mama pleaded with him to stop, but the beatings became worse as Simcha grew older and more unruly. For days on end, Simcha was sent to his room, where he ate alone, ordered to dwell on an appropriate penance, all the while shunned by Papa.

By the time of the pogroms, Simcha spent more time outside the circle of our little family than in it. Still, I remained devoted to my brother through it all, bringing him treats of freshly baked rugelah or, better yet, Russian books that Papa ordered from Minsk. Simcha loved to read and we enjoyed reading aloud to each other, playing parts from Chekhov.

My sister didn't appreciate it when I helped Simcha. "Don't fall for his escapades," she said whenever I climbed the steps to his bedroom with a new book in hand. "He's bound to get you in trouble," she cautioned. Masha was too dour for my liking, practicing her music day and night; worse, she competed with me for Papa's affection. But I was the eldest child, and nothing could come between Papa and me, no matter how diligently Masha tried to outperform me.

When the Red Cavalry arrived, they broke the windows of our home, smashed the grand piano and cut my sister Masha's angelic face with a sabre. Always a quick thinker, Vine pulled me down the basement stairs and out the trap door from the cold cellar. All the way to his house we ran, while I wept hysterically.

How could I abandon my family? How could he leave his? All these years later, it still haunts me.

At Vine's home, his mother hid us in an enormous wicker trunk in the attic, praying that the Cossacks, exhausted and starving, wouldn't bother climbing the narrow steep steps to our hiding place.

Vine's papa was a shoemaker, the best in Nesvicz. He ran his business from a storefront attached to their house. He was hiding under the counter when the cavalry officer with the golden curls whipped him with the butt of his pistol.

Vine's mama was right to fear the soldiers who were exhausted from war and plunder. When the Cossacks found her, they threatened to beat her head to a pulp in front of her youngest children if she didn't light a fire in the huge ceramic stove. Vine heard his mama's pleas for mercy from upstairs and leapt from the attic trunk to race down the stairs. Yitzhak, his older brother, the *Yeshiva boy*, was stowed inside the stove.

"Do you think I'm not wise to the tricks you Jews play?" the golden-haired cavalry officer roared when the stove was opened. His voice was so loud it echoed up the stairs to my hiding place in the attic. "Get out of there," he shouted at Yitzhak, "or I'll shoot you."

I was shaking with such intensity inside the wicker trunk that I thought the entire house was rattling. I didn't know if the invaders were Reds or Whites, but I did know whoever was down in the kitchen was sure to murder me if I didn't do exactly as ordered and then more. In what I thought were the last moments of my life I asked God why I hadn't had the sense to remain with my own family rather than running to the shoemaker's cottage with Vine. Surely, my papa would fend off the Cossacks with his fine tongue and the bulbous leather satchel of kopeks he kept hidden in the attic.

Why hadn't I remained by Papa's side? But there I was, stuck with Vine in the poor shoemaker's house. Vine suddenly began shouting for me, demanding that I come out from hiding. "Come downstairs," Vine ordered me. "Now."

Covered in dust from the musty trunk, shaking and whimpering, I stood in the kitchen beside Vine. The colonel was amused by my timidity.

When Vine took a step toward the officer to offer him a full bottle of cherry schnapps, I thought the Cossack would kill him. Instead, he smiled.

"Get your mother to feed us," he ordered Vine while his eyes turned to me.

Vine's mother, doing as she was told, set a table of salted fish and roasted chicken, sweet noodle pudding and bread from Friday's night *Shabbat dinner*. The Cossacks ate until there was nothing but a few crumbs of bread remaining on her white tablecloth.

"Now, it is your turn, to do something else for me," the colonel, sated with food and wine, said to Vine. "You seem like a clever young man. Go and collect the village doctor and bring him to the railway platform where my wounded men are dying. We must have a doctor, and you, my fine young man, friend to the people's revolution, you are going to lead him to us." He was pointing a silver pistol to Vine's temple. "If you bring your Jewish doctor to the station, I won't kill your brother, the one we found hiding in the stove. Perhaps I should have my way with your pretty girlfriend instead." The colonel pointed his silver pistol away from Vine's head and turned it toward me. "You Yids think we don't know your tricks?"

I began to sob while pulling my shawl tightly across my chest. I still believed the colonel would murder us all, no matter how hard we tried to appease him. The doctor, who was a selfish man, would never agree to follow Vine to the railway platform. But Vine was adamant that we try. "Stop crying," he ordered me in Yiddish, which the colonel appeared to understand.

Vine looked at the colonel and then at me. "Can't you see the soldiers need our help?" he roared. That was the moment I saw Vine change. A man so devoted to God suddenly wished to be a part of the grand struggle. By the look on his face, I also knew he wanted the approval of the colonel more than he had wanted anything in his life.

Vine grabbed my arm and pushed me toward the door. As we were about to cross the crooked stoop, he shouted back to the officer. "The girl comes with me. I won't leave her."

The colonel smiled his wide grin and stood before me. "You should remain with me. I'll take care of you," he murmured, loud enough for me to hear him.

I shook my head in absolute terror. "Let me go," I begged.

The colonel thought twice then slapped Vine on his slender back, sending him out across the stoop and into the chaos outside. "You win." The air smelled of burning timber, horseflesh and death.

We headed to the doctor's house and, as much as I resisted, Vine would not let me escape his grip. "Don't look back," he shouted above the bedlam of soldiers destroying our village, dwelling by dwelling, storefront by storefront. "Can't you see how that colonel looked at you?"

I'd never again witness anyone display such bravery, such chutzpah, as Vine did then. He had been destined for rabbinical school before everything changed for him that night, as it did for me. I walked untouched through the village with Vine, his head held high, yelling, "The colonel has sent me to fetch the doctor." And he did. He found the doctor hiding beneath an enormous stack of discarded cornhusks and potato peelings piled next to his summer kitchen. Vine tied a rope around the doctor's waist, grabbed the medical case beside the front door and pulled the doctor, in his Sabbath slippers, to the railway platform.

Wounded soldiers were lined up in rows on the platform at either side of the ramshackle station house. It was on the outskirts of the village, with the tracks winding into the forest. I couldn't see where the lines of the wounded ended, there were so many, cursing or crying out for their mothers. Some were screaming in pain; others suffered silently, a cigarette dangling from a torn, blood-soaked lip.

When the colonel appeared on the platform, Vine was helping the doctor to staunch the bleeding of a soldier whose leg had been blown off. I turned away, but I could hear the colonel and Vine talking. "You've got the idea now, my boy," the colonel said. "Join the modern age. Be a man. Do you want to be a shtetl Jew all your life?"

I saw the eagerness in Vine's eyes that all but answered the question.

The colonel paused to take in the gory mess laid out across the station's floorboards before he continued. "You can't stay here. Go," he said, pointing to the shadowy woodland that edged the village. "Things are changing. There will be nothing here for you by morning. If you leave now, you should make it. Take her with you, the girl," he ordered, pointing to me.

"My brother?" Vine pleaded. "Can I go back for my brother?"

"It's too late," the colonel replied. "Return to Nesvicz now, and you're as good as dead."

At that moment, I was only too relieved to flee the station and the wounded and dying Cossacks it was overflowing with, and I especially wanted to escape the colonel. Yet Colonel Zabotin's words rang in my ears. I didn't wish to be a shtetl Jew. I wanted to emerge from the confined world of religion. I wanted to be a person who discovered her own way, made her own decisions.

But I was afraid, and I never could understand why Zabotin let us go. Not then, not now. Why save us, when so many others were slaughtered? It all came down to luck or fate. No matter how tenaciously I struggled to find a definite answer, one that fit with a religious or even a political doctrine, it was impossible. I was let off the hook.

If I were to ask Nikolai now, as we sit cross-legged atop a picnic blanket below the shade of a horse chestnut tree in the Chernobyl forest, he might smile and claim that he fell in love with me the moment he saw me. "So young and unspoiled," he might say. "I saved you because I loved you. Right from the beginning. Nothing has changed." Or at least, I hope that's what he would say.

On our voyage to the New World, I met an old lawyer from Minsk. He took an interest in me when he saw me praying, beseeching my God to let Vine live when he fell ill with typhus.

"What your boyfriend requires is fresh air and water and not to be huddled in blankets in your cabin deep below the sea. I've seen you with the boy. He's very sick. He must breathe the sea air or the fever will burn his brains as sure as the Whites are setting fire to the villages of our people," the lawyer said.

So I dragged Vine from the hull and onto the deck. The old lawyer gave me his great woollen coat to cover him. For two days Vine did not eat or drink. I sprinkled water on his cracked lips and put cool compresses behind his neck. The fever burned his cheeks red, and then orange splotches broke out on his skin. He was covered in them. I held him close, not caring if I caught the typhus from him, knowing I would do anything to save him.

Aside from the lawyer, we kept to ourselves on the ship, not speaking German or Polish. All we had for money were the rubles Vine kept in his pocket. If I hadn't understood Vine before we left Nesvicz, I came to know him on the ship as I watched him fighting for his life, whispering that he wanted to survive to be together with me. If Vine died, I had no idea how I'd survive without him, a girl from the Pale entirely alone in a strange country.

Afterward, when Vine recovered and was sipping a glass of sweet tea, the lawyer found us again and began talking about Socialism. He knew a thing or two about the modern world. He thought it strange that I'd begged God to save Vine when, in the lawyer's mind, God wasn't concerned about either of us.

"What a waste of time," he said. "You think He listens to you, *shayna meydl?*"

I didn't answer, knowing that whatever I confessed would be wrong. And I still worried that if I took the name of the Lord in vain, an interfering Baba on the ship would give me the evil eye.

Insistent, the lawyer asked me if we were going to family in Canada. When I said all of our people were back in Nesvicz and that we would be alone in the New World, the old lawyer devoted more time to us.

During the long, lingering days of our passage across the Atlantic, Vine started to warm to the lawyer. He recounted the story of the terror in our village and how his brother had hidden in a ceramic stove. And when the lawyer asked Vine if the soldiers who came to his home were Whites or Reds, Vine answered: "They were the Red Cavalry."

"Didn't you wish to join them?" the lawyer asked Vine, incredulously.

"Yes and no," Vine replied. "But there was Freda to consider. What they might do to her." Vine evaded my eyes. "I did bring the doctor to the train station to help the wounded soldiers."

"Don't be timid," the old lawyer taunted Vine. "Think big. You protected your girlfriend. In Canada you must stand up for yourself and for her." He pinched my cheek with his right hand and patted Vine's covered head with his left. "Do you want to be nobodies all your life? Afraid of everything?"

We both shook our heads. We didn't wish to be nobodies, but we couldn't imagine how we could be anybody in Canada. No one outside of our shtetl even knew our names.

"*Sha*, don't worry, my little lovebirds," the lawyer said, assuring us that in the New World we would learn English. "I'll give you the names of my comrades in Toronto. It's like Minsk, only Canadian. A modern city. You can make a difference there. You'll meet people just like you; men and women who are trying to break free of the old ways. They'll teach you everything you need to know and what you need to forget."

And the lawyer from Minsk was as good as his word.

Chapter Four

1922
Toronto

During our first year in Toronto, Vine and I shared two rooms in a cold-water flat on the third floor of a lodging house on Beaconsfield, just off Queen Street in the city's west end. Toronto was stretching out in every direction from Lake Ontario. The rich were moving farther away from the lake and from the burgeoning immigrant neighbourhoods where we landed. Most of the people on our street occupied large homes that had seen better days and were broken up into flats, one or two to each floor. The paint on the Victorian gingerbread trim that decorated the eaves was no longer white and the painted doors were streaked with mud.

The landlords lived on the main floor. Some were elderly ladies who'd been born in the master bedroom upstairs and depended on the rent to survive. A few crones offered room and board, dividing their dilapidated homes into more than ten tiny rooms. I was young and accustomed to living in a fine, clean house where the sofas were piled high with silk embroidered cushions and the carpets were soft and woolly and not threadbare. I was full of ambition for myself and for Vine, and viewed the landlords harshly, never considering that I might turn out to be much worse than any of them.

At the time, I believed Vine and I would be together forever; that we'd marry and have children. In my head, I made plans for our wedding: me dressed in white, standing underneath the hoopa as we pledged our souls to each other. It never crossed my mind that Vine might look for someone else or that he'd desert me after bringing me to Canada. I was his girl from the old country and I expected him to bring me with him wherever he went. It felt like being born again.

Toronto was a huge net, catching all of us—those who ran from the barrel of a gun or those who left in search of wealth and security in a distant land. For Vine and me, it would be impossible to forget the Red Army colonel's silver pistol pointed at Vine's temple, or the colonel's amused looks aimed at me. But for all that terror, the colonel had also lit a fire in Vine's belly. I felt the same way and I was determined to work hard to become the person Vine wished me to be, whoever that might be. One thing I knew for certain was I would be entirely different from my mama, more like a person with Papa's brains and his eagerness to be modern. The old country seemed claustrophobic, while this one felt wide open with thousands of possibilities for a girl like me.

Our landlady, Mrs. Meretsky, was a Communist Party member who'd emigrated from Vilnius at the turn of the century. She was an old friend of the Minsk lawyer. He'd provided us with her address when we parted ways at the pier in Halifax.

"We should rent this flat," I said to Vine when Mrs. Meretsky showed us the two rooms with peeling paint and broken furniture. "You'll paint the walls a bright yellow, and I'll make curtains."

Vine was skeptical. He didn't care for the other tenants. They weren't Jewish and the landlady didn't keep kosher.

"I thought we agreed with the lawyer from Minsk," I reminded him. "We must be open-minded and try new things."

Reluctantly, Vine agreed to rent the flat. He coughed up his first breakfast of bacon and eggs that our landlady served, but I didn't. I enjoyed the new taste of the salty, smoked bacon on my tongue and the aromatic scent of coffee wafting through the kitchen. I drank my coffee with cream and I didn't gag as Vine did, even though I'd never before mixed milk with meat.

"Next thing you know, you'll be eating *treif* in restaurants," Vine said, not convinced that my open-mindedness was to his liking.

"Why not?"

Mrs. Meretsky's husband was a layabout and a *shiker*, a drunk, who stirred himself only to take the tram eastward across town to Greenwood

Racetrack. After a few weeks on Beaconsfield, I realized how dependent she was on our rent and how her husband often squandered it on the horses before she could buy groceries. A few times there was only dry toast for breakfast.

Right from the beginning I knew I never wanted to be in Mrs. Meretsky's position, with a lazy, evil-minded husband who used her without thinking twice about it. I was dependent on Vine, yes, for a time, but that didn't mean I couldn't judge people and situations on my own. I admired the courage Vine had shown in Nesvicz, but I expected him to pay a great deal of attention to me and not to ignore me as Mrs. Meretsky's husband ignored her.

When Vine held me in his arms, his kisses were passionate. I'd never kissed a man before, but I fell in with his advances. I grew ready for him to take me if that was what he wanted, but he didn't need me, not in that complete way.

Our rooms weren't far from Kensington Market, where most people spoke Yiddish and kept kosher. Vine found a job slaughtering chickens in the butcher shop where the shoichet blessed the meat to make it kosher. On warm days, I walked over to meet him at the shop when his workday came to a close. Most of us in the market were greenhorns and the local adolescent boys who played road hockey in the alleys beside the storefronts taunted us for our old-country garb and our timidity when we walked by with eyes pointed downward.

"Greenhorn," they shouted, in their gruff Canadian voices, throwing shards of glass at us. I was frightened of them and so was Vine, although he tried to show his courage by not avoiding them and finding another route. The boys were known to beat up new immigrants.

"Remember the Red Army colonel asking me if I wanted to be a shtetl Jew my entire life?" he inquired.

I remembered. I didn't wish to appear afraid either. Every day it was becoming easier to forget the way we'd lived in Nesvicz, immersed in the day's schedule of prayers and evocations to a God who now appeared to have forgotten about us.

"The colonel was talking to me, too," I said. "He looked straight into my eyes."

"No, he was talking to me." Vine never liked it when I put myself on the same level as him.

"I don't want to be that girl anymore," I told him. "But I can't figure out how to be a person here in Canada."

"We can learn, we can change," he said. "Become real Canadians."

And so I tried, but it turned out to be more difficult than I'd imagined. If I became more of a Canadian perhaps Vine would find me more desirable. During our first months in Toronto, we'd stroll uptown searching for real Canadians, not the ones living in the market or along Queen Street. We walked past the big university and the government buildings and up into the proper neighbourhoods where families resided in their own brick homes, not in shabby flats.

No one called us names or threw glass at us, but they never met our eyes or came close. Not once. When I stood directly in front of an exquisitely dressed woman and her two fair-haired daughters, rather than face me, the woman turned the corner as if I might contaminate her.

"She won't look me straight in the eye," I said to Vine.

Vine stroked his long beard. He hadn't been able to bring himself to shave it off, even though it made him look like he'd walked off the boat that morning. He answered, "These fine people, with their good manners and their lofty voices, they'll never accept us. They'll never let us in. We must try to find others who will accept us. We should consider what the Minsk lawyer advised, to talk to Mrs. Meretsky. She could introduce us to the right people. Talk to her, Freda. See if she will take you under her wing. She can instruct you. Show you how to act and what to look like."

"You mean to act like Communists?" I asked. "That's who she gathers in her parlour for meetings. They're Reds, the same people who broke into our homes, who threatened us. They want to topple the government and set up the same system as in Russia. Is that what we came to Canada for?"

Vine didn't answer me, but the next night, he sat on the stairwell landing intently listening to Mrs. Meretsky and the comrades talk about revolution. Before long, he never missed a meeting, and since his English was improving more quickly than mine, he gave me his interpretations of their speeches once they departed.

I did as I was told. After the meetings adjourned, I offered to help Mrs. Meretsky with the cleanup. All the comrades smoked, the women too, and the ashtrays were overflowing by the end of the night. Together we rinsed out the coffee cups, swept the remaining crumbs of strudel into the wastebasket and washed the kitchen floor so the house no longer smelled of tobacco.

"You could join our meetings," Mrs. Merestsky coaxed. "No need to hover in the stairwell."

I couldn't muster up the courage to sit in the parlour with the comrades. "Not yet," I whispered in Yiddish. "My English, I can't speak."

She was a kind woman with a generous heart. "Of course you can speak! We'll practice, you and I. You'll learn. Everyone does. Do you think I could speak English when my parents brought me over? You're smart and you're pretty. The Party could use someone like you."

In our rooms, Vine and I forced ourselves to speak English. I was cooped up on the third floor on Beaconsfield when Vine was working, so I needed to practice my English more than he did. I stacked library books under our three-legged table to keep it steady, replacing an unread book with a read one every few days. Mrs. Meretsky called me down to her kitchen in the afternoons, to drill me on what I'd learned from the library books. She was a gifted teacher, helping me to understand the nuance of the words. We started with simple picture books for children and later moved onto primers about the history of Canada, and eventually pamphlets by V.I. Lenin, who my landlady revered more than anyone else.

Vine slept on an army cot in the makeshift kitchen, giving me the single bed beside the window in the tiny bedroom. I'd keep the kitchen tidy for him, polishing the aluminum tea kettle that I placed on the gas ring to boil water for tea. Back home, we called a kettle a tshaynick. "*Hak mir nit keyn tshaynick,*" my mama cried when I was annoying her, begging for another slice of buttered black bread. In English it meant "Don't bang the kettle at me," which, like most things in translation, sounded absurd.

In Toronto, I was a girl in translation. Awkward but imbued with potential usefulness: like a plain metal tshaynick. I began to sit beside Vine during the comrades' cell meetings, listening to the speakers rise, one after another, explaining why revolution was necessary. Lenin was their hero. Without his insistence, the Revolution would not have been successful, they said once or twice at every meeting.

The comrades shared news from the Soviet Union, a letter from Uncle Yosel, another from Auntie Faiyge. Everyone back home was delighted with how they were prospering. In the new Russia, Jews were included in everything, members of the Central Committee, and at the highest level of the military. There were Jewish generals in the Red Army, something I found almost unimaginable, but the comrades could name them, officer by officer. For the first time in my life, I felt enlightened, as if what I knew about the changes in Russia counted.

When we were invited by Mrs. Meretsky's comrades to join the Party, both Vine and I were flattered. If wealthy, established Canadians didn't want us, the comrades did. Before long we began to throw off our old country ways. Vine shaved his beard and cut off the long, straggly ringlets that had framed his face since childhood.

Mrs. Merestsky took me shopping on Spadina, where the garment factories were open day and into the night. She had friends among the foremen, some of whom were organizing for the Party. She ordered two dresses cut for me, one yellow and one navy. "Modest," Mrs. Merestsky ordered. "She just arrived from the old country." The girls sitting at the machines whispered about me and giggled. I was wearing the same black skirt I'd worn when we boarded the boat. Peaking out front under my skirt were scuffed brown boots with torn laces, and on my head was a paisley kerchief tied tight under the bun at the back of my neck.

"Don't pay attention to them," Mrs. Meretsky said. "Pay attention to me."

She'd taken a shine to me, as Vine hoped she would. She had no children of her own and spent her days cooking meals for her lodgers, washing sheets and towels by hand and then hanging them out to dry on the line in the back garden. There were no servants as my mother had in Nesvicz and my landlady's life was harder than ours was back home. Yet she devoted whatever spare minute she had to the Party, calling the comrades from the phone mounted on the kitchen wall, hogging the party line and only hanging up when a neighbour on the same line threatened to report her to the telephone operators.

At first, I was curious where her husband went each day, before the track opened. He was rarely home even in the mornings when I awoke, and Mrs. Merestsky came and went as she pleased, never bothering to cover her head when she left the house. I admired her independence while convincing myself that a husband like hers was worse than no husband at all.

Inside the Pale, Jewish women were Orthodox and that meant covering your head. My mother did, keeping only a tiny fringe of dark hair showing under her scarf. She kept covered in front of everyone except her husband. Mama and I visited the mikvah, the ritual bath next to the synagogue, once a month to purify our bodies after menstruating. There might have been mikvahs in Toronto, but I didn't circulate with the devout women who frequented them and Mrs. Meretsky, as far as I knew, wasn't interested. For certain, the comrades would have laughed at me if I'd asked about a mikvah. None of the old traditions mattered to the modern Jews who befriended me. Party members ate pork sausages in front of the Minsk synagogue in Kensington Market on Yom Kippur. They taunted the Orthodox believers and imitated their fussy old country ways.

I was among those who accompanied the protesters to the Minsk on High Holy Days during my first year in the Party. At first I hung back, not touching the pork sausage. Not in front of the synagogue, but soon I joined in. Worshippers standing on the steps outside the front door shouted down to us, calling us bad names. "*Momzers,* bastards," they cursed, shaking their fists at us. The comrades shouted back, promising the day would come when the workers revolted and the temples would be boarded up forever. It was mayhem. Everyone was screaming at each other, until a comrade in a black cape pulled the trigger on his pistol. "Religion is the opiate of the people," he declared as the excited comrades sang "The Internationale," raising the red flag high above our heads, while throwing pigs' feet at the Orthodox Jews.

Two policemen were sitting on enormous horses, watching us, doing nothing. "Leave the Yids alone," I heard one shout to the other. "Let them murder each other." They were snickering at us. This dispute was a joke to them. It was supposed to be better in Canada. Tall men riding horses were meant to protect everyone, even immigrants, even Jews. But it wasn't better. The excitement back in Russia about the new society the people were building felt tangible to me. The comrades described it in detail. In Canada only the Party took our side and made us feel equal.

The early days in the Party were thrilling. More like a rollicking costume ball than a political movement. After my sheltered upbringing, I was startled by the absence of rules concerning modesty and proper feminine behaviour. At the Canadian National Exhibition fairground, I watched a girl, no older than me, being shot out of cannon and landing on a net beside the grandstand. The audience gasped in disbelief and then applauded loudly when she stood up to take her bow. I believed, at that moment, that I, too, could get away with anything, even though I was only fifteen.

Vine was more cautious. On Labour Day, I convinced him to return to the CNE with me, but he wasn't about to pay the five-cent admission to ride the Ferris wheel.

"Come on, let's try," I was speaking English more often.

"Communists have no time for silly things," he said sternly when a comrade from Mrs. Meretsky's cell group sidled up next to me.

"I'll go with you, Freda," he offered.

"Come, you too, Vine. I can't go without you." I reached out my hand but he pushed it away.

Vine held his ground, standing beside the giant wheel as I waved to him from the top. The young man next to me had wavy black hair and spoke without an accent. His face was clean shaven and he wore black and white shoes, not boots. His name was Leonard, but he insisted I call him Lenny. As we rose and fell with the movement of the Ferris wheel, he placed his arm around me, holding me tighter each revolution. He was the second man to touch me.

When the ride was nearing an end, he turned to me and asked, "Would you let me take you out? We all meet at a speakeasy on King Street not far from the exhibition grounds. Just on the other side of the tracks."

I had no idea what a speakeasy was.

"It opens after hours," he explained. "The police turn a blind eye. Nothing bad will happen to you, trust me. I could pick you up at Mrs. Meretsky's around ten tonight."

The Ferris wheel was slowing down. We were about to disembark when I agreed. "Sure, ten o'clock."

I discovered that the Canadian-born comrades were not as serious as those of us who'd come over by boat to start a new life. They took having fun as a given, not as a transgression of the rules. Mrs. Merestsky encouraged me to spend evenings with Leonard whenever he called.

"Don't you like Vine?" I asked her.

"He's not for you," was all she said.

I took to dancing the Charleston in a short, flimsy dress at a speakeasy down along a back alley off Spadina Avenue below King Street. It was Prohibition in Canada, and I felt like a fairgrounds' daredevil, dancing long after midnight with comrades older than me. I quickly lost interest in Lenny, finding men who were more prominent in the Party, and offered to buy my drinks.

Usually Vine eschewed the speakeasies, but from time to time, he'd rush in, sit down at the bar and order a shot of rye whisky. He never offered to buy me a drink. I asked him if he thought our brothers and sisters back home in the Pale were having as much fun as we were.

"Don't joke. It's been over a year since anyone has seen my brother Yitzhak," he replied. "Mama says the Red Army colonel took Yitzhak into the cavalry and she doesn't know if he's dead or alive."

I danced away from him, wiggling my hips in time with the piano player, crossing the speakeasy's rough-hewn floor to grab another soda. The floor was littered with empty cigarette packages and chewing gum wrappers. No one cared if I was underage. I was young, unattached and beautiful. A comrade from the Central Committee pushed a drink toward me. It was the first time I tasted their Canadian whisky, and I spat it out. A woman from the Party looked at me disapprovingly.

"*Meydele*, listen to me young girl," she said. "Time to grow up. You must learn to drink like a man if you want to be a good Party member." She shoved another glass of the golden liquid before me. "Try again," she coaxed.

Over time, I came to relish my new-found liberties. I was free of the Talmudic rules that my family and all others in Nesvicz imposed upon me. What surprised me was how easy it was to forget who I once was, and where I came from. All the ancient observances began to appear pathetic, like a discarded teddy bear after a child has matured to adolescence.

As the lawyer from Minsk promised, I started to believe that I could be somebody in Canada and that the comrades were the only ones who could turn me into the intoxicating woman I now wished to be. There were young women in the Party who I came to emulate. They spoke up at meetings, letting their strong opinions be heard. Soon I would have the nerve to speak up too, and to argue for what I believed. Until then, what I desired most was to speak without an accent and to dress without one, too. If I could look like an independent woman, I believed I could be one.

Before long, I depended on the comrades for everything. If they decreed that I should eat pork in front of the synagogue, I did. If they said I should dress in shorter skirts and remove my shawl, I did that too. If they said, I should apply pink rouge to my cheeks and cherry lipstick to my mouth, I did as I was told and repeated the revolutionary slogans I knew they wanted to hear. They became my family, when I had no other.

It was only in the early hours of the morning, alone in my room that I yearned to retain a little of myself apart from the Party. After a night of dancing and drinking, I found I couldn't settle down. When I thought about Mama and Papa, I cried silent tears. How disappointed Papa would be if he knew how I'd spent the night drinking and dancing. And Mama. She would weep and ask me why I was turning out to be a bad girl, not at all like the child she'd raised to be an obedient, modest wife and a good example to my children.

In truth, I was a little shocked at how loose the Party women were. One night they went home with one comrade, and the next night, with another man. Some lived in large houses that they called communes where couples were together for only one night. I wasn't certain I could be like them, no matter how politically educated I became. I wasn't even certain I wanted to be like them, although taking risks felt wonderful.

Vine, on the other hand, was unconcerned about Party romances. He was worried about whether his brother could survive riding with the Cossacks, and even admitted that his father's letters were not nearly as flattering to the new order as the Canadians comrades' proclamations. Why wouldn't the Red Cavalry officer, the one who'd let us escape, who'd practically ordered us to leave Nesvicz, not allow Yitzhak to return home after completing his service? Was it up to the colonel's discretion to release the boy, or was it an edict of the politburo to keep young men from the Pale in the military once they'd trapped them? I didn't wish to exchange one brutal regime for another, but I kept quiet, not willing to take the chance of antagonizing the comrades with my doubts or putting my new-found life in jeopardy.

Chapter Five

1923–38
Toronto

When I joined the Party, it was busy sanctioning free love and open marriage. Monogamy was considered bourgeois, and the Party leaders encouraged me to lead my own private life and not to be unduly attached to Vine. They said they had plans for both of us that didn't include marriage, at least for now.

On weekends, we went up north of the city to a camp called Naivelt. The comrades pitched tents next to the Credit River. Single girls like me in one large tent, and single men in the other. The tents were made of tan-coloured canvas with sticks in the earth for mooring their high ceilings. Each of us was assigned a cot, also covered in tan burlap. Early in the summer, one of the men came by to light the wood stove so we'd wouldn't freeze.

I'd met some of the unattached girls in my tent at the speakeasy in Toronto. A few bleached their hair with peroxide to become blondes. It looked fake, and I vowed never to change my hair colour. During the day, the women with young children waded in the river, their chubby arms flapping against the water, a babushka tied around their heads. They couldn't swim, but they were adamant that their girls and boys would learn. They hired a lad from a farmhouse near the camp to be the swimming instructor and watched intently as he entreated the children to hold their breath and put their head under the swirling water.

The older women set up card tables to play mahjongg while the men played poker or debated the issues of the day. They often argued so loudly that their wives reprimanded them. "Sha, sha!" they cried and then returned to their own game.

I preferred to walk along the perimeter of the camp enjoying sightings of the graceful deer who roamed through the bush or listening to the birds who chirped and twittered with abandon. The cardinals were my favourite. Elegant red birds with their haunting call. After a lengthy walk, I'd hole up on a rocky ledge next to the river and watch the rushing brown water cut through the landscape. The giant maple and birch trees loomed over the water creating a cool, shady spot. Sometimes I took a book with me.

The camp reminded me of the forest surrounding Nesvicz, and being alone outside in the clear air gave me room to reminisce about Mama and Papa and Simcha. I could do without Masha, but I missed the others terribly. I wondered if Simcha had settled down or if Papa was still beating him, or if Masha had won Papa over so much so that he'd forgotten all about me. I worried about them. Even Masha. I told myself I would do anything to return to them, even give up my membership in the Party, and time at the summer camp.

"Why are you crying?" Vine asked me on the day he found me sitting beside the river with my head in my heads.

"None of your business." I was learning to talk like a Canadian girl.

"Tell me," he coaxed gently.

I was surprised he was bothering with me. The other girls were sunning themselves near the gazebo when I'd left the breakfast table, and Vine was admiring them.

"What do you care?"

"Don't be childish," His voice sounded sincere.

"Could we bring our parents over, sponsor them? The comrades talk about how wonderful conditions are back home, but I'm not so sure."

"Don't be ridiculous." Vine enjoyed correcting me. "We don't have our papers yet. We're not even citizens. How are we going to sponsor them?"

"We will be citizens. Only a few more years. Surely you miss your family. Don't you want to bring them over?

"My father is not like yours. He would never allow it. He'd never adjust to Canada. He'd never leave the *shul* behind and his old ways praying from the moment he wakes in the morning until he goes to bed at night."

"You could persuade him to come. Help him."

"No, I couldn't. I have other priorities."

"For instance?" I asked.

"Union organizing. That takes precedence over personal affairs."

I thought he was going a little crazy but I kept my mouth shut. I believed I would never sacrifice my family for a cause. Never.

In Chernobyl I think about how Vine and I once were on the boat crossing the Atlantic and how we are now, separate but together. We followed each other across the water twice, from Russia to Canada and back. We understood too much about each other, but the distance between us was too far to breach.

At Naivelt, everyone ate together under the shelter of a huge gazebo. Supplies were brought in by truck from the market in Kensington, and men and women alike participated in preparing the elaborate, tasty dinners. The older women wore colourful housedresses with aprons atop. They rolled their heavy stockings over their oxfords. They were hard workers. The men wore short pants with socks and sandals and talked more than they chopped the vegetables or peeled the potatoes. The mosquitoes were vicious and we were all covered in oozing red bites by the end of the night.

The Leader of the Party, Tim Buck, showed up on Saturday night to deliver a speech about the grand progress the Soviet Union was making and how working people and farmers were no longer going hungry as they had under the czar. Afterward, musicians carrying guitars made their way to the open fire pit to lead the campers in one labour song after another. We sang in Yiddish or Russian.

I met more men who were interested in me and I noticed that some of the girls ran off with their boyfriends to the forest at night, or stayed behind in the tents when everyone else was gathered around the fire.

That never happened with Vine. I tested him to see how far he'd let me go, but there turned out to be no limit. He was spending less and less time with me. At Naivelt, after our discussion about bringing our families to Canada, he tried to ignore me and only came near to me if I approached him first.

Vine agreed with the Party leaders that he and I should keep our distance. He was always more willing to fall into line than I was, first as the most devoted Talmudic student in Nesvicz and then as the most ardent young Communist in Toronto. Tim Buck and labour leader Sam Carr were his idols. The more engrossed he became with the Party, the less he mentioned his missing brother back home. And he barely touched me after Buck took us aside at camp to emphasize that marriage was not in the cards for us. Still we continued to share the rooms on Beaconsfield.

In the city, Vine purchased a used phonograph player from a junk shop on Baldwin Street and a new 78 recording of *An American in Paris*. He played it over and over again, lifting the arm on the phonograph when the record was done and placing it back at the edge of the black shiny surface to begin again.

"Gershwin is a Jew, like us," Vine said, his eyes glistening with optimism. "He came from nothing, and now he's met all the bigwig composers in Paris—Ravel, Prokofiev, Poulenc—and they like him, think he's terrific, that his music is the best." He pulled the arm of the player back to the beginning once again. Vine lit up. "Listen, listen. It's Paris. I'll take you to the Eiffel Tower one day," he promised. We waltzed around the room and I felt myself sinking into his chest.

"Couples get married there," I said, but Vine pretended he didn't hear me.

I often think about the first time Vine played Gershwin for me, and how the magic of the composer's enthusiasm made him imagine he, too, could change the world. We'd only been in Canada for a short time, and anything seemed possible. As I watched Vine dancing, I understood that like most immigrants, he was forced to make a choice. The music was so fresh that I believe he felt free from the past, if only for a moment. What if he threw away the burden he carried with him, the need to believe in something bigger than himself? What if he truly believed in himself, as Gershwin must to write music of this kind.

But Vine, more than me, or Zabotin for that matter, couldn't stop himself from being a true believer. Communism became his new religion, as demanding as Judaism had been for him in the old country. Once he joined the Party and spent his summer weekends at Naivelt, he forced himself to become a re-invented man, and on the surface it worked. After that day, I never heard him play Gershwin again.

There were other young women who attracted Vine, ones who spoke English better than I and who pitched their own tents at camp. When we were alone late at night, I asked him in Yiddish about the other girls in the Party. "Do you think Betty is prettier than I am?"

"Speak English!"

Betty attended the evening cell meetings, and not just the ones in Mrs. Meretsky's parlour. She was at Camp Naivelt for most of the summer. If the topic was more sensitive, top secret, the group met in a musty basement in the city on Cecil Street. I'd never been invited to those gatherings, but once I arrived afterward to walk Vine home. The proceedings hadn't ended, and Betty was singing "The Internationale" in a rich contralto voice.

Arise ye pris'ners of starvation
Arise ye wretched of the earth
For justice thunders condemnation
A better world's in birth!
No more tradition's chains shall bind us
Arise, ye slaves, no more in thrall;
The earth shall rise on new foundations
We have been naught we shall be all.

Everyone in the room quieted down to listen to her performance and agreed that Betty belonged in the opera. When she concluded, Betty raised her arm and made a fist in the universal sign of solidarity.

I concluded that I'd need to work harder on my English. After watching Betty perform for the comrades, I stopped pinning up my hair and allowed it to flow over my shoulders, even on the street in broad daylight.

After the next cell meeting, I asked Vine again: "Do you think Betty is prettier than me?"

"Don't ask silly questions," Vine said, annoyed with me. He left me to walk home alone along Dundas Street, where the rough-voiced men called out foul words to me from their front porches. As I hurried away from them, I could smell their cigar smoke lingering in the night air.

I was ashamed that I was abandoned to walk home by myself. The next night, I didn't bother coming for Vine. In retribution, he didn't return to Beaconsfield, and I slept by myself, for the first time in my life. Afterward I felt stronger.

When Vine did appear early the following morning, it was only to shave and change into clothes suitable for cutting the heads from squawking chickens. I was in bed. "If you get up make sure not to get in my way," he said, standing at the little basin in our kitchen. "Make the tea, I'm in a hurry."

I wound a sheet around my naked body, since I had no dressing grown, and allowed the front to slip down exposing my breasts.

"I'll always care for you, don't worry," he said, dropping his razor to kiss my neck and caress my breasts. "But the Party wants us to lead separate lives for now."

I grew impatient with Vine, not understanding why he was so diligent, so subservient to the Party. He needed to idolize someone more than I did, or to rhapsodize over a cause, be it Judaism or Communism. I kept my judgment reserved and would remain that way.

As summer turned to fall and Camp Naivelt was closed for the season, Vine spent fewer and fewer nights sleeping on the cot in the kitchen while I grew accustomed to my own company. Most days I was alone. Vine was my only connection to the past. I had nothing to occupy my days until a woman from the Party came to visit me on Beaconsfield. She said Mrs. Meretsky was concerned about me, that I wasn't leaving my room until late at night to go to the speakeasy. The woman promised she would enroll me in secondary school at Harbord Collegiate. My English was good enough to start my Canadian education.

I was sixteen and terrified that the other students would make fun of my English pronunciation and the way I looked, but that's not how it turned out. There were other Jewish girls who wore lipstick to school and short pleated skirts called kilts. These girls had crossed the ocean with their parents fleeing from the Communists and they invited me into their circle.

My new friend, Rachel, tried to convince me that "it was much worse back there than it was in Canada," but I could hardly believe her.

If she was forbidden to stay out late at night drinking and smoking with her boyfriends, she did anyway. Rachel's parents were permanently exhausted from working at the Tip Top Tailor garment factory near the market. Her father and mother also gambled at all-night poker tables with the fancy Chinese men on Huron Street. Like me, she was on her own. Many of the girls were in similar circumstances. They hardly saw their parents who worked long shifts at the garment factories; unlike Nesvicz, where the family took three meals together, day in and day out.

At school, I excelled in English while at the same time discovering that it was becoming more arduous to write home in Yiddish. Since arriving in Canada, I wrote to Mama and Papa weekly, assuring them that I was safe, residing in the back room of the rabbi's house. His wife, I claimed, was supervising my every move. I told them that Vine visited me every day and that he continued to study at the Yeshiva in Toronto. I was ashamed to reveal to my parents how I was behaving now that I was becoming a Canadian girl, staying out late at night, joking with my classmates under the streetlights in Kensington Market.

When Rachel became pregnant, she was sent away from school and I never saw her again. Mrs. Meretsky explained to me that's what happened to girls who took risks. Next day, she took me to her doctor who fitted me with a rubber suction cup to insert before having relations, as she termed it. I told her that I'd do that after I married and not before, but Mrs. Meretsky insisted.

As for my parents, they wrote to me every week. Their letters were held at the Soviet border and then again by the Canadian postal service. At times, I would receive five or six on the same day and Mrs. Meretsky would shout up to the third floor, announcing that letters from Nesvicz had arrived. I cherished my parents' letters, but it took time for me to understand that my family was hiding as much from me as I was from them. They never complained. Occasionally they asked me if I could convince the rabbi to send them cloth for coats, and when they did, I approached the leaders in the Party, who wondered aloud why my parents needed anything from me, being that they were residing in a Socialist paradise.

Vine stayed with Betty of the gorgeous voice, who kept a room above a shop on College, just north of Kensington Market. As far as I was concerned, living without him had its advantages. Let her take care of his every need, make his tea in the morning, boil him an egg and iron his shirts. To my mind, I was becoming an independent woman, with opinions of my own and better things to do than cater to Vine. I knew from Mrs. Meretsky that the Party brass had plans for me. It was my landlady who repeatedly confirmed that I was more useful to the Communist movement as a single woman than as Vine's wife. I was only eighteen when I was selected to befriend men on behalf of the Party. It was weeks after Mrs. Meretsky took me to her doctor for the fitting. After that the leaders flattered me, and explained that they couldn't afford to waste my beauty.

"Don't be shy," Party leader Tim Buck instructed me. The woman who'd enrolled me in high school came to my room with Buck and convinced me to drop out. At the school, she posed as my mother, claiming that her husband was injured and I needed to work to help support the family. Then she instructed me on how to behave around older men, and to never act childish in their company.

When I asked Mrs. Meretsky if she thought I was doing the right thing, befriending men, she turned away and I could see there were tears in her eyes. "It's not for me to say what's right or wrong," she replied. The way Mrs. Merestsky uttered those words tipped me off that she was against the party's orders, but it was not possible for members to go against our leader.

I was not so naïve that I couldn't decipher the direction the leader was pushing me. At first I didn't believe I would actually need to sleep with men to turn them into sources of information, or that it would become my profession, my enduring contribution to the Revolution. I'm not certain any girl who enters this line of work does. Not the first time at least. I thought I could just talk to men, have coffee or drink some Canadian whisky, and they would open up.

In Nesvicz a bride didn't meet her groom until the marriage was arranged. If I'd stayed there, my father would not have chosen Vine for me. His parents were poor, and my father had ideas about me. Papa never said anything in front of Mama. He was a lawyer, smart in the ways of the world, and he mentioned to me, just before the pogrom that I would excel at the gymnasium, the secondary school for clever adolescents in Russia. I never had that opportunity to find out.

I've often wondered if Vine fully understood the Party's intentions for me, or if he set me up. He knew I had been schooled to never think of being with a man who wasn't my husband.

The first older man I befriended was a Jew from Odessa. He owned a haberdashery on Augusta Street in the market. His store was crowded with well-to-do Jews who came to him for tailored suits. I was under orders to find out if he was connected to the rebel Whites back home.

"They are class traitors who oppose Stalin," Buck told me. "Find out if there are Jews, living in Toronto, who are sending money to fund the White's cause. Find out who the courier is."

It didn't take long with the Odessan before I discovered that men were willing to tell me their ugly truths and their exaggerated lies at the drop of a hat. The haberdasher was a master tailor. He'd lost his wife years ago in an accident and never remarried. I'd hang around his shop when he was closing and ask him for work. I told him I was alone in Canada and I needed to support myself.

"I can do anything. Mop the floor. Iron the suits."

He knew from the beginning what I was angling for, but couldn't fathom why. Mr. Klopot didn't hire me, but after I spent a day with him in the shop, polishing the display cases, he escorted me back to his apartment. It was two blocks from his shop, a drafty place atop the local dentist on Augusta Street. He asked me to undress although he came to bed with his clothes on except for his trousers. Afterward, he was apologetic. "I had no idea," he said, seeing the stain of blood left on the sheets.

We drank coffee and nibbled on sugar cookies from a tin he kept beside his bed. Klopot paid me. He invited me to come back twice a week, every Wednesday after his store closed and again on Sunday afternoons when the market was deserted.

When I returned to Beaconsfield, after that first encounter with Klopot, it was very late. Mrs. Meretsky, who was listening to the radio in her kitchen, had waited up for me. She turned down the music as I approached her, but she didn't want me to kiss her cheek as I usually did before going to bed.

"You could have warned me. Right from the beginning you knew where this was headed," I said to her, my face flushed with shame.

I didn't start to cry until I was under the covers in my bed. If I hadn't run from Nesvicz, I would be married, living with a husband and a child by now. My parents would be down the road to help me whenever I needed them. I hated Vine for bringing me to Canada, and then, leaving me to fend for myself. Who would want me now that I was spoiled? At eighteen, my life was ruined. There was no getting away from the sin I committed.

I did my work for the Party and didn't complain. When I ran into friends from high school, I either pretended I didn't see them or manufactured stories about living with my uncle and aunt in an enormous house in the Annex, a luxurious part of the city. I even had the street name and number of this imaginary haven memorized. Supposedly, I'd dropped out of school to tutor their little children. If anyone asked me for my telephone number, I lied and said the phone company was changing it and would they mind giving me their own number first. "I'll ring you," is what I promised.

The person I'd become was someone I couldn't have imagined just three years earlier. I'd be walking along Spadina, peering into the shop windows overflowing with ladies' dresses and I'd need to stop and catch my breath, feeling that my heart was about to stop. The world was one I didn't understand. I couldn't believe who I'd become, seducing men for information the Party wanted. The Leader found me one day leaning against a dress shop window. "You're pale as a ghost," he said.

"I am a ghost," I replied. Tim Buck didn't bother inquiring what I meant. He took me for a drink, saying it would put the colour back in to my cheeks.

I did try to find my high school friend Rachel, who'd disappeared after getting pregnant, but no one in the market had seen her. Like me, she was spoiled before she'd even started.

Chapter Six

Klopot's bedroom was painted red and decorated with a shiny black satin bedspread and gilt lamps with flowered shades. He said he liked the colours because they reminded him of Odessa.

"Do you still have associates there?" I asked him.

"Not many, a few," Mr. Klopot said, blinking up at me.

We were lying in bed smoking cigarettes and drinking Coca-Cola from the bottle. Klopot had presented me with a beautiful red silk Japanese kimono to wear when I was with him. He liked to pull apart its silky folds and to put his head on my breasts when we talked. "Do you help them out, with money?"

"Sometimes," he said. "Life is hard in Odessa. People are starving."

I encouraged him to talk. It wasn't difficult. He created a role for himself that was much more important than it actually was. All he did was collect cash from his wealthy customers. A fellow with a heavy Russian accent came to his apartment to pick up the cash. He carried the money back to the Black Sea port. I never knew exactly who Klopot's allies were and why they mattered, but the Party was ecstatic when I gave them the dirt on Klopot. He was a dupe for the Whites, Tim Buck assured me. I could even name the courier. After that, I was ordered to forget about him and move on to bigger fish.

Months later I was buying bread from the bakery on Augusta Street when I bumped into the haberdasher. He admitted that he wasn't surprised that I'd disappeared from his life but seemed oblivious to the real reason. "You're the most beautiful woman I've ever known," he said softly. "I knew it wouldn't last."

After my victory with Klopot, the Party brass started to include me in their important meetings. All their dreams for me were coming true.

As another reward for naming the courier, I was allowed to return to Harbord Collegiate. The Party thought it best that I sound like an educated girl rather than an ignoramus. After I graduated from high school, the Party Leader found me a well-paying job as a finisher in a coat factory east of Dufferin Street and south of King Street. I could afford an apartment at the Inns of Court, a four-storey building with ornate balconies facing east toward the morning sun. A tiny elevator sporting a brass-grate door carried the tenants from floor to floor. My apartment was across the road from Mrs. Meretsky's lodging house, where Vine continued to pay rent. His girlfriend, Betty, had moved to Detroit where she sang in a choir.

I asked him if he missed Betty. "No, I have more important things to think about than women," he assured me. Vine was working for the Party, learning to be a leader.

Now that I had my own place, he visited me from time to time. Vine knew what I was doing for the Party, but we never spoke about it. I fixed home cooked meals for him rather than the fried hamburgers and greasy potatoes he usually ate at the diner around the block. We toasted the Revolution with shots from the bottle of Russian vodka I kept in the cupboard above the icebox.

I demanded more from the Party after my next encounter with an older professor of Russian history. More respect and more compensation for my talent. The first thing I did with the extra money was to buy white linen drapes. At Mrs. Meretsky's I'd never been able to sew curtains for the windows. Those rooms were dowdy and I always felt it was Vine's place more than mine even though he was rarely there. He made me feel that I was beholden to him, by incessantly reminding me: "Where would you be without me? Back in the dark ages in Nesvicz, that's where."

On my own, I shopped where the Canadians shopped, at Simpson's department store at Yonge and Queen. An extremely gallant salesman, showed me how to select a quality sofa, and two matching armchairs, not the junk the furniture dealers sold in the market. The upholstery was tasteful and the manufacturing solid. I ordered a tall wooden bookshelf for the books I intended to collect. The Party paid for everything, the furniture, the books, and the new clothes I purchased whenever I wanted to look fashionable.

It would have been understandable for me to sink into a melancholic state if I'd compared the new me with what I had been brought up to be: a devout, modest girl with no need to feel important or look special. But what choice did I have as an immigrant? Vine had all but vanished from my life, I had no family in Canada and I knew no one except the comrades in the Party. If I'd tried to speak with Mrs. Meretsky, and beg her to help me, she'd decline. She was loyal to the cause.

I convinced myself to enjoy the stylish furnishings and my fashionable outfits. I told myself that one day I would either return to Nesvicz and take up where I'd left off or I'd meet a good man, my own age, who would get me out of the state of servitude I was in. But over time, instead of trying to find a way out of the Party, I just dug myself in deeper. By forgetting the rules of my upbringing in Nesvicz, or by dismissing the true nature of my work, I convinced myself that I was doing the right thing for the Party. I was sewing the seeds of revolution. It helped that I was constantly praised and coddled. I became a big macher, a big deal, in the tightly-knit inner circle of the Party, the ones who knew what my job entailed and who communicated my discoveries to Moscow. Before long, I was allowed to leave the coat factory and concentrate on my duties for the Party.

During the third summer in my apartment, I boarded the trolley to Sunnyside beach whenever the weather permitted. My days were free. I worked for the Party during the night. It was safe shallow water in Lake Ontario, but not for Jews. On the beach a sign declared, "No dogs or Jews," but I went into the water anyway. I swam out until the bathers on the shore became black stick figures outlined against the sun.

No one ever again could accuse me of being a timid, uncouth greenhorn. As I floated out atop the lake water, I thought of myself as a rebel and a trailblazer. I reminded myself how fearless and committed I'd become in Toronto and how I was willing to grab at any chance to make a better world.

For the first time I started to wonder what could happen to me if I was exposed, if I was betrayed to the authorities. I realized, as young as I was, I could be deported for collecting secrets for the Communist Party. I pushed the notion to the back of mind and left it in the dark for years to come until I was forced to face the truth.

On a steaming hot day in July, Vine accompanied me to the beach. He wore bathing trunks, but he'd never learned to swim and wouldn't venture into the water past his ankles. Instead he sat on a blanket under an umbrella to ensure his pink freckled skin didn't burn while mine turned nut-brown.

He was watching me, so I swam out devilishly far, testing fate. A big wave pulled me under the current until it pushed me back against the rocky shore. My legs and arms were scratched when I emerged.

"Why don't you sit by me?" he asked as I was moving my own blanket away from him. "You're dripping in blood."

"I don't want to sit in the shade," I replied. "Why don't you try to wade in? Don't be a chicken!" I'd heard the older boys swimming in the lake, calling out to the smaller ones, the ones afraid to venture out. They called them chickens and mama's boys.

I closed my eyes to lie flat on my blanket after brushing off the sand and wiping the blood from my arms and legs. But Vine tricked me; he didn't appreciate it when I called him a chicken so he snuck up beside me and kicked sand on my face. Bits of it landed in my mouth and nostrils. For a brief moment I couldn't breathe. Then I grabbed the pail from the little girl playing next to me and dumped lake water on Vine's head. He sputtered like a drowning cat.

We never went to Sunnyside together again, but I still went; still continued to swim out far into the lake and battle the huge waves, taking my chances with fate.

My work became urgent as the possibility of a second great war loomed in Europe. I was busier than ever before. If I had been an artist I could have made a fortune sketching and selling drawings of men's bodies. Older men were my specialty, and if I could draw their bulging stomachs, yellowed toes nails, backs sprinkled with moles, ears sprouting with hair and shrivelled penises, I'd be rich.

LAST NIGHT OF THE WORLD

By 1935, the Party began testing me with men of serious influence. They concocted a mission where my target was a bastion of society, not like Klopot the haberdasher. I was to befriend the dean of the law school at the University of Toronto. We needed a man of distinction and influence, an expert in jurisprudence, to bring the Party out of obscurity by openly supporting our cause. If I failed, I'd be downgraded to men of Klopot's calibre. The Dean was a test of my usefulness to the Party.

In the West, we didn't know, then, how Stalin was ruining the Soviet Union: the midnight arrests, the show trials, the Siberian gulags. Only a few suspected, and they were expelled from the Party when they raised their concerns. For the rest of us, Russia was nirvana, a land of miracles. Those belonging to the inner circle in Toronto became a mirror of the Soviet Politburo, the pinnacle of a self-made hierarchy, and although we gushed over the ordinary members in the Party, they had no influence over how we operated. Orders came straight from Moscow and if Tim Buck disobeyed, he'd be replaced. My missions were classified. Even Vine didn't know about the luminaries I was convincing to come over to our side.

It took many years for me to admit what was actually transpiring in Russia. When my sister Masha wrote to tell me that the famous Russian poet Osip Mandelshtam was arrested for writing a poem that attacked Stalin, it was the first time I started to question things. "Mandelshtam has been punished, sent into exile for three years." She was stating a fact, so the censors didn't black out her words. She added, "our brother has moved to Łódź in Poland."

"I'm slim as a reed," Masha wrote in her next letter. "Mama and Papa are also on a strict diet. You should see how active they have become. Mama walks in the forest everyday to gather berries for dinner."

I couldn't discount that they were suffering, but I was powerless to help. In my parents' letters, there was no mention of the famine. In my mind, I could still picture their gracious home with the enormous cast iron stove in the kitchen and the enamel bathtub off the pantry. Mama was as beautiful as ever, Papa as clever. She spoke a cultured Yiddish, while he roared in his rugged version of the language, overpowering the rabbis when they came to settle the petty disputes that proliferated in Nesvicz.

After a while the letters from home dribbled to one every two weeks, then every few months.

"We should go back," I urged Vine, but he was adamant that we had important work to do in Canada and that Stalin would outsmart Hitler.

Vine wasn't lying. He had become the maven of union organizing in the garment factories and made a name for himself, which made me quietly proud of him. I never stopped caring about him, not entirely. He was my only connection to home, although I blamed him for what was happening to my parents. It was not easy to love and hate a man at the same time, to try to make him jealous without revealing a glimmer of interest. I would agonize over him anytime he came down with the flu, and then I would fantasize that he would develop a more serious illness, as he'd done during the crossing to Canada.

By 1939, when the Molotov–Ribbentrop Pact was signed between the Nazis and the Soviets, and the Party became illegal in Canada, the letters from home stopped altogether. I never heard from my parents again.

* * *

Chernobyl journal
1988

Now that I am an old woman living in a ramshackle cabin hidden deep inside the Chernobyl forest, I try not to condemn myself, both for what I did and for what I didn't admit to knowing.

I was used by the men who saw themselves as world leaders, who intended "to take the country," as soon as Canada was ripe for revolutionary war. Yet I believe, to this day, I made the only choice open to me given the circumstances.

In the forest, everyone is equal. If you are healthy, you count your blessings. My old comrades, Fred Rose and Sybil Romanescu reside in their own hut across the path from our cabin. She is sick and lies in bed. The radiation affected her more than the men or me. Then again, Sybil always was the weakest link.

LAST NIGHT OF THE WORLD

Although Vine and Zabotin barely speak to each other, we've discovered a way to co-exist in our little abode. I cook. Vine tidies up when he is able. Zabotin, still spry as a teenager, hunts and fishes. He and I are in remarkable shape for people of our advanced age.

In early spring I planted my first vegetable garden. The potatoes, cabbage, carrots and onions grow to unearthly sizes, as if they are exploding with the poison in the soil. Nothing, not even the greatest nuclear accident of all time, can kill me. Vine is another story. It is his heart that slows him down. Whenever he walks more than a few paces, he must sit down to catch his breath.

Fred Rose, who was imprisoned for six years in the Kingston Penitentiary, accused of divulging nuclear secrets to the Soviets during the war, is as healthy as can be expected. He contracted tuberculosis in prison, but he can still walk quickly and play the balalaika for an audience. Before Chernobyl, old comrades from Canada sought him out. They revered him for his great sacrifice and devotion to the Revolution, and as the first and only Communist elected to the House of Commons in Canada.

We have each returned to type, to the way we would have turned out if we'd stayed on in Eastern Europe and there'd been no Russian Revolution. Zabotin is the charming aristocrat of this godforsaken fiefdom, aged but dignified. He is pleased with himself. Vine is the hesitating shtetl Jew, heavy-lidded eyes pointed downward toward his untamed beard. And I am the old crone; grey mangled hair streaming down my back, gnarled hands, fingernails black from digging in the earth. But when I peer at myself in the mirror, my eyes are as bright and knowing as the stars in the sky.

Although I have the countenance of an old woman, inside I am as youthful and fresh as when as I came out of Europe. I am dancing on the grave of the ideas that almost obliterated me, all of us. After what I've witnessed and what I've done, I am one of the lucky ones. If my body is withered and my skin marked with brown spots, dry and thin as rice paper, I remain, brimming with hope for the next generation. I haven't given up on mankind. How could I when the world might have been destroyed by unlocking the power of the atom? Each time, mankind has stepped back from that precipice, each time good people have made their way through the darkness.

It's fortunate that Zabotin's dacha is exactly sixty-two kilometres from here, just north of Kiev. And although it is still overrun with Party officials from the city, Zabotin drives in his Lada to hunt there, where the terrain is most familiar to him. After the snow flies, when the apparatchiks return to their heated offices, he sneaks into the dacha to nap on the sofa. He maintains that he doesn't regret joining the Red Cavalry during the Revolution, nor does he have qualms about sending Vine and me away from our home in Nesvicz. He maintains we would be dead if we'd stayed. Zabotin does not apologize for much. About his actions as rezident in Ottawa, he simply boasts: "I saved the world. Who knows what would have happened if Stalin had got the A-bomb in 1945."

After Reactor Number Four failed, it was Zabotin who rushed the five of us into his old Lada. We escaped to his family's dacha on the morning after the meltdown, a full two days before the officials came around to officially evacuate the citizens of Pripyat. Once again, he saved us.

When I look back, regret is much too simple a word for what I feel. It is a gnawing torment, like the festering of a war wound the doctors can't heal. My heart is Zabotin's mutilated right hand. But there is also triumph. I survived it all: the Russian Revolution, the Second World War and the Gouzenko betrayal—when the entire world was introduced to the fact that I helped the Soviets steal atomic secrets from the Americans. Ethel and Julius Rosenberg fried for it, but not me.

Chapter Seven

1939
Ottawa

I lived alone in my apartment on Beaconsfield until 1939 when the Party sent me to Ottawa to befriend the head of the National Film Board, John Grierson. He was at the top of my list, along with a handful of journalists and government insiders. I was thirty-two, and the Ottawa posting mattered to Moscow now that all diplomatic relations between Canada and the Soviet Union had stalled.

It was easier than I expected to make government men confide in me. I turned out to be the Party's expert, and the leader, Tim Buck, relied on me. With bureaucrats, those with ponderous titles but insignificant work, all it took was flattery. They were surprised that I was interested in them; me, an exotic and a Russian journalist. They wanted a break from the banality of their monotonous days.

My first target was a Canadian government official, an assistant Deputy Minister in the Department of Defense. He reviewed the files that the Mounties accumulated on illegal Party members after 1939. It was remarkable how little the Canadians knew about Communism before then. It wasn't until Comrade Molotov signed the pact with the Nazis in 1939 that the RCMP went into full gear, gathering information about our activities. The Canadian wing of the Party was deemed illegal. To cover my tracks, I was made a reporter for TASS, the Soviet News Agency. I was no longer a card-carrying member so I could continue with my covert activities. In Toronto, I'd done my job well. I'd made friends with the right people. In Ottawa I was run from the Soviet Embassy and I thrived in diplomatic circles. All that mattered was how much information I could squeeze out of my sources and how useful it ultimately was for my handler, Nikolai Zabotin.

Zabotin took a special interest in my triumphs. "You are a success story," he said after I obtained some key information from the Department of Defense. "You're ready to meet John Grierson. You're the only one who can do it. It will not be easy like some of the others. Grierson is nobody's fool."

By then, the Party was my only connection to those who would protect me from the dangers of a cannonading world. I had no one else, and unlike the way I'd treated my own family, I was willing do anything to keep the comrades on my side.

Vine was transferred to Ottawa at the same time I was, but I rarely saw him. Zabotin preferred it that way. He never warmed to Vine even though they were landsmen, from the same village, and Vine was assigned to the most perilous operations of espionage. I suppose I was the reason the two men distrusted each other, but apart from their interest in me, their characters were diametrically opposed. While Zabotin was enjoying the comfortable high-flying life of a diplomat, Vine was on the constant lookout for action. He wanted to distinguish himself as a fighter for the cause. Zabotin had already proven himself in the revolutionary war and he was content resting on his laurels.

My liaison with Zabotin was different, of course, than my other trysts. I worked for him and we had history. Shortly after arriving in Ottawa, I found myself flirting with him at embassy soirees. He was the most attractive man in the room and he took a discernable interest in me.

At my first Soviet Embassy gathering, I'd recognized Zabotin as soon as he entered the room. He'd changed, the blond curls were greying, and his step was slower. But the beaming smile, the aquiline nose, the aura of power surrounding him was the same as the day he threatened to kill Vine and accost me in Nesvicz. He didn't even appear surprised, or ashamed to see me.

I was frightened as he approached, dressed in his full military uniform. I noticed that he wore a glove on his right hand and he didn't offer it in a handshake when I faced him straight on. "It's been too long," he said to me in English as I asked myself what he could do to me now that he was my handler.

However terrified I was, I looked him in the eyes. Of course, he remembered me, and what he'd done back in my village of Nesvicz. He was the reason I'd fled Europe in the first place, he and Vine. If I mentioned the Red Cavalry pogrom, I was certain he would find a way to hurt me.

I remained silent, as Zabotin guided me to the bar. We stood together for what seemed like hours, as he recounted his tales of bravery with the Red Army. He was proud of himself.

"How did you approach that bureaucrat in Defense?" Zabotin asked me after we'd both had too much to drink. "Tell me, Freda," he said putting his good hand on my shoulder. I shuddered. This man was familiar to me, I knew what he was capable of doing and how he wouldn't hesitate to harm me if I disobeyed his orders or lied to him, or worse, exposed him.

"I just talked and asked questions. I'm a curious person. A journalist. I convinced him," I said, presenting a bitter smile.

"That's it? You talked to him."

"They are bored, these bureaucrats," I explained.

"And…"

"I could show you, if you'd really like to know." The words tumbled out of my mouth. He was so powerful; he overwhelmed me. I needed to protect myself and this was the only way I knew how.

That night we left the embassy together. Vine was at the soiree too and I looked into his startled eyes as Zabotin ushered me out of the room and into his limousine. He took me to the safe house where we were to meet regularly during the next six years.

Chapter Eight

August 30, 1945
Ottawa

The safe house on the Rideau Canal was three storeys in all and one of the best addresses in Ottawa. The servants' quarters were on the third floor, the six bedrooms on the second and the massive parlour, dining room and library on the first. That night in August I met Zabotin before midnight, as instructed, entering by the back door on the first floor adjoining the mudroom, where the maids stored their buckets and mops. This is how we did it throughout the war, as the Soviets turned from an illegal enemy to Canada's ally. Still, Zabotin didn't want diplomatic Ottawa to know about us, so I dressed plainly, not in heels or a feathered hat, as was my style during the war years. "Without make-up," he ordered. Then he remembered to add, "You're pretty enough without being made up." I wasn't certain he was being sincere.

The master bedroom faced east toward the canal. The bay window was constructed of a hundred panes of glass. I relished making love with Zabotin in this room. I came to think of it as our room. It was opulent and different from the bulk of the rooms where I'd operated since spying for the Party. Not seedy, the sheets freshly washed and pressed. The carpet vacuumed. The walls were ivory with blue velvet drapes adorning the window. Many times I'd imagined sharing this room with Zabotin, just the two of us as man and wife.

But Zabotin had other ideas for us. He'd concocted a script during the war and on that cool, peaceful night, he wished to adhere strictly to the pre-scribed ritual. I reminded myself that although Zabotin was not an inventive lover, he was an ardent one. I was certain he admired me, but it was entirely possible that he also loved me from time to time, most often when were in bed together. I was moved that he could still feel such a tender emotion, a man who had seen what he'd seen, and done what he'd been ordered to do.

I tried to concentrate on my performance for him, but my mind wouldn't keep still. Since our conversation in the park the day before, I understood that Zabotin would be contacting the scientist Alan Nunn May, the Soviet asset at Chalk River, for new intelligence about the bomb to send to the Cen-tre. As usual, Vine would be the conduit between the reticent British scientist and Zabotin.

Begging his patience, I disappeared into the washroom, stood in front of the mirror and stared at myself. I thought back to the day the Red Cavalry invaded my home, and recalled each of Zabotin's words to me and Vine. He had allowed us—no ordered us—to run away. "You two will never survive the Bolsheviks," he'd said, with his silver pistol aimed at Vine. For a moment I had caught his eye and he looked back with a smile I would come to know intimately.

When I returned to the bedroom, he was naked lying on the bed. He toasted the Revolution as he popped the cork on a bottle of Veuve Clicquot. "*Nostrovia*," I said, as we clinked the crystal flutes.

My handler was the most spectacular person at the Soviet Embassy, I had to admit to myself; not at all like the drab officials that Moscow usual-ly sent abroad. The Centre preferred men who all looked the same: short, stocky, with tight brown curls and a five o'clock shadow.

"Why did you say that I'd never survive the Bolsheviks?" I asked.

His mouth became a thin line. "You remember everything," he replied.

"I remember what I need to."

"In deference to your great beauty, undress." A cigarette dangled from his lips.

"Tell me, Nikolai. Please." I took another sip of champagne. "Why not me? Did you think I wasn't worthy to build the new society?"

"You wouldn't have survived to see it. You're not the type," he said. "I could see it in you then. Your earnest boyfriend, Vine, he might have managed. He so wanted to be part of how the Bolsheviks were transforming Russia in our region. He'd have supported the making of the autonomous regions. Ours was to be Polish. But he's too pure. Stalin would have had him murdered for treason long ago. An enemy of the people. The autonomous regions were blamed on the most dedicated comrades, those who tried to create them and failed."

I was stunned. We often talked openly, but not like this. "And I'm not the type because?"

"Because you want too much. You crave beautiful things. You want romance and intrigue. The Soviet Union is not the place for any of that. You'd wither away trying to turn peasant villages into Party centrals."

"Now you and I spend every minute ensuring the Soviet Union survives. Now more than ever, with the Americans dropping the A-bomb. Yet you seem…"

He was perpetually surprised when I hit upon his truths.

"Don't be afraid. Disenchantment is normal. We each have a job to do and mine is to get the correct formula for the bomb so Stalin can use it at his will."

I looked up the ceiling. "The room is bugged," I said.

"Not tonight," Zabotin assured me. "We can talk freely."

I blushed in front of his frankness. He removed the glove from his right hand and I stared at the mutilation of bone and flesh.

"Now undress. Enough talking."

I turned my back to remove my blouse.

"Except for your garter belt and the silk stockings, leave them on" he ordered.

"Do I ever refuse you?" I asked him.

"Never. You wouldn't dare."

He was completely aroused by the time I was naked except for the black garter belt and stockings. He sat on the bed and pulled me down by my waist. I was to face the wall as he entered me, holding one breast in his swollen hand. With his good hand he rubbed between my legs until I cried out. It never lasted long, these sessions with Zabotin.

The ashes of his cigarette glowed in the room, illuminated by the street lamp suspended outside the window. "Why won't you admit it to me, say that you love me? Don't I satisfy you?" He was reclining on the pillows, stroking the flesh of my inner thighs. He was so proud of himself.

It was the right question to ask me. Over and over again, I'd asked myself the same one. If I told Nikolai I loved him, would he leave his wife? What would the Party say? Moscow was no longer interested in free love. They claimed it was "bourgeois." I could be in hot water if the Centre blamed me for a divorce. Appearances counted in the diplomatic service, even the Russian one.

Instead I uttered the wrong thing. It didn't matter what I said or what I did. I couldn't erase the past. I couldn't stop thinking about what I'd left behind. I couldn't decide if I deserved to survive. Why was I alive when so many disappeared? For all my manoeuvring in Canada, I was beginning to admit that my contribution hadn't saved a single soul, certainly not one Jew.

"I won't tell you I love you," I said, and Zabotin took offense. "Your Cossacks killed every young Jewish male they could get their hands on. Or kidnapped them into the Red Cavalry. I can't forget Nesvicz —what you did, what you did to Vine's brother. I can still see you, the dashing young officer, dressed in the crimson uniform with the silver stripe winding down your pant leg. You gloried in it, battled against terrified undefended Jews." Hadn't he conquered enough? Why did he need to add me to his empire of accomplishments?

Zabotin was surprised. I'd never spoken to him in such an impudent manner. It was difficult to tell if he respected me for it, or wished to punish me as only he could. But by then, I knew so much about the Ottawa operation that I counted on my belief that he wouldn't dare expose me. It would only open the entire espionage ring to scrutiny and implicate Zabotin himself. Like Gouzenko, he'd be heading back to Russia with not much to show for his time in Canada. How did he expect to collect the nuclear plans for the scientists back in the Soviet Union? He needed my help.

"I saved you, didn't I?" he asked. "You and your boyfriend, Vine. Don't forget it was me who set you free from the shtetl and all that religious nonsense your people worshipped."

"And your family didn't bow down to Orthodox icons?"

He chuckled. "We're not going to get anywhere arguing whose religion is more ridiculous."

I admired him, but I couldn't let him off that easy. "I'll never forget it, how you and your men galloped into Nesvicz. It was you, no, who whipped Vine's papa with the butt of your pistol? It's the same one you keep beside the bed. I've seen it."

Zabotin stared at me, as if I were a ghost. "I'd forgotten that old cobbler," he admitted. "Why must you bring everything back to Vine? A shoemaker's son."

I didn't know myself why I did it, enrage Zabotin. I loathed Vine for forcing me to follow him to the shoemaker's house on the day of the pogrom, but I couldn't let him go, either. I wasn't content unless both Vine and Zabotin were in my range, and sometimes I believed they felt the same, that they needed each other as much as I counted on them. Our affinity was based on what we'd forsaken and not on our expectations for the future. I realize this now, living together in the Chernobyl forest, how much we still need each other. Survivors cling to each other and can never let go. It's all that we have of our former selves, before everything dear to us was destroyed.

I pulled my camisole from the collection of clothes on the floor. "You promised Vine that you'd leave his older brother, Yitzhak, alone, but you kidnapped him into Budyonny's Red Calvary. How did he perish? Of exhaustion? Or did you fling his ravaged body in the forest and leave him to freeze in the snow? Did that make you feel like a man?"

If Zabotin was who he pretended to be, I'm certain he would have shot me. The silver pistol was pointed toward my heart. He'd removed it from the night table drawer beside the bed and cocked the trigger.

"Why have you bothered with me?" I cried. "It would have been better for me if you'd shot me in Nesvicz instead of putting me through this charade."

Zabotin aimed the gun at the floor.

I knew then he was ashamed of how his men in the Red Cavalry had decimated Nesvicz. He was smart enough to understand that the pogrom was part of a system of terror that would never end in our corner of Europe. Stalin's excuse for a government was the secret police. Zabotin was tired of excuses. We both were, but couldn't admit it to each other. If we were truly honest, we'd have to try to stop the Russians from getting the atomic bomb before they used it against Stalin's enemies.

"You are impossible," Zabotin said. "Nothing is good enough for you. You find a way to spoil it." He placed the silver pistol in the drawer beside the bed. This time he wouldn't murder me.

What was my life worth? Since seeing the news, I wished to put myself in harm's way. Why should I live when so many had died? When the cause I'd devoted my life to did not stop the slaughter. I wondered how anyone who lived through the war could ever be themselves again or make themselves whole.

I changed the subject, not willing to consider what measures I would need to take to make Zabotin hurt me. Vine was a superior choice if that was truly what I wanted; he'd behave ruthlessly if I got in the way of Stalin's plans to tame the western countries.

"Talk to me of pleasant things," I said to Zabotin.

He put his hand over my eyes. "Neither of us can change what is. Let's talk about my dacha. It's north of Kiev and lovely in late August. The climate is much like it is in Ottawa. It would suit you, the dacha."

Zabotin wished to forget about the war, the one that began for him in 1914 and continued until the Bolsheviks defeated the Whites. He wished to forget about the humiliation of the Ukraine when half the people starved to death because the commissars confiscated the kulaks' seed grain. Through the black market and his high ranking in the Red Cavalry, he'd kept his parents alive in their dacha. By the end of the Nazi occupation, they were dead. Even he could not save them. Zabotin wanted to dissolve into the landscape in a place where no one would remember what he had done to survive. I was beginning to understand who he was becoming.

"Why do I bother talking to you?" he asked suddenly, as if his story was over.

"Continue, please." I grabbed his head in my hands. There were more streaks of grey among the golden curls. "Tell me everything. If I am to love you, I must know who you are."

He sat up; his large feet perched on the carpet. The feet were discernably

Russian, wide with bulging big toes. Not unlike my own. We are all peasants. With his back turned to me, he declared, "We could just live, as we once did, as humans."

In the darkness of the safe house, Zabotin told me of his dacha in the woods, but he did not twist his long body to face me. He spoke softly as when he made love to me.

"The walls are wooden, made of polished pine. The windows open like hawk's wings onto the green yew trees. There is a ceramic stove where *Baba* keeps the samovar boiling and the blue porcelain cups ready for the steeping tea. There are always fresh lemons candied with caster sugar and cookies made of sweet dough and almonds."

He might have broken down. If I could have seen his face, I'd have known if his blue eyes were clouded with tears. Zabotin continued after a long pause.

"The wooden planked floor is always water stained after the winter melt. When I enter the cabin for the first time in the spring, the horsehair sofas are damp although they are covered in fox fur rugs and Baba's crocheted woollen throws. The feather beds sag dreadfully. I don't mind. It is always warm and cozy under the layered quilts.

"Inside the pantry is a huge meat locker where my father stores the kill from the hunt. The brothers plan our spring hunt as soon as we arrive.

"My mother's books cover the walls although they, too, are stained by the melting ice of the spring thaw. *Matushka* has taken to reading and rereading Chekhov."

I loved it when Nikolai referred to his mother by the old-fashioned and polite term for Mama.

"*Matushka* knew before Papa that the end was near. Just before the Revolution, she arranged for a production of *Uncle Vanya* on the verandah of the dacha, but our neighbours, the gentry of Kiev, didn't appreciate Chekhov's prescience, or Mama's for that matter.

"I noticed the broken snow skis and tins of wax left open from the previous winter. Remnants. Throughout the performance of *Uncle Vanya* the dogs barked. Old Victor Alexievich, he served us faithfully from before time began, he could not quiet them, the dogs objecting to the play as much as our guests.

During the Revolution, Victor was shot for being a class traitor and the dogs starved to death. Some say the animals ate Victor's rotting flesh before they, too, expired. It was during the great famine when nearly everyone perished. Poor Victor had no idea how to survive without the count and countess."

I wrapped my arms around Zabotin and kissed his neck hidden by his golden, greying curls. I pressed my breasts into the curves of his fine, straight back. I kissed the shoulder scar where the bullet aimed at his heart had emerged. "But your parents were lucky, they survived the famine."

"Only by trading on the black market. Until the Nazis came, they survived."

"Tell me more about the dacha."

"In the corner cupboard, Papa keeps his vodka and cognac. The crystal chandelier hangs in the centre of the room. After the civil war, I discovered it was miraculously still intact, the candle holders caked with wax from before the Revolution."

Perhaps if we'd made love one more time at that very moment, Zabotin would not have revealed his worries to me. "You must know that important papers are missing from the cypher room, Freda," he said, covering his bad hand with the good one. "Some filled with the usual nonsense that Gouzenko encrypts for the Centre about the Party's victories in Canada. But others are from the Centre's mole in Washington, wired to me, to forward to Moscow. Hundreds of cables."

"What else?" I asked.

"You know about the diagrams for the bomb that Vine brought back from Fuchs at Los Alamos in the spring?"

Zabotin was testing me.

"Yes, I know."

"I'm certain Vine would have revealed that to you by now." Zabotin understood everything about Vine and me. He always had.

"Did Gouzenko wire Fuch's diagrams? The instructions Moscow needs to build the bomb? Did Gouzenko send them to the Centre?" I could hardly believe I was asking Zabotin these questions.

He shook his head and said, "No. I haven't sent the diagrams to the Director. No one but me and Vine have seen them."

"So, Gouzenko never saw them, the diagrams for the bomb?" I asked again.

"Freda, always one step ahead," he said. "No, I didn't order Gouzenko to send them to Moscow."

"Why not?" I inquired.

"It was too early for the Kremlin," he explained. "At first I waited until after the bombs were dropped on Japan and afterward, the destruction, it was beyond what could be imagined. That's why the Director is hounding me for a sample of plutonium. He needs plutonium to make a bomb like Fat Man, the one that vapourized Nagasaki."

"You decided to wait?" I was incredulous that Zabotin would take matters of this nature into his own hands. "Why did you wait?" If Zabotin were recalled to Moscow for this crime, he'd be labelled an enemy of the people, stripped of his wartime medals, and ordered to stand before a firing squad at first morning light.

"The original information from Fuchs might have been flawed," he said clutching his bad hand in his good one. "I'd be crucified for sending the wrong formulations. I didn't want to take that chance in June. That's why Vine will need to verify the formula with Alan Nunn May at Chalk River. And to retrieve an actual sample of plutonium. Then I can courier the package to Moscow."

I wasn't convinced by Zabotin's story. He was covering his tracks, concealing the reason why he had not immediately sent Fuchs' diagrams to the Director. Fuchs was the most reliable Soviet mole inside Los Alamos. He was close to Oppenheimer. There was no reason why Zabotin would doubt Fuchs' recipe for the bomb, nor was there a reason for concealing it from the Director, for holding back.

"Why did you wait until after Nagasaki? How would you know the timing?"

"Homer, " Zabotin said.

Back then, I didn't understand fully how desperate the situation was. I couldn't have known that Zabotin acted as the crucial link between the GRU's key operative in Washington and the Director in Moscow. The operative's code name was Homer. He was a Cambridge man who operated on behalf of the Soviets. When it appeared that Churchill would not bolster Stalin's

effort to defeat the Germans on the Eastern Front, Homer cautiously lob-
bied for the Soviet war effect. At the same time, he spied for the GRU. Once
the war ended, Homer provided the Director with all the latest news about
atomic advances at Los Alamos. Homer's information was first passed to
Zabotin in Ottawa where it was encoded and transmitted to the GRU. If
Homer was exposed, Soviet atomic espionage would crumble, and it would
be on our heads.

"Why did you wait? Why didn't you send the diagrams to Moscow immediately?" I demanded to know. "It might have changed the course of the
war. The Americans might not have bombed the Japanese if we'd had our
own bomb."

For the first time, Zabotin looked frightened. "You're wrong. Our scientists aren't close enough. They couldn't have pulled it together between June
and August even with Fuchs' diagrams. Only now will Stalin be devising a
plan to bomb the West, now that the war is over."

"And Gouzenko never saw the diagrams?"

"Let's hope not," said Zabotin.

Neither of us mentioned what would befall us if the Canadians got their
hands on the hundreds of cables from Washington or learned about Fuchs' diagrams. First Ottawa would alert the Americans and next the British. All those
working for Zabotin would be implicated in the conspiracy to steal the formula.

I kissed away the tears from Zabotin's face. We both recognized that he
could be sent to the Lubyanka prison for retaining documents of such shattering importance. Vine would be under suspicion at the same time. He had
brought them back from Los Alamos, so he too was implicated by their delay.

"Was there music at the dacha?" I asked, not able to continue.

"Oh, yes!" Zabotin was openly weeping by now. "A gramophone. Matushka adored Schubert."

How he longed for the old Russia! Whatever drew him to the Red Cavalry was something I'd never understood before. Like Vine and me, caught in
the mayhem of the civil war, he wished to survive, but Zabotin was already
powerful before the Revolution. His family could have escaped Russia unscathed and lived in Paris as exiles. Perhaps that was it. He couldn't tolerate
deserting Mother Russia when she needed the bravest to fight for her. Zabo-

tin yearned for something beyond simple survival.

"Mine as well. Schubert was her favourite," I said, recalling Mama sitting at the grand piano in the drawing room playing Schubert in our beautiful home in Nesvicz.

"You see, Freda, we are not so very far apart. Both of our mamas loved Schubert."

To comfort him, I suggested that the secret cables from Homer in Washington, alerting him to the bombing of Japan, might have been destroyed, burned, and not stolen, but he retorted that only he could have given that order.

"Lydia," I suggested.

"My wife does not have the key to the cipher room," he said, clearly annoyed at the mere suggestion it could be his wife. "Only myself and, Gouzenko have keys. We are the only ones."

When Zabotin turned his body to kiss me, I allowed him to hold me in his arms for a long time and then I said cautiously, "I think you must keep me in the dark on Klaus Fuchs or Alan Nunn May, and nothing about the atomic bomb. It is too dangerous…"

"Dangerous, yes… well."

"Do you think it is Gouzenko who stole the papers? Is that why he's being recalled to Moscow? Is there anyone else you suspect?"

"Look, if you don't wish to know, don't ask so many questions. And do not, under any circumstances, let Vine know that I just couriered the diagrams to Moscow. Can I trust you?"

It was a naïve question, and one he probably didn't believe. We both understood how impossible it was to trust anyone, not even each other.

"Have you couriered them, Nikolai? How can I believe you? You want me to tell Vine that Fuchs' formula, the one he risked his life to bring to you, is in the Director's hands. I don't trust you. You are making things up for me to relay to Vine. You fear that he will go above your head, and expose you."

Zabotin laughed his grand, hearty laugh. "You are too clever for your own good," he roared and then pulled me down harshly upon the rumpled sheets.

And after making love again, he tried to fool me into believing that he was sleeping soundly, a look of calm spreading across his spectacularly handsome face. But I was wise to Zabotin and his blatant tricks. Perhaps he realized that he'd recounted much too much to me about the missing cryptograms and about the bomb.

I was wide awake. I moved from the bed to the dressing table and then back under the quilt to lie beside him. In the diffused moonlight, I saw him barely open his Slavic eyes.

"You are a disembodied spirit," he said to me. "Pretending to dance the dance of the living."

"Didn't we die many years ago?" My mind descended to dark places.

Silently and to each other we wondered how many more splendid nights we would enjoy together before the entire ruse was up. Perhaps this might be our last.

By early morning I fell into a deep, dream-laden sleep and when I woke Zabotin was standing naked, a silver tray in his good hand, a linen napkin folded over the other. On the tray was herring in dilled cream sauce, black bread and tiny bubbles of caviar spread artfully across crisp round toasts. He'd cracked a raw egg for us to mix with the black sturgeon eggs from the Caspian. He placed the linen napkin on a round table beside the bed, set the tray upon it and helped me to sit up. I wore only a peach-coloured camisole, which I knew displayed my complexion to its fullest.

"Your eyes are cloudy," he said. "How did you manage last night?" Zabotin brought an Imperial porcelain demitasse filled with steaming espresso to my lips.

"Perfectly." I'd dreamt about Nesvicz and a small boy I was tutoring in Russian literature before we escaped from the civil war pogrom. The boy wore a broad black felt hat whenever he appeared on my doorstep. I could barely see his eyes, hidden under the brim of the fedora, but they were the brightest eyes in the world and a smile that mixed sublime innocence with mischief. His carrot-coloured hair fell in traditional ringlets framing his freckled heart-shaped face. He reminded me of my younger brother, Simcha, the little devil, the teller of tales. If only he could be as real as the red-haired boy in my dream.

As I sipped the luscious coffee, I closed my eyes, imagining that the boy was dead, buried in a mass grave, the one that the Soviet liberators would unmask at the edge of Nesvicz, as they had done in so many of the shtetls inside the Pale.

Zabotin swept back the drapes. "Open your eyes, Freda," he ordered. "Come back to the land of the living."

On the streets below, industrious public servants rushed to work. Some pedalled their bicycles, trousers neatly encased in wire clips, some with bulging briefcases scurried to catch the morning's first Bronson Street bus. Canada was a new country teaming with boundless post-war opportunity.

"Would you help me find my family?" I asked him plaintively. "I have pictures in my handbag that my family sent me. The old street address in Nesvicz. Perhaps our brick house is still standing."

Zabotin looked at me as if I was talking nonsense. "How can I be of assistance?" he asked, buckling the metal belt on his trousers and sitting beside me on the unmade bed.

For a moment I wished to cover my eyes in shame, to pull the quilt over my head, to hide from his sympathetic gaze. "I've written to Mama, so many letters. Never a word." I imagined an enormous pile of unopened envelopes burning in an open field. Black shards of feathered parchment floating up to the heavens. "I am the oldest of the three children and it is on me to return to Europe to find the others."

I pictured my mother, the loveliest woman in Nesvicz, with her dark eyes, white skin, a tiny nose and high cheekbones. Long fingers that babied the keys of the piano, as she babied her children.

"Open your eyes," ordered Zabotin once again. He grabbed my chin and pointed my face toward him.

"That might prove difficult," Zabotin said. "Displaced persons are scattered in refugee camps across Europe, across Russia all the way to Alma Ata. Try to be realistic."

The living graveyards, I thought. But he was calling our home Russia. It would always be Russia to Zabotin. And to me. What had happened to Russia during the war was too terrible to investigate, but for my family, the least I could do was to find out if any one of them was still alive. Zabotin must understand. His brothers were in Russia, as was his only son, and he ached to see them again now that the war was over.

"Try to help me. You are connected to all the Soviet embassies."

"It would be like finding a needle in haystack," he said, attempting not to be cruel. He and I both understood that only a few lucky Jews had survived the Nazis: an inventive forger, a brilliant machinist, an original dressmaker, or a talented violinist, who by chance served a purpose in the camps.

"You are pleased with my work, with my sources, aren't you? I've done everything you've ever asked of me. I know so much. No one can criticize the stories I file for TASS. I am, as the Americans say, a star reporter. Who else but me could wrangle interviews with the most important men in this town? For God's sake, I'm friendly with Drew Pearson, the American journalist with ties to the White House."

"I know that, but don't threaten me." Zabotin shook his head. "I'll see what I can do, if there is anything at all to do. Don't expect too much."

"Whatever you say. Forgive me. But shouldn't I be able to hope that I might reunite with my family?"

"Don't apologize for wanting what we all want," he said curtly.

Zabotin rang the embassy, calling for the limousine. As in capital cities across the world, diplomats were ferried about in black limousines every hour of the day and night. Surely no one would notice him leave the safe house as he slipped into the back seat, holding the morning edition of *The Ottawa Citizen* up to his eyes.

Before leaving, he ordered, "Lock the door behind you and hide the key. You may need it some day."

* * *

Chernobyl journal
1988

In the contaminated Chernobyl forest, there are no limousines, only broken down Ladas, the Soviet Union's contribution to the automobile industry. Nikolai keeps one running, for his own use, a yellow-two door with one working headlight, for when he wishes to hunt at his dacha or visit old friends in Kiev. When I accompany him, we often talk about our days and nights in Ottawa, the luxury of the safe house on the canal, the starched white sheets, the black caviar and Turkish coffee. How we'd tried to fool ourselves into believing that our louche life in Ottawa could continue. Now we drink ground chicory root in the mornings and wash our rough linen in the river.

From the bedroom window of the cabin, I watch the huge grey-stained raindrops fall from the trees. The thick foliage is so intertwined that it camouflages our home. We haven't bothered cutting down the flowering bushes or the burgeoning branches of the birch trees. The grass is overgrown. The birds are free to hop from their perches high in the trees to peck at the rubbish littering the ground. When we are feeling energetic, we bury the garbage, but most days it sits atop the radioactive earth.

There is an enchanting variety of birds I have not seen anywhere else: huge muscular birds, colourful, coated with fat and feathers and chirping deliriously joyful songs. A mother deer and her babies feed by the window. The smallest colt has only one eye. It is either heaven or hell in Chernobyl, depending on your point of view. The sound of the rain lulls me back to my memories of Canada.

Chapter Nine

August 31, 1945
Ottawa

On that Friday morning in the safe house I didn't bother summoning a taxi, although Zabotin left me ten dollars on the armoire. Generous to a fault, but indiscreet. When he told me that he'd been withholding information about the atomic bomb from the Director in Moscow, he was putting his life in my hands. Why hadn't he sent the diagrams to the GRU earlier, the minute Vine brought them from Los Alamos? Even knowing about the stolen cryptograms was out of line. I couldn't be certain if he needed to confide in me, if he trusted me that completely, or he was drawing me into the abyss with him. I was certain the Director would discover that Zabotin had held back the diagrams since June, a critical time since the Americans had only tested their first atomic bomb that July in New Mexico.

I left the safe house through the servants' door. On one of the last Fridays of summer it was the best kind of August day: shining blue sky, hot and dry, with the faint scent of a northern wind bristling in the air. I had plenty of time to return to my flat, wash, drink more coffee and apologize to Harry Vine. To be with Zabotin, I'd skipped out on dinner with Vine and the other comrades who lived in my building. I'd neglected to let Vine know in advance I wouldn't be joining them. When I returned he would be waiting for me, figuring that I hadn't come home because I was with Zabotin. Vine didn't care for Zabotin anymore than the rezident appreciated him.

And, still I deferred to Vine's moods. For years, I wasn't certain why I did, but what I figured was in some corner of my mind, he made me feel smaller than I was, as if he owned me. Without him, I'd never have survived the invasion of Hitler's army. He got me out. Stories of entire villages of Jews rounded up and shot were circulating. Without him, I'd be nothing. I'd be dead. Another ghost.

In some way, I also admired Vine and his undying devotion to the cause. When the Communist Party of Canada was declared illegal, Vine lived on the lam, only coming out of hiding after the Soviets declared war on Germany. After that, he continued to sleep wherever a comrade offered a sofa, not wishing to find a permanent home.

Now that the war was over, Vine couldn't adjust. He never admitted that he relished his unconventional life, but he did say he couldn't imagine living any other way.

Only yesterday, he'd sighed, half smiling, "Too old to change now." None of us knew how to return to normal, if there was such a thing for old hands like us. The temptation was to make matters worse, more dangerous, rather than fading into the woodwork of a typically serene Canadian existence. The more I came to learn about what happened to the Jews in Europe, the more vulnerable I felt; less innocent, and more indebted to Vine.

I'd suggested to Vine that he could change, get a job and start a family. "It's never too late," I told him.

He shook his head as if I were a madwoman gibbering nonsense. "What makes you think the Party would even allow it?" he asked me. "You want to try it, settling down? One of your contacts must be looking for a good wife."

After leaving the safe house, I walked along the canal all the way to the lift-iron bridge, the one I'd crossed with Zabotin a few days ago, before he'd told me about the atomic diagrams and how he'd concealed them from the Director. I continued on to Elgin Street. Smug-looking men and women were rushing into government offices, civil servants with safe jobs and humdrum lives. For a moment, I felt the old sensation I'd had when Vine and I were first in Canada. I wanted to be seen. I wished to scream that I'd slept with dozens of men, strangers to me, on behalf of the Party, on behalf of peace.

I carried on across Somerset, crossed at the light at Bank Street and over to my second-floor flat on Florence. The walkway to my apartment was shaded by a canopy of pink climbing roses in the final blush of summer. I felt like an unfaithful bride returning home to her cuckolded husband. As always, I was the guilty one.

Vine made me feel that way. Under his critical eye, I felt shame, unworthy of his praise or even of his companionship. No matter how hard I tried, I wasn't good enough to stand on the same carpet as Harry Vine and his great martyrs to the Revolution. How could I continue to pretend that I hadn't contributed to the mayhem? That I was innocent of the evil that had overtaken the world?

When I turned the key, he was waiting for me in the vestibule. Either Vine had been peering through the keyhole or he heard me climb the steps and scrambled to meet me.

He was shorter than me by a few inches. Small and wiry, with the same straight hair, as fiery red as it had been on the day we left Nesvicz. Now he combed his hair directly back from his high forehead. Steel-rimmed spectacles didn't begin to camouflage his critical eyes.

Vine didn't ask me where I'd been. It was not in his nature to inquire or implore. Long ago, we'd established that it was dangerous for either of us to know the precise details of each other's clandestine work. That was the way it was between us. His eyes did not meet mine, nor did he address me directly. He'd never admit to being jealous of Zabotin, but I knew he resented my special friendship with our rezident. He believed that Zabotin was interested in me only because of my work for the Party, and that the personal attention he paid to me was false and without true feeling.

"You are making a fool of yourself, with Zabotin," Vine said as I entered the living room of the flat on Florence. He sneered at me. "Is this why I brought you out of Europe?" he scoffed as if he was newly scandalized by my activities, as if I was the dirty one and he was above the sacrifices the Party ordered us both to undertake. "Zabotin is using you."

"You think you are so much better than me?" I asked him.

On the wooden table in the living room that served as a desk and a dining table, a coal-black Remington typewriter sat uncovered. Vine had been up all night, as he often was, composing Fred Rose's next speech to be delivered in the House in Commons.

We were amazed when Rose took the Montreal riding of Cartier for the Party. When the election results rolled in, I thought it was a mistake. The first Communist Member of Parliament in Canada! We adored him for winning and for his affable and humble manners. Fred didn't frighten people the way Vine did, but it was Vine who wrote his speeches and weekly radio broadcasts for the Montreal riding that voted Communist. In fact, it was Vine who engineered the entire election campaign. While Rose was occupied with Parliament and his frequent meetings with Zabotin, it was Vine who condensed the missives of our clandestine ring into intelligible, and I must admit, creative reports for the rezident who handed them over to Gouzenko to encrypt and submit to Moscow. That was how the chain worked throughout the war.

While Vine was up nights interpreting our cell's activities for Moscow, Zabotin and Rose were found drinking vodka together in the bar at the Château Laurier. Zabotin enjoyed Rose's humorous tales of life in the Montreal Jewish ghetto. When I was sitting at a separate table with a contact in the Château's bar, neither Rose nor Zabotin paid me any attention. They only waved and looked the other way. It was crucial that they not appear to be in cahoots with the reporter from TASS.

When there was a dangerous mission, it was Vine who Zabotin chose, sending him to Los Alamos and Chalk River to collect information about the bomb for the Director.

"Sit down," Vine said, pointing to the straight-backed chair he'd used throughout the night. "Why do you resent me, Freda?"

"I don't. This is childish. What do you want?" I needed to get ready for work. I was late already.

Vine sat in another chair facing me. He pulled it close. "You think it would have been better for you in Nesvicz?"

"Different. I've sacrificed everything for the Party."

"You would have married a Yeshiva boy and had eight children, of which at least two would die or be taken in the army as my brother Yitzhak was. Your life would be small—no, minuscule, living inside a backward community that was bound to be destroyed."

There was truth to what Vine said, but instead of acknowledging it I replied by saying, " Your Yitzhak was a Yeshiva boy. Maybe a young man like that would have been a kind and faithful husband."

Vine was on the verge of a confession, but he was holding back. "He died. Either Zabotin killed him or riding with the Cavalry did him in. He was never strong and I've noticed that you prefer strong men."

He was right. Weaklings didn't do much for me.

"You can sit back here and wonder all you want about what happened in Nesvicz, but I'm going to find the truth. I'm going to find my family. Don't try to talk me out of it."

I'd kept secret from Vine, my plan to rescue my family. I believed he would denounce me, his index finger in the air, demanding that I do my duty in Canada working for the Soviets.

Instead Vine looked at me incredulously, and a little sadly, as if I were a naughty child. "How might they have survived the war? Aren't you reading the news? What happened over there, it can't be changed. You think you've sacrificed everything, but what have you done?"

Vine didn't want to understand. He could never admit that I'd done as much for the Party as he had. More so, he was afraid of finding out what actually happened to our people back home.

"In Nesvicz, you and your little children would be dead by now," he sighed. "You are dreaming of a world that no longer exists."

"Then what are we fighting for?" I asked. "I'm going to find them."

Vine pulled his chair closer to me, so near I could feel his breath on my face. "You are still beautiful."

I thought he would take me in his arms after so many years of resistance, but instead he said, "I can smell Zabotin on you. Go wash. Get to work."

When I rose to leave, my face flushed, he squeezed my hand. "I've already spoken with Zabotin. He's called off my trip to see Nunn May at Chalk River. He says it's too delicate now. Too dicey. What do you think? Is he lying?"

Zabotin had ordered me not to mention anything to Vine, but it was impossible. "He is telling the truth. Don't go now. Don't get any crazy ideas to disobey his orders either." Vine needed to know about the missing crypto-grams, about Gouzenko. It would stop him from acting on his own.

I couldn't be sure if the rezident had enlightened him. They were al-ways at odds and lately it was worse. It was Vine's idea to bring back the formula for the atomic bomb from Los Alamos. Zabotin only directed Vine to report on the activity in New Mexico, but he came back with the prize in his hand. If he was searched at the border, how would he have explained the drawings? But Vine returned safely with them. I expected Zabotin to treat him like a hero, but he did nothing, not even send the diagrams to Moscow.

"I'm telling you this, but you must never repeat it. Not to anybody—especially not Zabotin. Do you know about the cryptograms?" I murmured. "The ones that Gouzenko sends to Moscow."

"Of course. He encrypts my reports for delivery to Moscow, as he has done throughout the war."

"They are missing."

"Missing? Well, I don't believe anyone will notice. I try to make them sound more important than they are. I crib stories from the newspapers to satisfy the Centre's appetite."

"But they will notice. If they fall into the wrong hands, your notes will incriminate all of us—Rose, Zabotin, you and me."

Vine didn't know that Zabotin hadn't sent Fuchs' formula to the Director. That was something he'd neglected to tell him.

"The Canadians consider the Soviets their best friends. Why would anyone bother stealing these cables?" he asked.

I had no answer—at least not one I could admit to Vine. "I'm going to dress," I said. "You figure it out."

I was relieved that Zabotin, for now, had cancelled Vine's trip to Chalk River, but worried that he'd decided to keep him in the dark about withholding the atomic diagrams from Stalin. But it wasn't my place to fill in Vine. That bit was the responsibility of our rezident, and I knew better than to overreach my standing in the Party.

Chapter Ten

I cherished my flat on Florence Street, which was only a mile or so south of the Parliament Buildings. My books were piled high on roughly hewn boards balanced on mustard yellow bricks. Alone in my flat, I felt Bohemian, what I might have been had I arrived in Canada and not joined the Party. I'd painted the entire flat white to make the space appear larger, except for the galley kitchen, where I'd inherited purple-wisteria-decaled wallpaper from the old woman who lived here before me. In the mornings, it suited me and reminded me of Nesvicz; of my mother's little desk beside the stove where she wrote Yiddish poetry to read to me and sister Masha.

In my apartment, a window opened outward from the kitchen. Ivy grew clinging to the wooden frame and stretched across to my bedroom window. By August the windows were overgrown with dark green foliage that kept the rooms cool. My friend Sybil, who shared an apartment in my building with her mother, had crocheted a blanket for me, and I kept it spread across my bed that summer. It was such a hot summer, the nights smelling sweetly of pine and roses, the blanket was all I needed to be cozy. Under the mattress, I hid two hundred dollars alongside the code names and numbers of the comrades I would call if the time came. I also kept a picture of my family that Masha had sent before the Russian post stopped for good.

My bed was a feather mattress on an iron frame, but it was all that I desired. Rarely did I bring my contacts back home. It was much too plain and I never knew when Vine would turn up. Although it seemed now that I shouldn't be expecting him to drop by anytime soon. That morning, after Vine and I had spoken about the missing cryptograms, he decided to stop speaking to me, as if it were my fault that they'd gone astray.

Sybil lived below me on the main floor of the building, and when she would enter my flat, she used the fire escape. Her flat was a two bedroom that overlooked the garden. She and her mother had entered Canada illegally, after the Canadian government slammed the door on those fleeing Hitler. Sybil and her mother Zsuzsa were Romanian and stalwart members of the Party. I think Zabotin liked the idea that the two kept on eye on me when he couldn't, although I wasn't certain how accurate their reports were to my handler on my nocturnal comings and goings. At the same time, Sybil, who was fond of Vine, knew instantly when there was trouble between us, like she did that morning when she came up via the fire escape.

"Yowzah," she said and whistled through her teeth. Sybil was like a carny barking from the big top. "What gives with you two?"

I entered the front room, where Sybil's head poked through the window.

"Can't you two stop talking and let a girl get a word in edgewise?" she shouted in her greenhorn English. She sensed there was trouble between Vine and me whenever the room went silent. This wasn't the first time Sybil had found us at odds.

As she descended from the wrought-iron fire escape to lower herself to the living room floor, neither he nor I uttered a word. Sybil's kimono rode high over her generous hips. I was dressed for the office and Vine, who wasn't on speaking terms with me, offered a polite hello to our visitor

"Why don't you join us for a nosh?" she asked us. "Mama's made cherry blintzes with sour cream and sugar." Sybil's hair was chestnut, lush, and tied in a swirling chignon. Now in her cabin in the Chernobyl forest, she wears a babushka over her thinning grey hair, but that morning in Ottawa she wore a pink silk kimono decorated with flowers. I remember it because she brought it to Europe with her from Canada.

"You skipped dinner last night," she said to me. "Fred was here and Vine too, weren't you, fella? Mama made chicken paprikash and veal roulade and potato knishes. You should have been here. Fred says you're too skinny."

I looked kindly at Sybil, who enjoyed her mother's food.

"C'mon downstairs," she said. "I'll pack you a lunch of leftovers from dinner." She sounded as if she'd just stepped off the boat, and there was something about her openness about her past that reminded me of the way we'd talked back home.

Until that day, I'd never spoken publically about the people I'd left behind in Europe, and I couldn't understand why Sybil felt the need. Her father and brothers were captured by the Fascists and drowned in the Danube. It was better to remain silent and to be strong. Tim Buck taught me that when I joined the Party.

"Give the leftovers to Vine," I said.

Without looking at me, Vine knotted his tie tight while standing in front of the mirror above the gas fireplace. "I won't be having breakfast this morning, thank you," he said to Sybil while ignoring me completely. "Or lunch, for that matter." He claimed he had important writing to do and didn't have time to eat or gossip with women. I followed her down the fire escape to her apartment.

Sybil's flat, unlike my own, was awash in colour. Landscapes covered the walls. She painted them when she wasn't fussing over Fred Rose. Most of the canvasses were dreamy depictions of the Gatineau Hills, northeast of us and across the river, in Quebec.

"How is Fred doing in the House of Commons?" I asked Sybil as we sipped Turkish coffee and nibbled at chocolate halvah at her dining table.

"*Vey iz mir!*" she shouted, holding her head in her hands. "Busy. That man will perish slaving for the Party. In the summer, he can't breathe. His asthma. He can't sleep."

"Vine doesn't sleep. I hear him crying at night." The words tumbled out of my mouth.

Sybil put her hand to her heart.

Her mother's grand piano stood in the adjoining drawing room dominating the apartment. Before the war, she was a rather famous concert pianist in Bucharest. Her husband, György Romanescu, owned the city's finest department store. Before the Nazis took over, he shipped the piano from their luxurious home to Canada. He wanted his wife to play after his demise.

"Last night I was with Zabotin," I confessed to Sybil.

"Lucky you."

"He promised to help me return to Europe. To find my mama and papa, my sister and brother. I shall board a ship to Danzig and go by train to Minsk. From there it is not far to Nesvicz. Zabotin will arrange for passage. He promised."

Sybil looked at me disapprovingly.

"He gave me his word," I dissembled.

"*Gay, guzunta hiat.*"

Sybil spoke Yiddish when she was vexed or frightened. It was the perfect language to talk of catastrophes. It annoyed me that she lapsed into Yiddish so often and didn't attempt to enlarge her English vocabulary. I was perpetually reminding her to speak in English. I wanted her to be more Canadian than she cared to be.

Sybil spent her days caring for her mother or scurrying between the apartment and Fred Rose's office in the centre block on Parliament Hill. She ran errands for him, often to Montreal, with instructions for the comrades who were also engaged by Zabotin and the GRU. Rose didn't need to pay Sybil. The Romanescu women had money. It was rumoured they had smuggled diamonds into Canada sewn inside the hems of their skirts.

"Aren't you scared to go back there?" she asked, making a face and running her index finger across her throat.

Before I could respond, Zsuzsa Romanescu swept into the room. Unlike her daughter, she was petite and small-boned, elegantly wrapped in an ivory sateen dressing gown that perfectly matched her tinted hair. "Are you out of your mind, Freda?" she asked, jumping into our conversation, on which she clearly had been eavesdropping from the next room. "Give it a few years, and the Soviet flag will be planted on Polish soil. Then you can go safely. It's too dangerous for a woman on her own right now."

"Thank you for your advice, Madam Romanescu," I said politely. "But I must leave soon. I can't wait. My family might be alive. I could get them out. Zabotin wouldn't arrange the trip if he didn't believe I would be safe."

Zsuzsa clicked her tongue.

"I have to go. Nesvicz haunts my dreams," I spoke softly to the women.

LAST NIGHT OF THE WORLD

I didn't wish to alarm them, but I couldn't control myself. "It's all I see at night." The two woman said nothing and I continued. "I am standing at the kitchen window with Mama and Papa. A little musical band of Jewish men, dressed in black, is crossing the icy river that flows through the village. Our elderly rabbi with the long white beard is leading his troupe through the blowing snow. Some of the players are smiling, some frowning. The butcher is carrying his cello over his shoulder. The baker is smoking a pipe as he taps his tambourine. A black bird flies overhead. Beside the rabbi walks a skeleton, but the band members take no notice, not even the red-haired young triangle player who lags far behind."

Sybil put her hand on my shoulder. "Vey, vey. What are you talking about?"

I stood up to leave.

"How about a *bisl* poppy seed cake from last night?" Zsuzsa offered, an ocean of her concern floating in my direction. "Sit, sit. You've been working hard. Too many assignments, too many long nights." She sighed and looked toward the heavens where the God she didn't believe in must reign.

Sybil noticed Vine first. As soon as I saw him kneeling on the fire escape landing outside the Romanescu's apartment, I sank into a chair and turned my back to him. I was not able to face him. He was on his hands and knees while he listened to me recall my dreams, his ear next to the open window. His face was white and I could tell he knew exactly what I meant about the skeleton, marching behind the rabbi. He never admitted it, but I knew he'd snuck in the cinema to watch the newsreels of the walking skeletons released from the camps. I heard him through the thin walls of my apartment, calling out for his mother and brother in his sleep.

On those nights I covered my head with a pillow to block out the noise. I slept fitfully and could not fall back asleep in the wake of Vine's nightmares. I imagined the pictures in his mind when he cried out, but I, too, carried visions in those days before I knew with certainty what had happened to my family during the war. I never comforted him in the night. I couldn't. If I had gone to Vine, sat on the side of his bed, placed my hand on his forehead, wiped his tears away, my world would stop. I would crumble.

I was late for work. I forced myself to stand up straight and walk out the door. I reminded myself that some got away, all of them unsuspecting, never knowing why they'd cheated death. Why couldn't my family be among the chosen few?

* * *

Chernobyl journal
1988

In the forest, I met a woman named Elka who looked much older than me although she must have been ten years younger. She dyed her white hair with henna until it turned a ghostly pinkish grey. Her face was a map of Eastern Europe, indented with smallpox scars deep as ravines. The lurid blue veins in her nose ran wild in all directions.

During the war, Elka had fought alongside the partisans, existing in makeshift shelters in the forest, summer and winter. She sided with the Communists since they were the only ones unyielding enough to outlast the Fascists. Only the Communist cadres could muster up the unbreakable courage to confront the Wehrmacht, she repeated many times.

She told me that when she returned to her village after the war, not one Jew had survived so she decided to walk into the Dnieper River to drown herself. Admittedly it was an act of cowardice, she said, one the Party would condemn; but for that moment, she soared above politics. A young Soviet officer pulled her from the current just as she was going down for the third time. He threw her in prison where she languished for weeks until a stranger from Jewish Rescue Services discovered her and sent her by ship to the port of Haifa.

Elka couldn't stand the Levantine heat or be bothered to learn the Hebrew language. It was impossible for her to share in the optimism at the founding of the new state of Israel where she lived with a small sect of religious Jews. They took her on, more as a matter of conscience than as a convert.

"They sensed that it was too late for me and God," she said. "Because I was good at solving puzzles they sent me—on a scholarship for survivors—to the Teknion in Haifa where the most clever physicists and engineers were working on the atomic bomb."

After five years—she had managed to stick it out for that long—she booked passage on a ship to Piraeus. Athens delighted her. She longed to visit the Acropolis, having seen pictures of it in a book as a child. In the Plaka, she discovered a lodging house where everyone ate bacon and mixed milk with meat, something she missed doing in Haifa. After two months exploring the Plaka, she carried on to Kiev, satisfied that she'd finally experienced the louche life while schooling herself in the architecture of the ancient world.

"La guerre n'est pas finie," I responded when we first spoke in the forest, but Elka disregarded my warning with a brush of her hand. "I'd fought enough by the time I arrived in Greece. It's one of the reasons I left Israel," she said firmly. When I asked her what happened to her partisan comrades, she clamped her lips shut and drew a line across her neck with her forefinger.

In Kiev, she had continued her studies in nuclear physics at the university. She claimed that she preferred the climate in the Ukraine to that of Israel and relished hiking in the woods on her days off from the lab where she helped to build the Soviet nuclear arsenal.

"I've had a life," she said in her matter-of-fact way, as if what she'd experienced wasn't much at all. "Not that I'm complaining. It doesn't pay to whine. I've never wanted jewels," she added, stretching out her bare, gnarled fingers for me to inspect. "I've never needed a husband or children. They slow you down. I prefer it this way. No ties."

Elka asked me if I'd ever made love in the snow, and when I said I had not, she prodded me to try it. I thought it ridiculous that two old crones were discussing sex in the snow, but Elka insisted on giving me the details.

"I'm resistant to the cold," she said. "Nothing bothers me after spending long winters in sub-zero temperatures with the partisans. The winter of '42 was the coldest on record. God had forsaken us in more ways than one. How about you? Could you have stood it, the cold?"

"I doubt it," I admitted. "When my friend Zabotin first took me to his dacha, I was freezing even though there was a wood stove and fur blankets."

Elka thought it necessary that I toughen up if I intended to remain in Chernobyl, and when I argued I was tough enough, she smirked and I could see the gaps in her broken teeth.

She was excited by my mention of Zabotin's dacha. Her eyes became slits. "Are you referring to Nikolai Zabotin, the count who became a Red Cavalry officer? The one who ended up in Canada and then returned to Chernobyl of his own free will?"

"Not quite of his own free will."

"Ah. I thought there was more to the story." Elka clenched her teeth, satisfied she'd been correct all along. "I can't see him as the comrade he should have been. Wasn't he at Reactor Number Four when it blew?"

How did she know so much about Zabotin? It made me suspicious. I wanted to question Elka, but I was afraid.

The other day I bumped into her picking mushrooms in our Chernobyl forest. The plants were enormous, as broad and succulent as watermelons. Elka was intending to boil up a mushroom pudding on her wood-fired stove. She'd learned how to cook while in the forest with the partisans, she informed me.

There's a rocky path above the forest's steepest ravine overlooking a squalid hut. When it rains, mud creeps down to the water that collects in the crevice of the ravine. Elka squats in that hut, smaller than mine, and more Spartan because she chooses to live alone. The walls are covered with portraits of Soviet leaders, beginning with Lenin and ending with Gorbachev. She invited me in for nettle tea and blackberries, and I agreed to partake of her hospitality.

PART TWO

Chapter Eleven

Friday morning
August 31, 1945
Ottawa

It was after ten by the time I caught the Bank Street bus to work. I couldn't face going straight to the TASS office. Instead I stopped at Party headquarters, a stuffy two-room affair above a pool hall on the French side of town. If anyone took notice, there was nothing strange about a Soviet journalist visiting Communist Party headquarters, not that summer. Giant-sized, sepia-toned photos of Marx and Lenin lined the walls, along with rows of musty books: the complete works of Lenin, all of Marx and Engels, each bound in leatherette with gilt lettering. A green shade was drawn tight against the one window that opened onto the street. The office was airless, the ceiling low. Tea streaks stained the creaking linoleum floor; dirty cups were scattered around the room.

The head of the Canada–Soviet Friendship Committee was asleep at her grey steel desk, her head drooping backward, snoring. Two other matching metal desks were laden with books, pamphlets and twine-bound copies of *The Masses*, the Party's weekly newspaper. Above the fold of that week's edition a photo of Stalin shaking hands with Tim Buck stared up at me. Buck was smiling broadly, and it reminded me of how he'd looked when he first convinced me to turn informants for the cause.

I removed the loose brick next to the mantle above the gas fireplace where messages were dead-dropped for me. It was safer than leaving them at my flat. But the drop was empty. Nothing new from Zabotin. Sometimes he had a courier leave orders for me, but not that day.

Just before I'd left Florence Street, Vine jumped from Sybil's fire escape to land inside the apartment. "Convince Zabotin to send me back to Los Alamos," he pleaded, the desperation bringing to an end his vow of silence with me. "By now Fuchs will have new drawings for a bigger, more powerful bomb than Fat Man. Nagasaki was obliterated. By now, I bet, they'll have a bigger one. Why doesn't Zabotin realize he won't find anything spectacular at Chalk River?"

"How could you possibly know all this, about the bomb?" I asked him. Was Zabotin talking on the side to Vine, trying to play us off against each other? "It's too dangerous," I said. You can't be serious about meeting with Fuchs now?"

"I am serious," Vine said. "After Japan, there's no turning back."

He was ashamed I'd seen him falling apart at Sybil's window, and now, to make up for the shame of it, he was all bravado with his talk of returning to Los Alamos. I wasn't certain that he realized I'd also overheard him weeping at night. Yet again, he was determined to be courageous, to be bolder than a ghetto Jew. To fight back, no matter what the consequences. I admired him for his resolve to escape his past, but Vine was having a difficult time now that the war was over and the sloganeering of the Party was beginning to sound outdated. Chants such as "Workers of the world unite…" were sounding hollow. The soldiers were returning home to their wives and kids. What they yearned for was peace and quiet on a shady street in the safest country on earth. If Vine was posturing, I could understand. If he meant what he was saying, I could see why Zabotin believed the USSR would use the bomb if the scientists built it.

Now that Moscow was intent on stealing the formula for the atomic bomb, Vine would be the one to risk his life to get it, or he claimed he was. Yet, I was unclear about Zabotin. Would he send Vine back to New Mexico? If he did, he'd have to own up to the Director that the original drawings were missing.

At TASS, the atmosphere was light-hearted. My Russian colleagues were rejoicing now that the war was over. Somehow they'd survived when millions of patriots were dead fighting for Mother Russia. They were among the lucky ones, sent by *Pravda* to cover the war from Ottawa. Some were intending to bring their families to Ottawa. I was the only reporter working directly for the GRU, although I assumed that at least one other journalist was a NKVD operative.

My editor, Comrade Tabachnick, liked to tell racy jokes. He wired our stories about Canadian–Soviet friendship to TASS headquarters in Moscow.

"Miss Linton," he said, looking straight at my chest. "So glad you've decided to join us today." His wife and children lived on rations in Russia.

Everyone in the office laughed. I did too, not wanting to interrupt the jolly atmosphere. The only other woman at TASS was Irina, a twenty-eight-year-old blonde with chiselled features. She'd suffered from such severe malnutrition as a child that she was painfully bow-legged. "No protein in my diet," she explained. Her husband was among the first to die when the Red Army fought the Nazi invasion.

At my desk, I took a lipstick from the side drawer and slid it over my lips. I didn't need a mirror. I could paint my face in the dark.

Upstairs above my cubicle I heard the footsteps of the filmmakers, the editors and cameramen milling around the Wartime Information Office. John Grierson, the director of Canadian wartime propaganda, hadn't shown up. When he arrived, I would hear him. He shouted when he talked and the building was poorly insulated. I was waiting for him, but I was too impatient to sit still.

I climbed up the stairs to stand outside Grierson's office and stood facing the typing pool. None of the women smiled at me. The close of the war meant the end of their jobs and they were on tenterhooks for the word from Grierson. It was time for me to face this fact, too. Grierson had commissioned films to stoke up support for the Soviets fighting Nazis on the Eastern front. Now there would be no need for more documentaries from Canada. Perhaps the TASS office would close as well and I'd lose my cover. Then where would I be? I could only hope that Zabotin would send me back to the East to hunt for my family. Nothing else mattered, I reminded myself.

When Grierson turned up, I brought him his coffee, black, as I always did when I visited his office. He clenched the cup as he unlocked the door to his office, and placed his briefcase on the mahogany desk. The desk was a gift from TASS. The girls in the typing pool assumed I was interviewing Grierson for a story in the Soviet press. During the war, Canadians appreciated the attention given them by TASS, and more than ever, they wished to keep the news stories of Canadian heroism coming, now that the Americans were taking all the credit for winning the war. My stories made the locals happy.

As soon as Grierson settled in behind his desk, I snapped the door shut to the office and locked it. He wasn't a tall man, not like Zabotin, but he was confident. Curly brown hair parted neatly to the side, a strong chin and a wry smile. A filmmaker's curious gaze in a Savile Row suit and a black bowler hat.

Grierson was lured from Britain to launch Canada's National Film Board. The artsy community doted on Grierson, and so did the government. He was exactly the kind of Brit they wanted to manage their information services: suave, cultured, with inroads to tastemakers across the pond. When Canada declared war on Germany, the prime minister asked him to run the Wartime Information Office. At the same time, he was working for me on behalf of Zabotin and the GRU. A longtime fellow traveller from his Cambridge days, Grierson was a rebel with friends in the right places, and because he was creative and bold, he understood how film could be used as propaganda. He wasn't the first either. Sergei Eisenstein in Russia and Leni Riefenstahl in Nazi Germany had shown him the way.

Any news that I've picked up about Grierson during my years in Chernobyl showed that Canadians still called him the father of Canadian documentary film. He is revered. No one ever alludes to why he disappeared in 1946. Perhaps no one recalls or wishes to remember.

How the Soviets had manipulated cinema during the halcyon days of the Revolution was a never-ending revelation to Grierson. In Ottawa, he was fond of saying "Art is not a mirror, but a hammer. It is a weapon in our hands to see what is good and right and beautiful." For Grierson's sake, I hoped he was correct. He was my other choice, the man who might rescue me from the trap I was falling into. If I stayed in Ottawa, and Zabotin and I survived the Centre's response to the missing cables, I would never be free. The Party would own me.

Vine wasn't the answer, either. I feared at the time that he would devise a way to implicate himself or self-destruct trying to please his masters in Moscow. It was his only way of keeping the darkness at bay, of facing what happened to his family in Nesvicz, the little people he and I abandoned. That morning at Florence Street confirmed my fears.

"I rang you last night," Grierson said. "Vine answered. He's often at your place."

I was tempted to tell him about the missing cables and about Gouzenko's recall to Moscow, but I decided against it. The less Grierson knew, the better. That was how the game was played; that was how Zabotin and Buck had trained me.

From his open pack of cigarettes, I took a Sweet Caporal.

"Vine told me you weren't in and when I called back after eleven, you still weren't back," said Grierson. He was upset with me.

I wasn't in the mood to comfort him. Grierson had agreed, when I first convinced him to work with us, never to indulge in questioning me about private matters.

"Where were you, Freda?"

I shot him a disappointed look. A broken-hearted operative was a liability to the Centre. But I sensed that knowing the rules and then trying to break them on my account, made Grierson want me more.

I was never certain how far he would go. If he would disregard orders, and ignore Moscow's code of conduct. What he would do under pressure, would take time for me to know, but I understood that he was a true believer, as only a British-born Communist could be. Like other men of his ilk, Grierson would risk everything for the cause. It was more a calling for him than it was for me or Zabotin or even Vine. For us it was a historical necessity; we were born into it, the turmoil and the necessity to choose sides. Grierson was propelled by idealism rather than historical circumstances, and it made me pity him and think less of him.

In Chernobyl I am often tempted to tell Elka about Grierson, and how Moscow and Zabotin destroyed him, although Elka would applaud Grierson's overwhelming need to be a warrior for the cause. To fall on his sword rather than betray us. I don't believe he ever considered going over to the other side, or exposing us to the Canadian authorities. I knew from the beginning that jealousy would be his downfall. He adored me, as only a certain kind of man can love a woman, quietly and without much fuss, but with the deepest of emotion. Grierson confessed his longings and his dreams to me. I was his sore point, his Achilles heel.

When Gouzenko came clean, about the ring of spies run by Zabotin, Grierson might have gotten away unscathed. But when Gouzenko's revelations lit the spark that ignited the Cold War, Grierson acted on my behalf, as I knew he would. He never recovered.

"What else did Vine say?" I asked him. From the look in his eyes, I could see Grierson knew about my rendezvous with Zabotin, but tried to hide his anxiety that he could lose me entirely to our handler by pressing too hard.

"Just that you were out, probably with Zabotin, and that you would be home before eleven, but you didn't come home, did you?"

Grierson tried to cover his need to know everything about me by rising from his desk and looking out the window toward the Department of Defense.

"Do you think Zabotin will help me find my family? The people I left behind?" For Grierson's own sake, I wanted him to understand my motives.

"I'm certain he will. Zabotin is a man of his word." No matter how overwhelming his feelings for me, he admired our rezident. He turned to clutch my hand. "Do you think now is the time to return to the Soviet Union? I'd prefer you remain here with me. Or possibly I could accompany you, help you to find your people. You'd be surprised what doors are open to a filmmaker." Grierson sat on the easy chair facing his desk.

"Particularly one who has been such a brave supporter of the motherland," I added.

He rubbed his delicate hands together. "Stalin is making great strides," Grierson said, motioning me to sit on his lap.

How naïve this man was! Sophisticated and clueless at the same time. I thought about Nesvicz and how I would appear to him if I were standing in the village square today, me and the ghosts.

"Come away with me, Freda, this weekend, to Montebello. It's been months since you agreed to an entire weekend," he pleaded.

I understood that I was everything to him. In a moment of weakness, he'd confessed to me that he'd never felt for a woman the way he did for me. He'd admitted that his good friend, Preston Ellery, who was the Canadian Ambassador to the United States, had cautioned him about me, advising Grierson that an infatuation with a woman like me was dangerous business. Ellery would be back in Ottawa for the Labour Day weekend.

"Preston flew in last night and he wants to talk."

"Go," I said. "Spend the weekend with him. He'll be much better company than me."

By his expression, I could see that Grierson had expected me to put up a fight.

"Preston believes the Americans want me to come to Washington to run their new film board," he said standing up.

I straightened my skirt to sit on his desk. "Go," I said again. "Washington is important. The Centre would approve." I crossed my legs.

"Come with me," he said. "To Washington."

"Soon, if not already, the Americans will know that I work for the Soviets. I would be a huge liability to you."

Grierson didn't believe me. "Let's take the weekend to discuss a move to Washington. We would be in an envious position to help the Soviet Union. I would only accept the position if you were with me as…"

He was going to say as my wife, but I interrupted him. He was breaking the rules of the game. In truth, I could never leave Vine or Zabotin. I wasn't made that way. If the missing cables were discovered, I'd still press Zabotin to send me back to Russia. After the scandal blew over, I wanted to believe I could settle in Ottawa with my family, whatever was left of it. I'd never leave the country. No one would care about our little family from Nesvicz and how we survived the war.

I was about to turn the lock on the door and depart, when Grierson invited me to join him and Ellery for lunch. "Preston has his table at the Laurier Club."

"Preston won't appreciate my company," I said truthfully.

"To the contrary. He enjoys the company of beautiful women."

After I left Grierson's office I went back downstairs to TASS to use the short-wave radio in the locked cupboard to notify Zabotin I'd be lunching with Preston Ellery and Grierson at the Laurier Club. Zabotin fired back immediately confirming that his own man, Oleg, an undercover operative, would also be listening in on the conversation, memorizing every word. I knew Oleg from previous jobs he'd taken on for the GRU. He descended from a long line of memory wizards, his father having spied on Czar Nicholas II for the Bolsheviks, and his great-grandfather on the Decembrists for Nicholas I. His work was irreproachable.

Chapter Twelve

The Laurier Club, the private club for Liberals, occupied the corner of an elm-lined avenue, blocks from the University of Ottawa. It was on the old French side of town, where Catholic priests, dressed in billowing black cassocks, meandered along the shady streets in summer, and in winter walked gingerly upon the icy pavement between the university's austere limestone buildings.

A government limo delivered Grierson and me to the iron gates of the club. We were eager to avoid the burning afternoon sun so we quickly climbed the stairs to enter the grand foyer. The grey-haired maître d' directed us to the lounge where Preston Ellery was waiting, sipping a whisky and soda.

Ottawa was abuzz with the rumour that Ellery was the top contender for the Secretary-General's position at the UN. Before Grierson even sat down, he congratulated Ellery on his accomplishment, as if it was a foregone conclusion. Then he introduced me to Ellery who didn't bother to stand when he shook my hand.

Grierson and Ellery ignored Oleg, who stood at attention, ready to lead us to our table and serve lunch.

"I know who you are, Miss Linton. My friendship with John goes back to university days in England. We keep no secrets," confessed Ellery.

"How nice for you both, keeping no secrets. I wish I had friends like you."

"When John told me you'd be joining us for lunch I was pleasantly surprised. I've decided to speak openly in front of you. I require you to relay the nature of this conversation to your rezident, to Colonel Zabotin. Can you do that?"

I nodded my head in agreement. Ellery's voice was strained when he spoke.

"Some of this information comes from Zabotin so you might be familiar with it, Miss Linton," he added, not looking directly at me, but turning to Grierson.

"Zabotin tells me the key Soviet asset in Washington, a high-placed British diplomat who goes by the codename Homer, is worried that the Americans are close to breaking the wartime code used by Russian intelligence."

I was surprised that Zabotin had confided in Ellery, who I'd understood worked expressly for the Canadians. But things were never that simple during the war.

"If that is true," Ellery continued, "my connection to Moscow would be exposed. The Americans, and the Brits, will read the wartime cables between Zabotin and Homer. My advice to Homer is often quoted, according to Zabotin."

"Does it matter?" Grierson piped in. "Whatever you did, you did to beat back the Nazis and win the war."

"It matters, John. I must be careful. Lately, the Soviets have hinted they're hungry to bite off more of Eastern Europe," Ellery replied. "Atlee is a dyed in the wool Labour man and he loathes Stalin. If Harry Truman has his way, we'll be at war with the Russians before the year is over. In any case, the Soviets will nix my appointment as Secretary-General, believing I'd compromise their seat on the UN Security Council. I know too much."

Grierson trusted Ellery's judgment. "What's important is that Nazi scientists aren't running the show at Los Alamos," Grierson said, trying to calm Ellery. "Truman must acknowledge that Stalin won the war. Even Churchill knew the Allies couldn't have done it without the Russians. The fighting turned at Stalingrad. You could influence the Americans. Help them to see that keeping the peace with the Soviets is paramount."

Grierson's naïveté even surprised me.

Both men ordered sirloin steak, medium rare, green beans and mashed potatoes, while I asked for the chicken breast. Ellery selected an excellent Burgundy stored in the club's cellar long before the outbreak of war.

Over lunch, Ellery became increasingly perturbed. "Damn it, John. I can't let this nonsense with Soviet intelligence cost me my run for Secretary-General. I'm the modern choice. Canada, that is. We will become the world's peacemakers," he said.

"The Soviets, the Brits and the Americans will support you at the UN. You've done nothing dishonourable." Grierson was confident, but Ellery believed differently.

Oleg poured more wine for Ellery and Grierson as they spoke of the dangers Homer posed. I covered my glass with my hand. Homer had stood as First Secretary at the British Embassy in Washington for much of the war. In the summer of 1945, he was acting as Secretary of the Combined Policy Committee on atomic energy matters, a joint committee of Americans, Brits and Canadians in Washington. If, as Zabotin warned, it was discovered that he was run by the Soviets, Homer might crack.

Ellery explained to Grierson that although Homer didn't relay technical information to Moscow about atomic secrets, he did report on the progress of the scientists at Los Alamos, and his intelligence was encrypted, and sent directly to Zabotin, who in turn, transmitted it to the Centre. Ellery didn't know if the Soviet Embassy in Ottawa used the same Soviet encryption method as the one the Americans were about to break. If so, Homer's messages to Zabotin could be translated by the de-coders in Washington. "We'll be exposed," he whispered to Grierson, "on matters of atomic espionage."

Grierson took a long drink of his wine.

"You could help us, Miss Linton," Ellery said, finally turning to me and offering me more wine. "I'd be grateful if you could find out how Zabotin transmits his cables to the Centre. Does he use the wartime encryption code or the Soviet diplomatic pouch? Could you find out?"

I said I would try.

"Security at the Ottawa embassy is impenetrable, and even if the code is broken, we were working to defeat the Germans, not endangering the Allies," said Grierson, but again Ellery disagreed.

"No John, everything is up for grabs now that the Americans have exploded two atomic bombs. Understand that Soviet hotheads, excuse me Miss Linton, believe they must replicate the device to maintain the balance of power. What will happen to me, to us, if Washington cracks the Soviet code? Apparently the Nazis knew it for years. A pro-Nazi Norwegian decoded it for the Germans. That's how Washington got their hands on it, through this Nazi who needed to get out of Norway after the Germans surrendered. The Americans welcomed him." Once Ellery starting talking, it was hard for him to stop.

"Eventually the FBI or this new organization, the Central Intelligence Agency, will figure out that it was Homer who passed the information to Zabotin who in turn passed it on to Moscow. I helped Homer to gather that information and I assured Zabotin that he was safe to send it from Ottawa to Moscow. It was my duty. Churchill was holding back financial and military support to the Russians. Otherwise the Allies would have lost the war."

Ellery put his head in his hands. "My appointment as Secretary-General will look like a Communist plot. I've spent the entire war easing relations between the West and the Soviet Union. So did you, John. Now we'll be ruined."

"Did Homer send the actual formula for the bomb, or the drawings themselves?" Grierson asked.

"God no, not the drawings or the actual formula. As I said, nothing highly technical. I don't believe Homer or Zabotin or any other Soviet operator outside Los Alamos is privy to that."

Grierson threw back the remainder of his wine. "Freda, what about your friend, Harry Vine? Wasn't he in Los Alamos?"

Ellery was curious about Vine. "Who is he? One of Zabotin's boys?"

I couldn't believe our best-kept secrets were being discussed in front of Ellery.

"They go way back. Vine, Zabotin and Freda hail from the same village, a God forsaken place near the Soviet-Polish border. Could you elaborate, Freda?" Grierson asked me.

"John is correct. The three of us come from Nesvicz, a village inside the Pale, but it's not important."

"You're an odd triangle, aren't you?" John liked to talk. "Zabotin and Vine can't stand the sight of each other from what I've gathered."

"We're from a different world than you are," I commented, trying to put an end to this line of conversation.

Ellery asked me if I knew what transpired on Vine's trip to Los Alamos, but I said I didn't know.

"Could you find out, could you ask your friend Vine? Our continued anonymity depends on me knowing the facts."

"I'll ask," I assured him.

After that, the two men placed their linen napkins on their seats as they stood up to leave the Club. I followed suit. On the way out, Ellery invited Grierson to his lodge on Pink Lake for the Labour Day weekend. "Our sainted cook is spending the summer with Patsy at the lake house and you'll enjoy the roast beef and her storied maple syrup pie."

"How's Patsy?" Grierson asked kindly.

"I suspect she'll spend a great deal of the weekend in her bedroom," Ellery replied. Ellery shook my hand and disappeared into his waiting limousine.

Grierson's car and driver were resting across the street under the shade of a tree, and he offered me a lift back to the office, but I declined. "Spend the weekend with your friend," I said curtly. "I have work to do."

I walked back to the Party office where I painstakingly jotted down whatever I could remember from the luncheon conversation. Then I translated my notes into Soviet code and destroyed the originals. The Chairwoman of the Canada-Russian Friendship Association pretended that she wasn't interested in what I was scribbling and as I was stuffing the encryption in the prescribed drop, she looked down at her desk loaded with photos of a smiling Tim Buck and Stalin shaking hands. I told her to remain at the office until a courier from the embassy picked up the drop, and like the good comrade she was, she nodded her head in acquiescence.

Chapter Thirteen

The weather changed after I returned to my flat on Florence Street. The sun retreated behind the clouds and a blanket of hot, humid air was hanging over the Ottawa Valley. No one, except spies and journalists, worked late on Friday during the summer in Ottawa. It was the last long weekend of the season and the civil servants were heading up to their cabins on the other side of the river in Quebec. Parliament would re-convene after Labour Day.

I considered walking over to the Soviet Embassy, but Zabotin didn't appreciate it when I made unscheduled visits. Neither of us thought his wife Lydia knew about our trysts at the safe house or the Château Laurier, but there were others at the embassy who did. If Gouzenko was one of them, I didn't wish to give him more ammunition.

I found Vine at the Florence Street flat. I'd expected him to be gone or to give me the cold shoulder, but he opened a bottle of cheap red and a packet of liver pâté from Bousey's, the market on Elgin Street. We spread it on the black bread I'd bought at the Rideau Bakery on my way home from the Laurier Club.

By midnight the temperature inside my flat was thirty-three degrees. The living room was an oven, and with Vine and me attempting to be civil to each other, it became unbearable. I suggested we take our sheets and pillows outside onto my little balcony facing the Ottawa River. We both felt it that night: the improbable stillness. Zabotin hadn't contacted me, not since receiving my notes from the luncheon with Ellery and Grierson. The weather report said the summer heat was expected to break around midnight.

In the early hours of the morning, Grierson phoned from Ellery's lodge. I'd gone swimming there with him during the war when Ellery was in Washington. It was the most peculiar lake in Canada. The upper warm and lower cold waters did not mix. Only a three-spined sea creature was able to withstand the temperature shock of the disparate waters.

I asked Grierson why he was calling me at 3 a.m. He said Ellery's wife, Patsy, was raging and no one could sleep. Everyone in Ottawa knew Patsy drank and that the diplomat tried to keep her hidden away at the lake and far from cocktail parties.

"What else?" I asked Grierson.

"Convince Vine to stay in Ottawa. Zabotin wouldn't want him in Chalk River with Alan Nunn May, not right now. It could be dangerous if our scientist was seen with a stranger, a foreigner at that. We need to know what Vine found out when he was at Los Alamos and who's privy to that intelligence. Who has seen it other than Zabotin? Have you found out how Zabotin transmits his findings to Moscow? By wire, by courier? How?"

I didn't bother asking him how he knew that Vine had been scheduled to be at the atomic laboratory in Chalk River or if he knew the exact nature of the visit. "Why shouldn't he go?" I asked. Grierson didn't know that Zabotin had already cancelled his trip.

Grierson was distraught. "Homer claims it is not safe."

I assured him I would be speaking with the rezident before the weekend was over.

I wanted to tie it all together, Ellery and Zabotin's outpouring about the encryptions, Vine's cancelled visit to Chalk River, but I began to worry that the RCMP might be listening in. "I'll talk to Zabotin," I said again and hung up.

I was wearing a white cotton nightgown. Vine could see me standing beside the desk light with the receiver in my hand.

"It was Grierson. He thinks you shouldn't go to Chalk River."

"You didn't tell him that Zabotin cancelled my trip?" Vine asked.

"Not on the phone. Grierson is with Ellery at Pink Lake. They had lunch together. I was invited to sit in and Ellery claimed that Homer is worried that Washington will decode the cables he transmits to Zabotin. You do know about Homer?"

Vine was stunned by this revelation. "Fred Rose mentions Homer. It makes him feel important." Vine grimaced. "We're finished. We'll be exposed. Fuchs' drawings of the bomb, the ones I brought back from New Mexico, Zabotin must have sent them to Homer and to Moscow. And any information I've uncovered about a prototype reactor and heavy water at Chalk River from Nunn May, that will be exposed as well."

"It's possible." I couldn't tell him that Zabotin had never sent Fuchs' drawings to the Director, and he certainly would not have wired them to Homer as an afterthought.

I worried about how much we were revealing by speaking so openly. All this talk on the telephone and in my apartment had to stop. The world was changing so fast. I was trying to convince Vine to be more careful, when he unexpectedly began chanting in Yiddish, as if the old language would shield him from harm. "Since the destruction of the Temple, prophecy has been taken away from the prophets and given to madmen and children. I learned that long ago in Nesvicz," he sang, rocking back and forth as if he were praying.

Climbing back onto the balcony, we pulled the white sheets around us. Cold air was blowing in from the north. We were solitary ghosts, caught up in our private fears, careening in the black Ottawa night.

Chapter Fourteen

Before daybreak, Grierson rang again. This time he asked me to join him at Pink Lake, explaining that Ellery requested to speak with me in person and that it was urgent. Ellery offered to send his chauffeur in one hour and I agreed. Vine didn't try to stop me, but he did ask if Grierson knew about the missing cryptograms from the safe at the Soviet Embassy.

"If he doesn't, he will before long."

Vine shook his head in dismay. "Zabotin should warn Moscow so the politburo has time to react."

"Let Zabotin be the judge of that," I said firmly.

"He knows how serious the breach is," he urged. "He should not delay. It will only make things worse for us."

"Give Zabotin a chance to recover the cables before he alerts Moscow."

Vine didn't agree. "What if there's no time?" he asked. "Maybe we should pack our bags."

"Where will we go?" I asked Vine. "Who will take us in?"

"What if we return to Nesvicz?"

I couldn't believe my ears. "Sit tight," I cautioned him. "Wait until I'm back from Ellery's lake house. Zabotin will attend the Labour Day celebration at the Gouzenko's. Svetlana Gouzenko prepares the best potato perogies in town. We don't want to miss that." I was surprised at how practical I was becoming.

I wanted to hold my own at Ellery's, so I quickly curled my hair, applied my brightest lipstick and placed a double row of pearls around my neck. The ones Zabotin had presented to me for my birthday.

The drive into the Gatineau Hills gave me courage. Across the Ottawa River and into the sultry hills of Quebec, where the trees grew tall in a thousand shades of green and the lakes were cold and mysterious. How could anything go wrong amidst this delicate beauty?

I prepared what I should say while revealing as little as possible. I couldn't tell Grierson or Ellery that Zabotin hadn't sent Fuchs' drawings to Moscow. I didn't want this information to get back to Homer via Ellery and risk Zabotin being betrayed to the Centre. I took it for granted that by this time Zabotin would have reviewed my notes from the Laurier Club as well as debriefed Oleg. He would know everything of importance and would be planning his next move.

Ellery greeted me at the door and ushered me into the front room of the house where Grierson sat beside an open window that overlooked Pink Lake. He rose when I entered.

It wasn't a grand parlour, not the least bit ostentatious. For a second, I remembered my first conquest, Klopot the haberdasher, and his red-and-black bedroom, decorated in the taste of Odessa. Here the dimensions were shapely, the colours muted. It was expensive, filled with paintings of the Canadian landscape, accented by buttery-tan leather and maple wood furniture. The walls and floor were polished pine; the rugs Turkish and the lamps made of brass. Although it was warm, a delicate fire burned in the floor-to-ceiling stone fireplace. Shards of burned paper were disintegrating in the glow. A red telephone sat on the end table beside Ellery's rocking chair.

Since I was wearing three-inch heels, Ellery did not ask me to climb down to the lake with him. Patsy, his wife, was still asleep and "under the weather," according to Grierson.

He took my hand. He was too polite to mention my shoes, but I could see that he was amused by my attempt to overdress. I realized that I looked like a version of Klopot's bedroom to these men.

Before speaking again, Ellery closed the door to the kitchen and the window beside Grierson. "The situation is dire, my dear. Homer tells us that there is a mole at the Soviet Embassy in Ottawa and he's contacted British intelligence. The mole has been trying to persuade MI6 to get him out of Canada."

I felt the ground moving below my feet. The same sensation I had when Zabotin first told me about Gouzenko's recall to Moscow. What Zabotin didn't know was that the cryptographer had already made plans to defect before he was recalled by the GRU.

Ellery continued. "Apparently Homer's handler in London reports that the mole wants out of Canada on a diplomatic passport. He's looking for a safe haven in England, but neither Homer nor MI6 can promise that. We're fucked. Excuse me, my dear," Ellery said clearing his throat.

"I've heard worse," I admitted.

Ellery began to pace. "There's this clever young woman at the State Department in D.C. She's working with the Nazi who originally decoded the Soviet cyphers during the war. The Norwegian, I spoke about yesterday. The operation is labelled Venona and I suspect Washington already knows more than we could have imagined. For now they aren't letting on. Homer believes the mole here wants to expose you, your entire group in Ottawa. He can prove that atomic secrets have gone between the Soviet Embassy in Ottawa and Moscow." Ellery stopped when we heard Patsy calling to him from the bedroom.

"Put her down to sleep," Ellery ordered the cook, who came into the parlour looking for instructions.

"Homer will be exposed. I'm sure of it," said Ellery as he continued to pace the room. "The role he's played with the Manhattan Project, with Fuchs and Nunn May. He's the go-between for all that and Zabotin—and, ultimately, the Director in Moscow. Miss Linton, you must tell Zabotin to get Nunn May back to Britain, where he'll by protected by our friends."

"I can do that," I said immediately. "The mole must be Igor Gouzenko," I added. "He's in charge of the cipher room at the embassy. He's been recalled to Moscow."

Grierson's hands began to shake. "And you know this how?"

"Zabotin told me," I said.

"We can't be kept in the dark about this. Does Zabotin realize what danger we're in?"

"I don't know what Zabotin realizes," I replied. "How could I?"

Grierson and Ellery looked at each other. Grierson guessed that I'd spent the night before last with Zabotin. I suppose he'd told Ellery about my roaming affections.

"Do you understand how serious this is, Freda?" Grierson asked me. "And for Vine. What did he conclude from his visit to Los Alamos? Did he have information for Zabotin?

"I wouldn't know," I lied. "Why don't you ask Zabotin yourself, or Homer? You're such good friends." At that moment, I looked at Grierson with contempt.

"You can help us," Ellery stated.

"How? The two of you will be protected. Possibly Homer will be saved by his English friends. Like him, your lives will continue, perhaps with less grandeur, but they will continue. Particularly you, Mr. Ellery. The prime minister championed you. He'd have egg on his face if you were seen aiding the Communists. And John, how would the government appear if the head of the Wartime Information Bureau turned out to be a Soviet operative? I bet the Canadians will try to cover up their mistakes in your case."

The two men were silent.

"Have you thought about the rest of us? Vine, Sybil Romanescu, Fred Rose. Even Zabotin. And me. What will happen to us? Do you believe that Moscow will rescue us? They will blame us for being sloppy. Gouzenko, of all people. He's the clown who will bring us down." As an afterthought, I admitted that the code the Soviet Embassy used was, indeed, the same one as the wartime encryptions. "This mess will be over soon."

"Now, now," Ellery chimed in. "Let's not get ahead of ourselves. So far it is all conjecture. Homer doesn't know for certain how far the Americans have gotten decrypting the Soviet code. Perhaps Venona is something of a ruse. Homer seems to be having a bit of a break down. Perhaps he's overplaying the danger."

With that he tried to ignore his wife's calls from the bedroom. "Let's wait and see what Zabotin says. Let's make prudent decisions," Ellery continued. "If you would contact Zabotin today, Miss Linton, I'd be grateful. Warn him. Find out how much information he's garnered about the bomb. Possibly he can commandeer this defector, this man Gouzenko in the embassy, before anything critical leaks out. Defectors are the worst kind of people."

"I have contacted him and I'm waiting for his response, but you must mean send Gouzenko back to Moscow before he can do any harm? He'll be executed first thing," I reminded them.

Ellery and Grierson exchanged glances, but they did not dispute my claim. Stalin's enemies, the disappeared, were dragged from their slumber in the middle of the night and charged with treason—if only they could talk. I wondered if Grierson and Ellery knew about the show trials where every prisoner was found guilty. They must. Siberia became an enormous prison camp dotted with thousands upon thousands of graveyards, a nowhere land where the falsely accused were sent to perish. "If Zabotin returns to Russia, he'll be held accountable as well."

Ellery nodded in agreement. He clenched his fists and looked down to avoid my gaze. He invited his wife to join us as we moved into the dining room. Patsy became subdued once she was allowed to speak with her husband. She wore a ruffled, champagne-tinted peignoir with the top three buttons of the gown undone. I could see her breasts popping through the ruffles. After a meal of vichyssoise, and smoked ham and cheddar cheese quiche, I was escorted back to Ottawa.

There was no sign of Vine when I arrived at the flat. This time I wondered if he'd fled without me. He'd have escaped through Quebec, up the St. Lawrence River to Quebec City, where he'd book passage on a ship that would carry him across the ocean to the Baltic Sea, and then home. This time he would be travelling alone.

Chapter Fifteen

Sunday morning
September 2, 1945
Ottawa

During the early hours of the morning it stormed, a torrential Ottawa Valley downpour with the branches of the trees tearing at the latch of my bedroom window until it broke open. Rain seeped onto the floor. Shards of lightening, followed by bellowing thunder, turned the night into a violent display of natural force. The electricity went out. I hid under the covers.

After the storm passed, a waft of fresh, dry air streamed into my room. I turned the covers down and inhaled as if it was my first breath. The air smelled sweetly of the green Gatineau Hills on the other side of the river in Quebec. I wondered how Grierson and the Ellerys had weathered the harshest storm of the summer. I imagined Patsy Ellery wandering the rocky shore of Pink Lake under the booming crackles of thunder with a bottle of gin in her shaky hand.

I'd hardly slept during the night. Vine hadn't called. I considered going to the Party office to see if Zabotin had arranged a drop for me, but thought better of it. What if Gouzenko had already defected?

Instead I took down the wireless transmitter, stored in a suitcase on the top shelf of my closet, behind a box of hair curlers, to send Zabotin a two-line coded message. *Meet me at 3 p.m. at the railway station bar,* it read. Then I waited. It was impossible for me to fathom what Zabotin would do next, if he'd attempt to talk sense into Gouzenko, or if he'd confront him to frighten him into giving up. I secretly hoped he would alert the Director immediately and be done with the cipher clerk.

My options were limited. Being without Zabotin or Vine to lean on forced me to imagine what it would be like without them. Refreshing, like the northern breeze at my window, but lonely. For hours I felt that I was living in a bubble, disconnected from the tangible objects surrounding me. The desk was not real. The chair, a figment of my imagination. I could melt objects with a touch of my hand. I forced myself to drink a cup of black tea and settle down.

When the transmitter sounded with Zabotin's reply, I dressed. He would meet me at three at the agreed location. I figured that the train station would be close to empty, but when I arrived tourists were milling around aimlessly.

Zabotin met me at the entrance to the darkened bar. We sat at a table in the far corner of the room above the tracks where the trains pulled into the station. He ordered two double martinis and a plate of warm olives, as he always did. From the second-floor bar, we peered down at the tourists standing at the ticket wicket, clutching their children with one hand and their overstuffed suitcases with the other. How I wished to be one of them.

The tall lead-paned windows in the station were closed after last night's storm and the air inside was still sultry. Across the road from the station stood the immense Canadian Pacific Hotel, the Château Laurier. For years, Zabotin and I met behind the walls of that great pile of stone, marble and northern Quebec timber. It was the most beautiful building I'd known. There were mirrors lining the great halls and when I looked at myself, I felt beautiful and important, as if I were making a difference. I assured myself that Zabotin and I were on the right side of history and we would come through the war as good, conscientious people in a spectacularly improved world. I thought of myself, then, as a decent person who did what I did for a just cause. We all did, at the time. Until everything changed.

That afternoon in the station bar, Zabotin didn't act like a good person. He was not in an agreeable mood. At first we smoked cigarettes instead of talking. When Zabotin stubbed out his cigarette to speak, it was to order me to attend the Labour Day celebration. "Cancelling the event is the worst thing we can do," he said gruffly. "The celebration will be held at the Gouzenko's as planned. We must behave as if nothing is awry, as if we know nothing about the stolen cables. No cause for suspicion. Correct?"

"I don't see why we must meet at the Gouzenkos' apartment. Having us all there at once. It's too dangerous. What if he alerts the authorities?"

"He won't. I've spoken to him."

"He has the cables? Is it him?" I wanted to trust Zabotin, but I couldn't help myself from checking that his story hadn't changed.

"Yes, it is Gouzenko," Zabotin said. "Don't look so shocked. We knew it would happen one day. That we'd be betrayed."

"We did, but I didn't think it would be that little worm."

"I already know that Homer believes that the Americans are decrypting the Soviet wartime code. The project is called Venona. When the Nazis lost the war and their necks were on the line, they turned over the encryption key to the FBI. That was the bargain between them, the Americans and the Nazis." Zabotin had a funny way of telling the truth, as if he'd invented it.

"Ellery wants you to understand that Homer is coming undone. If the FBI discovers that you've been sending his reports from the Joint Committee on Atomic Advances to Moscow, you're done for," I said as calmly as I could. "Ellery knows so much, too much for my taste, and he's hinting Homer will break down if he's interrogated."

Zabotin ordered another martini. " I'm not concerned about Ellery or what he thinks. We used him when we needed him. Now his career is on the line. I could betray him, and Grierson." The rezident looked smug.

"Why would you do that?"

"He's not useful to us anymore.""

"Useful—I loathe that word," I said.

"The situation is more complicated than it first appeared. As you guessed, I'm holding back Fuchs' drawings from Moscow. I'm only trying to protect you. As for Homer's information, I'm not even certain our Gouzenko has his hands on Homer's transmissions. I might have kept them out of the cipher room. For my eyes only. What he saw wasn't very important. I made certain of it. I wanted Gouzenko to have only so much information."

Zabotin was vague about details but certain of final outcomes.

"When we were at the safe house, you tried to convince me that Homer's cables were of utmost importance and that they'd been stolen," I said.

"Things change," Zabotin said curtly. He wanted to keep me off balance, shooting at a target shrouded in shadows and fully reliant on his direction. "Keep in mind that Homer did not transmit the technical drawings of the atom bomb. Yes, he kept Moscow updated on the progress at Los Alamos. Yes, he could tell the GRU and the NKVD about the amount of uranium used in the Little Boy bomb, but not the exact formula. He doesn't have the new drawings for Fat Man and now he won't receive them, at least not from me." He was hedging. Not wanting me to see the picture as clearly as he did.

"But you have the formula for Fat Man," I said. "Vine brought Fuchs' formula with drawings back from New Mexico."

"Of course, but I didn't pass the drawings to Moscow, as I've already confessed to you. Gouzenko never saw the drawings. From Homer's information, the Americans were predicting the number of bombs their factory could build—and from that, the Director would know how many the Soviets needed to build to keep pace with them. Tit for tat," he said. "I still hold the key to building those bombs. The all-important drawings."

"Why didn't you send them to Moscow?" Zabotin was clever. By that time, he realized what mattered were the drawings. What shocked me was how easily he was slipping into a different persona. As the embassy's rezident, his ultimate duty was to ensure the Soviet Union would have its own atomic arsenal before it became impossible to catch the Americans in the race to world domination.

Zabotin looked at me closely. "Do you wish to survive, my darling? If you do, you must never repeat a word of this to anyone, not to Vine and certainly not to Grierson."

I drank my martini. I was more terrified than I'd ever been, more than when I was standing in the Vine's kitchen back in Nesvicz afraid that Zabotin would hurt me.

"I interrogated Gouzenko and I extracted a promise from him," said Zabotin. "He'll defect the day after Labour Day. To be exact, in the early morning hours following the celebration. If he refuses, I'll have our boys pick him up before he can get to the Canadian police."

"Couldn't Gouzenko run now?" Zabotin was certain about how it would play out, but I wasn't so convinced. "How do you know he hasn't already?"

Zabotin lit a fresh cigarette with the one he was finishing. "Freda, you must understand that Gouzenko has a wife and child. I have his apartment building surrounded."

I took another cigarette from Zabotin and waited for him to light it.

"The information in his stolen papers is essentially dribble," he sighed. "It's enough to incriminate us, but the papers don't reveal what Moscow really wants. They are Vine's overblown reports of my operation in Ottawa."

"Why do you call them overblown?" I asked.

"By the time the Director received Vine's reports, they were old news. The only piece he wants is the nuclear one. The ins and outs of Canadian Parliament are not that shocking."

"So why bother with us at all? Have me squeezing information out of petty bureaucrats?" So many wasted years. "Why bring me here from Toronto?"

"Grierson, of course. We needed him."

"And now?"

Zabotin took a drag on his cigarette. Little people milled around below us. Some were eating sandwiches and drinking milk. They had no idea, no idea. More than ever I wished to go home, back to Nesvicz.

Zabotin placed his good hand on my knee. "You must understand how this will work," he said. "I ordered Gouzenko never to keep a copy of Homer's cables in the embassy safe. I made certain of that by making my own handwritten copies and destroying the originals. When he's debriefed, he'll remember little of the exact details in Homer's notes. What he'll say to the Canadian authorities is that Zabotin was receiving information from a high-placed mole in Washington. That's all."

Zabotin's confidence in his plan told me that he'd been planning this escapade for months, to trap Gouzenko, who was the most vulnerable person at the embassy. When did he decide to go over to the other side, if that was what Zabotin was doing, after devoting his life to the cause of Marxism and the Soviet state? "Are we safe?" I asked him.

"Don't be silly. We're never safe. With or without Homer's cables both the Canadians and the Russians will want my head, certainly yours and your comrades. Our operation will be exposed and eventually Canada will be forced to take action, however reluctant its sleepy prime minister is." He looked directly into my eyes. "I'm going to need your help to pull this off. You, too, can make it out of this mess."

"I'm listening."

"Your sister, Masha, is alive," Zabotin said, letting the information sit with me before he continued. "She lives in Kiev."

"How do you know this?" My eyes clouded over with tears. Masha. Alive. Zabotin took his handkerchief from his pocket, but I pushed it away. "How do you know?"

"The other night you begged me to help you find your family, so I began the search. She survived."

"How?"

"Masha remained in Nesvicz. She wasn't far when the Germans invaded. My family helped her. Without the Zabotins she would have perished as the others did."

"My mama and papa? My brother, Simcha?" I was wringing my hands.

"I have no idea about them," he said gently, lifting my hands to his lips. "You can repay me now, for Masha, for all the count and countess did to keep her alive. I need your promise you will not say a word of this to anyone. Not one word about how Gouzenko came to defect. And there is more."

"What do you need?" I asked, praying that he would leave me be, if just for a minute. I wished to contact Masha, and figure out how I could return to the Soviet Union to be with her.

"You've always been clever," Zabotin said. "Think this through. This is the last mission I will assign you."

He was forcing me to hold my tongue and to contain my excitement over his news. If Masha was alive, perhaps the others were as well. A million questions welled up inside up, the first being how I could travel to Kiev. I wanted to leave that very day but I understood the game. God knows, I'd been in it long enough to never expect Zabotin's help until I performed for him. I must stick to the issue at hand and make his plans succeed.

"Where are Fuchs' drawings?" I asked.

"I have them," he told me. "If I send them to Moscow now, if Stalin sees them, there will be a war, the magnitude of which we've never imagined—a war of total destruction. Comrade Stalin will never hold back, not after what Russia sacrificed to beat back the Germans, and to stay in power. You must agree to join me. You know about the purges and the show trials and the gulags. We all do. We just can't admit they are real, how our grand experiment has gone wrong. Everyone we admired back home is dead. I haven't told you, but my brothers are missing, probably sent to the gulags. If Stalin didn't murder my friends in the Party before the war, the Nazis finished the job. It's over." Zabotin drew hard on his cigarette before extinguishing it.

At that moment, I couldn't distinguish with certainty if Zabotin was betraying his country or if it was something beyond loyalty to one ideology that drove him. Russia had turned into Stalin's nightmare, fraught with paranoia, an open wound emitting blood and pus. I thought about my own family and how they must have suffered first from the Soviet regime and then from the Germans. Masha would tell me everything once I found her, no matter how painful, and she would forgive me for deserting her and little Simcha, along with our beautiful mother and proud father.

For years they were my private concern and my shame. No matter how many times I convinced myself that what I did for the struggle was admirable, acts of bravery and principle, the gnawing doubt that I agreed to the Party's terms to feed my own desire for recognition, never disappeared.

I looked down to see Oleg standing at the foot of the stairs. I figured that if I didn't agree to Zabotin's terms, he'd take me back to the embassy for questioning. I must support Zabotin. If it was true the count and countess helped Masha to live, I owed him that.

"What about Nunn May? Didn't Vine mention the scientist in his reports?" I asked, trying to focus on what I needed to do.

"I'll have Nunn May out of Canada as soon as possible. It will take some time for the Canadian authorities to put two and two together. In Vine's reports there are snippets from the scientists at Chalk River, not much, but enough to implicate Nunn May." Zabotin's demeanour toward me changed. He knew he had me. "Together we can pull this off. "

"What will happen to us?" My life was in his hands.

"Moscow will react to Gouzenko's defection by recalling me. The Americans will have Homer's cables if or when Venona decodes them. The crisis will escalate, that is for sure, beyond Nunn May or you and me. The Director will blame me," he said, pounding his own chest. "He will want to interrogate me in the Lubyanka. I'll perish there and Lydia can put flowers on my grave." Zabotin shrugged. "If Venona takes more time, six months or a year, as I believe it will, Moscow will zero in on Gouzenko and the release of his worthless information. We will be able to buy some time. We might be able to escape. Or better still, perhaps I can cut a deal with Moscow."

"Do you want the Soviet Union to fail?" I asked him plainly and looked away.

Zabotin banged the table with his good hand, but thankfully the bar was deserted and not even the bartender took notice. "If I pleased, I could betray Gouzenko today and he'd be done for, but I don't wish to. You know that. My men could pick him up and escort him back to Moscow tonight. I have all the evidence to show the Centre that he was about to defect. Instead I prefer to watch how my plan plays out," he said, satisfied with himself and his manoeuvrings. "In my own way, I've given that little cipher clerk enough rope to hang himself. If he defects, he'll never be a free man. He will spend the remainder of his days in Canadian jail or tucked away in a remote hiding place. If he doesn't have the nerve, he'll return to Russia where eventually the GRU will blame him for the loss of Fuchs' drawings. It's too bad. I always found him hilarious."

We left the bar to walk across Rideau Street to the Château Laurier, where Zabotin asked for his usual room with a view of the Ottawa River. White light burned through the shuttered windows of the grand lobby while the overhead fans kept the halls cool. The gilt mirrors shimmered in the late afternoon sun. I was to take the key, as I usually did, inspect the room and then ring down to the house telephone in the chandeliered lobby if it was clean. Zabotin picked up the receiver at the appointed time.

In the room, there was more vodka and caviar for affect. Then he made love to me. I could sense he wasn't putting his heart into it that afternoon. Not once did he cry out swearing that he loved me. But he did want to talk. How strange that men wish to reveal themselves, to tell all, after the act. I suppose they are all lonely.

"The other day when we were in the park, you said we must stop deceiving ourselves about the past?"

"And you told me we have no past, only the present," I replied.

"No, you were correct. Where do the deceptions end? When I joined the Red Cavalry it was the only way to protect the Zabotin name. Do you understand?"

I understood. "By destroying Jewish villages inside the Pale? That protected your good name?"

"We always end up in the same place, Freda. You accusing me while I grow frustrated. Don't forget it was my parents who saved your sister."

"Forgive me. Of course, I am grateful."

"You have never done anything you are ashamed of doing?" he inquired.

He knew the answer. "I am ashamed of my entire life," I replied. "Everything I've done from abandoning my family, to working as a whore for the Party. That's enough, isn't it?" I was coming to terms with the truth.

Zabotin pulled me down until I was completely covered by his long body. "It's a risk what we're doing. If the Director discovers that you know about Fuchs' drawings, you'll be escorted to the Soviet Union and detained. You will be expected to betray me, which you will, after they're done with you. Everyone breaks. You must promise me that you won't inform Vine that I failed to send the atomic diagrams to Moscow."

"I'd prefer not to deceive him," I said, pulling myself out from under Zabotin.

"That's not your decision," he said. "Make up your mind. If you tell Vine, he'll report me. You know that."

"You make it sound like I have a choice. That giving the drawings to the GRU will end the world."

"You do have a choice. I won't force you to do anything against your conscience," he said. "This time, let's save ourselves while protecting our countrymen. Stalin has waged war against his own people. They die, not him, if there is nuclear war."

It was much too late for me to disregard his words. I knew too much to run from Zabotin.

"Grierson will help, I assume. He's a good man, an innocent, in love with you. He and Ellery can get you out of the country when the time comes, or better yet, I'll figure it out. I'll make my own way back to Russia. Freda, I promise to protect you."

I was beginning to convince myself that this daring man cared for me and that he would abandon Lydia for me. His intention was to outfox Gouzenko. Zabotin wouldn't betray him to the Director before he defected. The intelligence in the stolen documents would tell their own story, a story Zabotin wished the world to know. What he didn't wish the world to know, he would release in time or never.

It was a fantastical ploy. Zabotin allowed Gouzenko to steal the documentation that would implicate our small band of Communists in Ottawa. But the drawings for the bomb would remain in his hands, as well as the critical information in the cables from Homer, at least for now. In a sense, he'd leak the information as he chose, and by his own methods. Gouzenko was just the conduit. The great Zabotin had decided he could save the world from nuclear annihilation. When he invited me to join him in this scheme, I accepted. To this day, I believe it was the right choice. The only choice.

My life changed that Sunday afternoon. I began to realize the clandestine work I'd done for years was a waste. In the end, what information had I gathered that changed history or even saved one life? I'd lured men to my bed for their secrets. How important were they, these contorted confessions?

That afternoon I asked myself how the second world war had escalated into a bloodbath where millions upon millions of innocent civilians died. Men and women like my father and mother, and my brother Simcha who'd done nothing to deserve what befell them.

Somehow Masha survived. I would find her with Zabotin's help.

It was possible that Zabotin was the last reasonable man on earth. He was starting to exist beyond ideology, perhaps above loyalty to any cause, no matter how enticing.

He'd left me no option but to side with him. But I also asked myself what happened to people like me, those who have devoted their lives to a cause that turned out to be the opposite of what it preached? I didn't know if I could let go of the person I'd become and then re-imagine myself as a free being, unencumbered by the commandments that guided my life. First it was Judaism, then Communism. I had no idea how to live outside a strict regimen of thought. To re-invent myself.

In Russia, Jews from inside the Pale went over to the Communist side. It didn't matter that our villages were decimated during the civil war. For we Jews, it was the moment to escape the dark fate of our ancestors and join the Revolution, where we would be equals among comrades and encouraged to act outside the strictures of Hebraic law. There was a sense of relief and recklessness, of lawlessness when throwing off the confines of the Orthodox faith. It took years to realize that by taking up a new cause, we'd only exchanged one set of rules for another.

To Zabotin's way of thinking, you took sides as the circumstances dictated. When situations changed, he altered his thinking. I wasn't certain I could accept that there were no absolutes. It was in my bones to believe there was a right way and a wrong way. It was detestable to change sides. I'd done it once before when I'd joined the Party and my life was transformed. Now I was intending to change sides again, to help Zabotin keep the atomic bomb out of Stalin's hands.

Years later, when I met Elka in Chernobyl, I understood what happens to someone who fails to reconstruct her life after her worst fears come true. It is the descent into nothingness. I wouldn't stand for that. Not even in Chernobyl where the hopeless congregate and the afflicted die a painful death, I scratch my own way out of the darkness.

* * *

Chernobyl journal
1988

During my second visit with Elka, Zabotin unexpectedly knocked on her crooked door. The bottom hinge had come off and she had no one to repair it.

Elka pretended that she didn't hear the knock, but I knew better.

"It's Zabotin, my friend. He's hunting me down," I assured her. I always knew when Zabotin was searching for me.

Elka smiled knowingly. "You answer the door," she said. "He's your comrade, not mine."

Each time I saw Zabotin, I was gleefully surprised. How well he'd aged! How the thick curls, now white, cascaded down his straight back. How erect he held himself. The forest air intensified the brilliance of his ice-blue eyes and rose-coloured lips. His years in the gulag had only temporarily diminished him. To me, he now looked like the man he was in Ottawa. Handsome and defiant.

"How did you find me this time?" I asked.

Zabotin grinned. It was late August, the same time of the year when he'd followed me on my walk along the Rideau Canal in Ottawa, days before I threw my lot in with him, put my life in his hands, and betrayed the Soviet Union.

We both remembered that day with utter clarity. "This time, I've come on Vine's behalf," Zabotin admitted. "Not for myself. It's his heart. He needs his medicine."

More than forty years later, Vine still depended on me. When the Pripyat's People's Hospital was evacuated, I broke into the pharmacy to collect as much nitroglycerin as I could carry in my satchel. Nitro, morphine and glass syringes, the outdated kind that the hospital kept in circulation before the accident. I boiled the syringes to disinfect them before I injected Vine with morphine. Of course, the water was radiated from the accident but there are things that can't be fixed. Vine suffered from congestive heart failure and when the pain in his chest became too much for him to bear, I squirted nitro under his tongue to open the arteries and morphine into his veins to quell the pain. He wasn't able to inject himself. Zabotin refused to learn how to use the needles.

"You're on call?" Elka asked.

"In a manner of speaking. My other friend isn't well."

Elka didn't expect me to introduce her to Zabotin formally, although she knew who he was. She was only pretending that she didn't recognize him. She did, however, invite me to visit again and I promised I would.

Zabotin and I walked back to our cabin. He held my arm. "If you ask me to fix her door, I won't," he declared. "She doesn't deserve my help or yours."

I thought about the weeks directly after the accident at Reactor Number Four, when Zabotin hitched a wagon to the back of his Lada. We loaded the flatbed, he and I, with fine furniture from the chief councilman's house and made numerous trips back to the lumberyard for tools and supplies. No one stopped us, not even the head of the Chernobyl Communist Party whose house we also rummaged through. I never cared for the bureaucrat. He reminded me of a mafia boss, the swarthy type I saw in the American movie The Godfather, when the film reached Kiev in the 1980s.

During those early weeks in the forest, Zabotin and I built a large screen porch attached to the back of our cabin, one that faced the river and protruded into the green foliage of the ravine. The trees were birch, with slender white trunks, and round leaves that resembled silver dollars. The wind whistling through the forest was like silk brushing against the clouds. I could stare at the birches for hours, listening to the wind's song.

On the screen porch, we installed a ragged leather pullout sofa from the council member's house and that's where Zabotin and I slept in summer. Once the porch was ready, we dozed most of the day, during that first summer after the accident, believing our time had come and we'd be dead within months. It didn't happen that way.

The next time I saw Elka, she was lurking about our screened porch. I noticed her from my vantage point on the sofa where I was reading. I made weekly trips to the Pripyat Library, where the collection remained in pristine condition. Zabotin drove me to town in the Lada to exchange my library books, which I neatly stacked on the library's shelves for the next patron. I didn't want to steal books. They belonged to the people, I remarked to Zabotin, and he laughed, his belly laugh, the one I'd come to cherish.

Elka was as hesitant as a feral cat when I opened the screen porch door for her, but eventually, after some coaxing, she came through the portal. We drank coffee made from chicory, with a little peppermint schnapps I'd taken in Pripyat. I prepared a cucumber and onion salad picked fresh from my garden. "What do you normally eat?" I asked.

"This and that," was her cagey response. Elka was wearing a red paisley babushka around her head. Her green eyes sparkled when she grabbed my hand, and I was astonished by the strength of her grip. She was lean, but not emaciated. She didn't appreciate it when I asked her questions, although she felt she had the right to ask me anything.

"I know your brother, Simcha," she suddenly said.

Although I thought about Simcha every day, I'd never spoken about him to anyone in Chernobyl before or after the meltdown. Only Masha and I remembered Simcha, and Masha didn't like to speak about the past. She spared so few words about Simcha, and I couldn't force her to tell me more. How could Elka know who I was mourning?

My face turned red. "He's dead."

"Who told you that? Don't believe it," Elka stated.

It had been sixty-seven years since I'd seen Simcha. When I returned to Europe I discovered that he'd been in the Łódź Ghetto. "He must have perished on the death march to Auschwitz-Birkenau before the liberation. No one saw him after that," I said sternly, "or I would have been informed."

"I don't believe so," said Elka. "I remember Simcha quite well. He looks like you. Good looking. Same grey eyes. Red hair, though. Fine manners. He speaks a polished Yiddish."

My hands went numb with excitement. Simcha would be in his late seventies, only a few years younger than me. "Where did you see him last?"

"Do you really want to know or would you rather go on believing he died a honourable death?"

I wanted to tell her to stop right there, but how could I resist knowing the truth? I'd always feared that Simcha had been tortured by the SS, or something unfathomable that no one talked about, or more likely that he dropped dead on the prisoners' march to the death camp. There were no records of him, but then so many dead from the war remained anonymous.

My sister Masha claimed that she lost all contact with him after the Nazis invaded Poland. He'd moved to Łódź with his wife and children and died in the ghetto or during the death march. That's all she knew. After Elka's claim, I wondered if Masha had held something back but didn't wish to cause me pain. Many people couldn't talk about their wartime experiences. They were trying to forget or just get on with their lives.

As for Masha, she was residing in a suburb of Kiev. Zabotin claimed his parents saved her, but the real story turned out somewhat differently. When the Nazis marched the villagers of Nesvicz to the ravine behind the synagogue, they shot them. One by one they fell into the ditch or were pushed, but Masha wasn't in Nesvicz on that day. Count and Countess Zabotin had taken her on as the laundress at their dacha. Masha was healthy, a good worker, and they chose her.

The Zabotins appreciated her diligence and her honesty. She survived because of them. Masha did not steal from the count and countess. During the Nazis invasion, she faithfully scoured the countryside for food for the aged couple. After the liberation and under Soviet rule in the Ukraine, Masha became a security officer, who rose up quickly in the local Party hierarchy. When I first returned to Europe, she rescued me and it is because of her that I am alive. In 1988, she remains a true believer; even after the nuclear accident, Masha considers herself a good Communist. The only time she'd doubted the Party was when the Director ordered her to take me under her wing after Gouzenko's defection.

Elka sat beside me on the sofa, balancing a plate of salad on her knee. She was itching to tell me more. There are people like Elka, who feed off other's pain, but I wasn't prepared to give in to her.

I wanted her to leave and I told her so. "I'm busy Elka. I have better things to do than listen to your nonsense rumours about my brother."

"Your choice," she said and departed within seconds.

Elka didn't visit for a long while after that, and I believed she'd learned her lesson. I wasn't someone to be tampered with.

As with so many who'd survived the war, and its aftermath, I intended to be brave and good and honourable as long as I was alive. Yet there were certain things at my advanced age, I did not wish to know. Those closest to me, who remained loyal to Communism, saw themselves in a similar light. During the most dreadful times, they'd stayed true to the cause. Sybil and Rose never wavered, not like Zabotin or I. Vine returned to Judaism after seeing what the Nazis had done to Nesvicz. Each of us acted on our own without orders from on high. We all went our own way after Gouzenko.

Upon my return to Europe after the war, I met a Jewish couple from Poland. German SS officers had occupied their Krakow house after hearing that the wife was an extraordinary cook who could bake Sacher torte as well as the experts in the fabled coffee houses of Vienna. The woman looked after the Germans, and they brought her the best meat and vegetables to prepare for their sumptuous meals. Every night, the table in their elegant dining room, adorned with velvet drapes and crystal chandeliers, was decorated with tall candles and rare bottles of wine from the couple's private cellar. The husband descended from a wealthy merchant family. He'd inherited the house, but joined the Party shortly before the invasion and told me he had always intended to offer it to the Party as long as he and his wife could continue to live there.

By the time I met him, he wasn't so sure the Communist government was on the right course, but he remained in the Party because it was what he understood. He worked in the military police, and the couple received the treatment accorded to senior Party apparatchiks. They survived the Great Patriotic War; no one blamed them for what they'd done during the bad years, not even the small, remaining Jewish community in Chernobyl where this man and his wife ended up when the Party confiscated their home. As I said, the wife had talent; she was a celebrated cook, and the Party brass at the reactor wanted her to make the meals in their private canteen.

People did what they had to. They stopped asking questions. If the Party ordered them to relocate, they did as they were ordered. Everyone, like the couple from Krakow, had a story to tell. First the famines and then the show trials, followed by the Nazis, and finally by the long years of crushing bureaucracy. After the accident at Reactor Number Ffour, the husband, who'd been about to retire from his position as a security guard at the nuclear plant, joined us for a few short days in the forest, but he couldn't stand the primitive conditions, the aching discomfort. He and his wife immigrated to Israel, where I assume they adjusted to an entirely different life. I know I have; adjusted, that is.

It was easy to judge. Elka was itching for me to ask her more questions about my brother. Her tone when she spoke about Simcha was odious, as if he'd commited unspeakable acts. After the war, survivors were suspicious of each other. How did some make it while so many perished? Elka's distrust was understable, but whatever she might accuse my brother of doing to stay alive, I was certain he'd had his reasons. I wasn't going to allow Elka to destroy my golden memories of that clever little boy, although I was longing for the truth.

Chapter Sixteen

Monday
September 3, 1945
Ottawa

At the last moment Svetlana Gouzenko, Igor's wife, cancelled the Labour Day party. Their baby was sick with the colic and Svetlana claimed she wasn't up to preparing an elaborate meal with a screaming child in her arms. After Fred Rose rang to ask if she could cover for the cipher clerk's wife, Sybil bounded up the fire escape to give me the news. Sybil's apartment was smaller than the cipher clerk's, but she was flattered to be asked. Zsuzsa promised that their superior hospitality would make up for the lack of space.

I didn't mind. What did it matter where the party was held? Gouzenko would defect in the early hours of the morning, if he obeyed Zabotin. We had one more night for things to remain as they were. I preferred not to spend it at Igor and Svetlana's. I'd been to Somerset Street on the few occasions when Zabotin asked me to deliver messages to Gouzenko. It was a grimy mess, overflowing with the boy's dirty nappies, discarded whisky bottles, piles of half-eaten candy bars and unfolded laundry.

I wondered if the rezident might have engineered the move away from their apartment to allow the couple time to prepare for their escape, or to entrap them if Gouzenko disobeyed him. If Gouzenko, who was now barred from the embassy, left his apartment with his wife and child in toe, Zabotin's goons would pounce.

I arrived late to the party, after seven. It was sweltering in Sybil's apartment and the humidity made it feel like a greenhouse. Vine was there, standing alone, in collared shirt and tie, which in public, he was never without. I tried to imagine him in a T-shirt, but it was a distorted picture at best. I stood in the doorway, admiring his smooth peach-like complexion. It was remarkable how little Vine had changed over the years. Even during an Ottawa heat wave, he didn't wilt. It was only after he returned to Nesvicz that he became an old man.

Zabotin arrived after me, bold and colourful as a peacock, sporting a chest of medals awarded for the bravery. He was a war hero, severely wounded, who'd lived to experience the resurrection of the motherland.

Other comrades swarmed into the tight corners of the flat. Most were in attendance when Igor and Svetlana Gouzenko appeared. The crowd included Sam Carr, the labour leader and J.L. Cohen, known as "the people's lawyer." Tim Buck was in fine form and he slapped me on the back as soon as he saw the expression on my face. "You were always a worrier, Freda," he said. "Don't overthink it. We're winning."

These three men had driven up from Toronto. The Ottawa contingent included Kathleen Willsher, the English woman who worked in the British Embassy and regularly spied on the ambassador for the Soviets. Drew Pearson made an appearance. He was the American journalist who knew everyone in Ottawa that mattered and claimed he "got a kick out of his Commie friends." In the far corner of the room was Mildred Macepeace, a cipher clerk at the Canadian foreign office. She was a devoted Communist who memorized the contents of the cryptograms wired to her boss, the Minister of External Affairs. Mildred never missed a Party event.

That night her fading blonde hair was tightly curled and her eyelids were covered with thick turquoise shadow, her eyelashes coated in midnight blue mascara. She wore a tight-fitting shift of mauve and green striped silk shantung, which I surmised, was to make her appear exotic and desirable. Mildred's heart was set on Vine. I didn't know how he felt about her. As usual, he was impossible to pin down.

The last to arrive was Fred Rose, straight from his Montreal constituency office. He'd brought Raymond Boyer along with him, the soft-spoken chemistry professor who'd figured out how to make RDX, an explosive that was more powerful than nitroglycerin. From Vine, I knew that Boyer was fast working out how to produce RDX in enormous quantities. His research was done at the McGill chemistry lab where he taught, but he sent his findings through Vine to Zabotin, who in turn had Gouzenko encrypt them for Moscow. If dynamite could shake steel until it blew up, RDX was capable of cutting through metal and pulverizing it. Until the Americans dropped the bomb on Hiroshima, the politburo thought the RDX formula was promising. After Hiroshima, Moscow dismissed Boyer, but he remained true to his mission, claiming to Vine that RDX was more humane than atomic destruction.

Sympathetic professors with thirds from Oxbridge were heavily represented at the Labour Day event. The academicians were helping to found Carleton University over on Colonel By Drive. They'd all read about the international brigades of socialists fighting during the Spanish Civil War for the anarchists, and they wished to do their bit for the Revolution. Zabotin couldn't figure out how to make use of them since they were remarkably naïve English professors who specialized in Romantic poetry while coveting adventures as glorious as those they lectured about to their idolizing Canadians students.

Zabotin enjoyed their company, their deadly serious discussions about the imminent dictatorship of the proletariat. The rezident was particularly fond of Professor Roger Iron and his slender wife with the cherry-red manicured fingernails. In a moment of weakness, Zabotin once told me that her long powerful legs reminded him of Betty Grable's, the American movie star. The Irons attended Soviet Embassy events whenever they were invited and sometimes ran as couriers for the GRU when no one else was available. In Ottawa, other power couples considered them a debonair duo.

A comparative literature professor from Berlin, Dietrich von Schloss, who'd been on the correct side of the war from the beginning and wished to see the Reds govern all of a divided Germany, pinned me against the wall, trying to extract my telephone number. The muscular Professor von Schloss, with the bulging sensitive lips, was slated to head the new German language department at Carleton University.

In truth, Charles Haines, the portly Assistant Dean of Arts at Carleton University, was more of interest to me than von Schloss. Haines was spying for the Americans and Zabotin suggested I befriend him. His grey stringy locks surrounded a beaming, friendly countenance. When he smiled I could see his nicotine-stained teeth.

"Isn't it exciting that Harry Truman thinks Stalin is as evil as Hitler?" I asked Professor Haines. Men like Haines enjoyed a good pull on their leg.

"Oh, Miss Linton, how you jest! I prefer being on the winning side of history and I fear your moment may have passed." The distinguished professor, who was sweating profusely, took a long drink from his tumbler of Canadian Club followed by a draw on his Cuban cigar.

I noticed he was wearing tan loafers without socks, unlike Professor von Schloss, who preferred tightly laced black brogues with diamond-patterned silk stockings. I brought Haines a plate laden with Zsuzsa's veal rouladen and potato dumplings drenched in gravy, without once meeting von Schloss' entreating gaze as I passed him by. When the German's cool hand touched my arm, I pulled away. Professor Haines ate with abandon. He was more interested in his dinner than he was in me.

The young man I secretly found intriguing was a doctoral student in linguistics. Kent Hardman had recently returned from Havana, where he'd spent the summer improving his Spanish by working in the sugar cane fields with Cuban peasants. I knew him from Grierson's operation at the Wartime Information Bureau, where the linguist frequently translated missives into Spanish for the comrades in the Caribbean. According to Grierson, Hardman also volunteered at a left-wing bookstore on Bank Street called Red Star Books.

I appreciated the way Hardman allowed his russet hair to flow down to his shoulders, as a poet would, and how his sea-green eyes peered directly into mine when we spoke. Hardman was telling me about Cuba, the corruption, the grinding poverty of the peasants, who he believed would eventually rise up against their oppressors. As we spoke I could feel two sets of eyes on me, Vine from one side of the room and Zabotin from the other. I wondered if they were jealous of the graduate student who'd captured my attention.

They needn't have been alarmed. I understood Hardman. He was a New World thug. I turned to meet Vine and then Zabotin's gaze. They were my landsmen, my countrymen from the old world. I rolled my eyes and we silently agreed, as old friends often do. Hardman was the type of political monster we hadn't encountered before: coldly ambitious and oddly detached, while we'd wished to save our own skins at the same time as rescuing the world. Russia meant something to us. Zabotin couldn't match Hardman's need to destroy whatever he touched. He was a walking time bomb: a loner, no family and no real connections. When he had a girl, she never lasted long. After a few months, he was on to the next, each woman like a small Caribbean island waiting to be plundered.

In the crowded apartment, I couldn't help being curious about this young man as I watched Hardman chatting with Gouzenko. Gouzenko pointed to the brown over-stuffed handbag he'd left by his wife's feet, but Hardman turned up his nose at the cipher clerk.

Instead Hardman walked toward me and extended his hand. "Labour Day, Miss Linton, the People's Day. In ten years—less than ten—I expect we'll witness a display of Communist military might on Wellington Street, right in front of the Parliament Buildings. When we take the country."

"I'd love to think so, but how exactly are we going to manage that, Mr. Hardman?" I inquired. "Taking the country, that is."

"Well, armed struggle of course."

"Led by the Communist Party, no doubt," I said.

I thought about how Hardman was the type who might thrive under Stalin's rule. He was the kind of political animal the Party could promote. Maybe it needed him. In 1945, Stalin wanted only one thing: the bomb. Without his own atomic weapon, he'd be under constant threat from the American military. What the Soviets needed weren't Russian patriots, or idealists, but scientists, technocrats and more yes-men. I was thirty-eight, but my time was over. I recalled the girl I had seen at the Canadian National Exhibition, who'd been shot out of canon and how she landed on her feet. I was so young when I watched her bounce safely onto a net inside the stadium. I'd been thrilled. I wanted to be her. No longer.

I looked around the room that night and shuddered. Sybil had invited two displaced persons from the camps, survivors from Auschwitz, a brother and sister, both mathematicians. They'd snuck into Canada after the liberation. The two kept thanking Sybil and anyone else who'd allow them to tug at their sleeves. Before the war in Berlin, they'd been members of the Communist Party and they were Jews, so they were twice cursed.

I understood that Canadian immigration policy limited the number of Jews entering the country. It was Preston Ellery, in fact, who had pleaded with the government to allow in more. That's what it was like after the war. People's loyalties were divided. Ellery was a good man; he'd never have betrayed his country without a heartfelt explanation. He aided the Soviets when the Nazis were winning the war. Now we were all stuck with the choices we'd made before or during the war. Even me, who'd never thought about what joining the Party would eventually mean or how I'd end up in an airless flat in Ottawa on the last sultry night of the summer wondering if a cipher clerk from the Soviet Embassy could destroy my life.

Before dinner, Fred Rose led the group in singing the Soviet National Anthem and then the Communist "Internationale." Mildred Macepeace was moved, trying to hide her tears behind her dainty handkerchief. Zabotin drank to Stalin's health with a double shot of vodka as the platters of smoked fish, herring, trout and salmon, were sent around the room. Roast brisket and chicken came next, followed by potato puddings and mounds of peppered, vinegary coleslaw. We all ate so much in the suffocating heat, except Igor and Svetlana, who didn't touch a morsel. They sat, side by side in silence, their thighs touching, Svetlana's large handbag at her feet. She was heavily pregnant and looked as if she might faint. I brought her a cold glass of water.

"You don't look well," I said as I handed her the glass. "Don't feel you must stay. No one will mind if you leave."

"Thank you, that's very kind," she said.

"Put an ice pack on the back of your neck when you get home." I touched her forehead. "You are feverish. Go home."

The Gouzenkos rose form their seats, excusing themselves, speaking in Russian. When Svetlana approached Drew Pearson, she pushed her handbag at him, but Pearson withdrew and turned away. Igor saluted his boss, Zabotin, and strangely his wife did the same. Zabotin raised his mutilated hand to his temple, and they were gone.

After the couple departed, I removed the white lace collar that accented my dress. The night was so humid. I sunk into Svetlana's place near an open window. I could feel the lingering heat of her body. From the window, I noticed Zsuzsa, ignoring the crowd, tending to her flower garden as the evening light faded to a sultry grey haze. In her sixties, she was still beautiful, a small woman with pearly skin, slender shoulders and dainty narrow feet.

In her garden, there were yellow roses in second bloom, purple delphiniums, pink hollyhocks and white asters. She watered her plants after the sun set, and tonight was no different. A limestone birdbath sat in the middle of the garden and I could detect the shards of heat lightening illuminating the miniature stone statues of frogs and chipmunks that Zsuzsa had hidden among the tall flower stalks. In a strange country, she had made this place her sanctuary. Like her, we were all displaced people, refugees from Europe with its conflagration of war and revolution.

A flash of lightening illuminated the garden. Soon it would thunderstorm and the earth would be drenched. From my seat near the window, I could see the electricity reflected in the glass eyes of the enchanting limestone animals. Roger Iron's wife suggested that the party move to the garden where the air was cooler. Hardman followed her, admiring her slim hips and muscular legs.

"More music," Zabotin ordered. "Louder!" He was drinking and appeared out of control. But I understood him, knowing that it was a performance. If asked, no one at the party would believe that Zabotin had allowed, no encouraged, Gouzenko to expose the Soviet plan to steal atomic secrets from the West that very night.

Sybil lifted the top of the record player nestled inside its wooden compartment. From outside, I could see through a mesh screen to the green tubes burning brightly inside the box. Carefully, she pulled a disc from its paper sleeve to play the *Concerto de Arunjuez*. I watched Sybil's expression of pure longing and knew she was dreaming that Fred Rose would spend the night with her and not return to Montreal before daybreak. If I were a true friend I would have offered them my apartment. It would be their final night of tranquility together for many years.

The music wafted through the living room. I continued to sit beside the window, where Vine joined me, leaving Mildred Macepeace to wait impatiently for him. He rarely sat still at parties or even at meetings, preferring to find a corner where he could stand and fidget and observe.

I didn't care who saw us. I leaned my head against Vine's shoulder and he kissed me, tenderly on the neck, as he hadn't done in years, not since we'd lived together in Toronto on Beaconsfield. His lips were cool. We clung to each other in silence for what seemed an exceedingly long time. Finally Vine rose, took my hand and led me to the garden where Zabotin was holding forth on Stalin's new five-year plan. In the rezident's presence, Vine stood back and disappeared into the shadows of the treed yard. I followed him out of loyalty, for old time's sake.

In my way, I cared deeply for them both, Vine and Zabotin, although it's hard to imagine how I could. These two men from my village. The three of us were all that remained. When I did return to the East, I discovered that not one Jew who'd lived in the shtetl on the day the Nazis invaded was alive. Nesvicz had become their graveyard.

Across the night sky, a great billowing cloud hung low above the trees. My view was of a menacing sky turning to the blackest of blue. Lightening shot across the heavens like an elaborate map charting the pathways of an ancient city. Rain pounded the earth. The music from the record player grew faint. From the building next door I could hear the CBC blaring on the radio. The announcer was informing us that a tornado had been spotted in the Ottawa Valley. It was heading our way and we were instructed to take cover if it reached the outer limits of the city.

I, who had managed to survive each maelstrom I'd encountered, considered what it would be like to be caught in a tornado, twisted and broken by the velocity of the storm. Each of us destroyed by the churning funnel's natural might. What would the destruction look like? Zabotin, the war hero, with his uniform torn open to reveal his scarred chest. Sybil and Fred locked in a terrified embrace. Vine and I, mangled by the storm and bloodied by the debris. Would it be easier, to expire that way? Was it better than what we were about to endure if Gouzenko followed through with his plans on the night Zabotin intended to save the world?

I returned to the flat. The lights flickered and went out. The air turned cold as the wind died down. Vine stayed by my side until the storm passed. Then he disappeared. When the power returned, an announcer on the radio said the tornado warning was over. The sharp scent of pine needles from the bush at the edge of the city filled the air. The CBC played a rousing fiddle tune from the backwoods. I dreamed of the silvery vodka never running dry or the music never coming to an end. I suddenly felt like I ought not to leave Zsuzsa's sanctuary on Florence Street. If we could remain exactly as were, mummified, the world would be kind to us, might absolve us for our inglorious betrayals, or offer us the time to forgive ourselves. But I was wrong. By morning, our lives were to be turned upside down, and I realized that I'd been right. A tornado would have been preferable.

The party was over. After the tornado warning, it couldn't be revived. Zabotin looked disappointed. He approached me and put both of his hands on my shoulders.

"Why so glum?" he asked. "It will all turn out the way I've planned."

"That's what I'm afraid of? Did you see Svetlana tonight? She was white as a ghost."

Zabotin didn't disagree. "It's Gouzenko's only chance." His eyes scanned the room. "Let's go outside."

The night sky was clear and the garden glistened under the light of the moon. Zabotin lead me to a bench.

"You need to know that the only original documents left in the safe for Gouzenko to steal were Vine's reports to Moscow. He had the combination to that safe. Remember, I enticed him to take the reports, once he was re-called to Moscow. So, stop worrying. Everything is under control."

"What about Fuchs' atomic drawings?"

"I told you I have them," Zabotin assured me again. But I knew, then, that he was lying. They were in Gouzenko's cache, in Svetlana's satchel. Why else would Zabotin have bothered with this entire operation if not to frighten the West into action?

"Why not include them? Aren't the drawings the proof that the Soviets have infiltrated Los Alamos?"

Zabotin pushed me away and for a moment, I thought he would tell me the truth. "I'll keep them with me for now as a safeguard. All in good time," he assured me.

"And the cablegrams from Homer?"

"Gouzenko didn't cable Homer's critical reports to the Director. I told you I sent them myself, and only I kept copies of the originals."

"Won't he realize that his stolen documents are of limited value?" I demanded.

"He's desperate. If Gouzenko doesn't go to the press tonight, I'll ship him back to Russia. His life hangs by a thread." Zabotin looked smug and it irritated me.

"Believe me, Freda, Gouzenko doesn't understand that his cache isn't as incriminating as he thinks. I'm telling you that I sent the critical ones myself to the Director. Do you think that I'm not able to decode and encrypt cables? When Gouzenko is debriefed by the Canadians, he can tell them intelligence was received from a source in Washington, but who knows what Gouzenko remembers or who he thinks Homer is?"

"Why are you doing this?" I asked. "Exposing us while Gouzenko stays safe in Canada?"

"You know it is not about Gouzenko and what he knows and what he doesn't know. I want to stop the Russians from making an atomic bomb."

I asked him if the papers in Svetlana's over-sized handbag were the stolen documents and Zabotin broke out into his most electrifying smile.

"So clever you are, darling Freda. Of course. I ordered Gouzenko to bring the documents with him tonight. He'd be mad to leave them in his apartment. That's why he tried to approach Drew Pearson tonight, but Pearson wasn't interested in the hysterical pleading of a lowly cipher clerk and his pregnant missus. Too bad for him. He might have broken the biggest news story since Hiroshima."

Chapter Seventeen

I t was after three in the morning when I fell onto my bed exhausted. Grierson had missed the Labour Day celebration, spending another night with Ellery at Pink Lake. I was intending to skip work that day or at least to sleep in as late as possible. Zabotin promised to alert me as soon as Gouzenko's revelations hit the news.

At seven-thirty, Grierson poked his head into my bedroom. "How on earth did you get in?" I asked him.

"Up the fire escape, like Vine does, he said. "I rang you over and over. I finally gave up."

Grierson's petty jealousies struck me as ridiculous. He was an original filmmaker, but lacking in other talents.

"Don't try to keep up with me, John," I said. "Allow me to shower and dress or I'll be late for work." Being at the office would be better than spending the morning with Grierson.

"I need to talk to you." Grierson was pleading with me.

But I was tired of hearing men's confessions. "Before you say anything, I'm going to put on a pot of coffee." My head ached from last night's vodka. "Then I'll listen." There were too many men in my life, and they all required immediate attention.

In the shower, I ran the water as cold as I could stand it. I was worried about Vine, where he'd gone to hide after disappearing from the party. He could still make me feel exceptional, the way he did last night when he kissed me. I couldn't say the same for Grierson.

I heard him as he opened the bathroom door, undressed and pushed aside the shower curtain to get in behind me. Grierson grabbed the soapy cloth from my hand and began to wash my breasts and between my legs. When he pressed himself against me, I turned to face him.

"Now is not the time, John." I stepped out of the shower and away from him, drying myself and twisting a towel into a knot to cover my soaking hair. "Give me a minute."

I was barefoot and wearing my red silk dressing gown, the one I'd brought from Toronto. It was a gift from poor Klopot. I poured two cups of coffee from the pot brewing on the stove. Grierson was looking sporty in brown Bermuda shorts and a yellow-striped golfing shirt, the clothes he wore at Pink Lake.

"I have no idea why Zabotin allowed Igor Gouzenko to work alone," Grierson abruptly announced. "I suppose he trusted him."

"We're all looking for someone to trust."

"When that worm Gouzenko left your party last night he walked over to *The Ottawa Journal* to hand the night editor a cache of secret documents."

I wondered if this was true. Zabotin hadn't alerted me this morning.

Grierson continued. "The fellow at the *Journal* thought Gouzenko was a clown, assumed he was joking."

"Unbelievable."

"Very late last night, the phone rang. I was exhausted by the endless conversation with Ellery at Pink Lake, but decided to pick up. It was my friend Andrew, the night editor at the *Journal*." Grierson drank his coffee quickly. Clearly he'd been up all night. "He said a Soviet national who could speak little English was talking rubbish to him. He had his pregnant wife with him and a huge handbag that resembled a diaper bag. Andrew laughed. He knows I'm close to the embassy, so he suggested I call the Soviet Ambassador, just in case this Russian joker got out of hand." Grierson was clenching his jaw.

"I know Andrew." I spoke softly. "Let me get in touch with him. I'll meet him for a drink tonight. Did he actually send Gouzenko away?"

"He did. The biggest story since the war, and he turned it away. Andrew told him to come back in the morning when the city desk editor was about," Grierson said. "He told him to take care of his wife and get some sleep."

"Are you joking?"

"No, I'm not. Gouzenko sent Svetlana home to tend to their boy. Apparently, he then decided to pace outside the Department of Justice's front entrance throughout the remainder of the night."

"Why would he do that?"

"He's was waiting for someone to show up and bring him inside. I'm told that when a guard arrived, Gouzenko demanded to speak with the Minister. Apparently he begged the guard to let him in, but the man wasn't having any of it."

"A man needs to follow orders, no matter what."

"The guard wouldn't budge. Gouzenko became more vexed and said he was carrying documents that proved that the Soviets were spying on the Canadian government. Later when the guard was questioned he admitted that Gouzenko swore up and down that a Member of Parliament was an intelligence operative for the Soviets. Even so, the guard was proud that he'd held his ground. Gouzenko wasn't allowed into the building until after nine.

"At about 10 a.m. the Minister of Justice heard about Gouzenko. He too, thought it was a hoax, and left Gouzenko cooling his heels in the hallway outside his office for more than an hour."

"How do you know all these details?"

"Zabotin contacted Ellery at the lake house and told him what was going to happen. He asked him to treat Gouzenko with compassion, as a defector. Ellery rang me directly afterward. Zabotin had said Gouzenko would be tried under Soviet law if he was returned to the embassy. He wanted Ellery to speak with the prime minister. Ellery was surprised that Zabotin wished Canada to accept Gouzenko as a legitimate Soviet defector."

"And what did Ellery do?"

"Tried to fix it, as he always does. He immediately rang Norman Robertson, the deputy minister at External Affairs, and pleaded with him to pick up Gouzenko. But Robertson wouldn't hear of it. Robertson didn't want to tangle with the Justice Department. It wasn't his territory and he'd didn't wish to step on toes," Grierson reported. "While Gouzenko was left sitting outside the Justice Minister's office, he threatened to commit suicide. Apparently, Robertson was on the line at that moment and he thought it appropriate for Gouzenko to approach the Ottawa police rather than the federal government A tender-hearted Minister's assistant sent him to the city police by taxi."

I could hardly believe what I was hearing, but Grierson wouldn't exaggerate such matters.

"Robertson should have spoken to the Minister, to St. Laurent, immediately. It's up to the Minister of Justice to offer safe haven to Gouzenko and Svetlana." I was livid. It was hard to believe that Norman Robertson didn't realize that Gouzenko was exposing a foreign spy ring operating right under the Canadian government's nose. I was nervous that Svetlana wasn't resilient enough to withstand this comedy of errors.

"The Ottawa police alerted the Mounties who transported Gouzenko to their headquarters. Robertson caved in then," Grierson said, "sending his own limo to pick up Svetlana and the kid. They've joined Gouzenko at RCMP headquarters. They're safe with the RCMP. Justice Minister St. Laurent never approved of the government's wartime love affair with the Soviets. Now he can prove that his suspicions were justified. If I understand Ellery correctly, he wanted St. Laurent to be the one to alert the prime minister. Ellery is already trying to distance himself from the entire affair."

I asked Grierson if he knew how many documents Gouzenko had delivered to the Mounties. I thought about Svetlana's bulging handbag, sitting at her feet during last night's party. I could have taken the bag and done what with it? Put an end to Zabotin's escapade. He was playing the hero again, but suppose he was acting honourably, as he was attempting to convince me? In 1917, he'd sided with the Bolsheviks. The old regime was rotten. His motives were admirable. In his eyes, little people like Vine and me and places like Nesvicz were dispensable, but if Stalin could make the atomic bomb, Zabotin was certain that he'd deploy it, after which the Americans would retaliate. It always came down to deliberately hurting those closest to us for the greater good.

"Ellery knows. One hundred and nine documents, two hundred and forty pages of material," Grierson said.

"Zabotin knew this exact count and he told Ellery?" By then, I understood that Zabotin had selected the perfect cables for Gouzenko to expose to the West. The rezident knew exactly what the authorities were about to discover.

"Yes," Grierson said. "Zabotin kept count of the number of documents in the safe and so he knew the precise number missing."

"How prescient of him," I said. "And he offered this information up to Ellery?"

"It was good of him to let Ellery know that the authorities at the highest level will soon realize that we are working for Soviets intelligence," he added. From the beginning, this was the chance we took."

"Did Zabotin say what was in the documents?" I didn't know whether to laugh or cry. "Was there intelligence about the bomb?"

Grierson put his coffee cup down on the table. His hands were shaking and he didn't want me to see how frightened he was. He was kicking the table leg with one foot while swallowing hard. I watched his Adam's apple move up and down. "Not exactly. Zabotin admitted to Ellery that he wasn't certain of the content of the cables and how incriminating they were."

I wondered how much Grierson would pay for his transgressions, or Ellery for his. I was tempted to ask Grierson if he thought it odd that Zabotin kept count of the exact number of missing documents, but not their content, but I knew better.

"There was probably no use in pushing Grierson for more information. He knew the least of all of us. Last night Zabotin tried to assure me that Fuchs' diagrams were not in Gouzenko's hands, but I was certain then he was lying.

"I'm going to work, John," I said calmly. "You should do the same."

"We need to take action," he replied, searching for an emotional response from me.

"And what do you propose? Kidnapping Gouzenko from RCMP headquarters?"

Grierson was disappointed. He'd wanted to shock me, to make a lasting impression. "You and Vine, Sybil, Sam Carr, Mildred Macepeace, Raymond Boyer. The lot of you will be exposed. They'll learn everything about us and that the one Communist Party Member of Parliament is working for the Soviets. They'll throw the book at Rose."

About us, I thought, but said nothing. As I sat smoking his cigarettes and drinking coffee, he offered to rescue me, to smuggle me out of Canada. If I married him, I'd become a British citizen. He would be my protector.

Grierson never understood me. "What makes you think I would run and hide?" I asked him.

"Zabotin will leave you behind, Freda," he said. "He's already been re-called to Moscow."

Perhaps that was why Zabotin hadn't contacted me this morning. "When?" I inquired.

"Well, not for some months. The GRU wants Zabotin in Ottawa for now. Possibly to defend us or to wait until the furor blows over."

Of course, Moscow would watch to see how the Canadians handled Gouzenko and how hard the Americans pressed the RCMP to dig deeper to expose the activities of Zabotin's spies. I wondered if the Mounties would round us up, interrogate us, demand to know how much we knew about Soviet intelligence and how it operated across North America. They would question us about Homer, if Zabotin was lying about the cryptograms from Washington. He'd given me his word that he had ordered Gouzenko to destroy the cables from Homer after transmitting them to Moscow. Only Zabotin kept copies of the critical ones. But still, the cipher clerk was certain to mention the Soviet mole in Washington. I never did believe Zabotin when he assured me that Gouzenko wouldn't be able to recall the encryptions from Homer.

Last night Zabotin also gave me his word that he'd retained the atomic drawings from Fuchs, that no one had seen them other than Vine and him-self. Yet, I couldn't help wondering if Zabotin had included them in Gouzen-ko's cache of documents. If he truly wished to stop a nuclear war, he would signal to the West how deep Soviet intelligence had permeated Los Alamos.

"What's the prime minister doing?"

"Probably what he always does, consulting his long-dead mother through a spiritualist, or so Ellery tells me." John looked grey and exhausted. "President Truman wants him in Washington tomorrow, and Ellery is to accompany him."

"Are others exposed, our comrades in New York and Los Angeles?"

"The old Marxists from the Frankfurt School, the ones living in L.A., who are advising the FBI how to handle the Nazis, are still sending cables to Stalin on the sly. Nuremburg was too easy on the criminals, they believe and rightly so. We aren't the only ones worried that the Yanks are going soft on the Germans."

"That's what Zabotin believes, too," I added, wondering how Grierson knew about the German philosophers. "And Ellery?" I was curious to know if Ellery would become the top man at the United Nations. "What does he think will happen to him?"

"Ellery expects he will be recalled to Ottawa. The Soviets will have to nix his bid for the top spot at the UN. He knows too much. Anyone could blackmail him."

I was surprised about how much Ellery revealed to Grierson and how Zabotin was using Ellery as the conduit between himself and the prime minister. "What happens to Gouzenko now?" I asked.

"The Soviets are desperate to convince the PM to release Gouzenko to them on diplomatic grounds. He is an employee at their embassy. But Ellery is in on it now, advising King not to act imprudently."

Of course, Ellery would become the mediator. He would be the only one close enough to influence the prime minister while trying to avert a diplomatic crisis. As Zabotin predicted, if the Americans got out of hand, or if they discovered that a British diplomat in Washington, the very one who chaired their atomic committee, had been flipped by the Soviets, they, too, might be capable of rash action. It was only weeks since they'd exploded two nuclear weapons over Japan.

I understood at that moment why the Director wished Zabotin to deliver a sample of plutonium from Chalk River to the Centre. It was why Zabotin was still considering sending Vine to meet with Alan Nunn May. He was under orders to obtain a sample of plutonium for transport to Moscow. Plutonium was the missing ingredient the hard-pressed Soviet scientists needed to make the bomb, as well as determine where and how to construct their heavy water plant, one modelled on Chalk River's recent discoveries. Without heavy water to refine uranium, there would be no Soviet atomic bomb. I wondered how much Gouzenko knew about this.

According to Grierson, Ellery had already been in to speak with Gouzenko. He was attempting to cool him down while trying to convince King that the best place for Gouzenko was in Canada. Gouzenko would give Canada leverage over the other Western powers.

"It looks like Gouzenko will be offered asylum in Canada," Grierson recounted.

"Who else in Ottawa knows?" I asked.

"By now, I expect a few people," he replied. "Fred Rose. Norman Robertson rang him right away as soon as his limo delivered Svetlana to join Gouzenko at RCMP headquarters. Rose and Robertson were chummy during the war when intelligence between Canada and the Russians was shared. Robertson needed to make sure that Gouzenko wasn't a crank before bringing him in. Afterward, Rose went directly to Zabotin. By that time, Gouzenko was under suicide watch by a cordon of Mounties. Ellery is surprised that Zabotin took it so calmly. Robertson is making certain the details of story don't get out, at least until the PM talks to President Truman. The Americans are livid that security in Canada is so sloppy. Zabotin is practically operating right under the prime minister's nose."

"Freda, do you have a passport you can use?"

"I'm not running. I don't want to disappear. I've done that once already."

For the next hour, Grierson strived to convince me otherwise. "The circumstances are entirely different," he pleaded. "I can get you into England. In London, you'll find friends; comrades who will protect you. Before long, I'll meet you there. We can start a family."

"I'm not interested in marriage or starting a family," I replied. "Not now, not until I find the one I lost."

What he never understood was that I couldn't be convinced that I deserved to be rescued. It wasn't the way things worked out for me. Years ago, Vine had been successful, and in the end, it was fruitless. Even when Grierson pleaded that he could get me into England without marrying me, I wouldn't hear of it.

Chapter Eighteen

A t the Wartime Information Bureau, Grierson was as fidgety as a man with his finger plugged into a live socket. I was back at TASS, hoping my work would distract me from the chaos swirling outside. I started to compose a story about the federal government's agricultural farm at Dow's Lake. I was trying to convince Grierson to shoot a short documentary about it but knew there was no chance it would ever see the light of day.

I went to Grierson's office to pitch him the story. Zabotin was on the line to him incessantly, calling over and over again. Through the receiver, I could hear his wife, Lydia, crying in the background. She was no doubt frightened about her husband's recall to Moscow.

I returned to my desk at TASS and waited for the rezident's message. It came at 4 p.m. He asked me to meet him at the bar at the Château Laurier. I suggested it was too public, but he just laughed. "What possible difference does it make at this point?" Zabotin had been drinking.

I locked my desk, checked to ensure that my passport was in my handbag and left the office. I crossed Rideau Street and stood back to admire the Château Laurier's grand sloping green metal roof. It was shining under the brilliant afternoon September sun. The air was cool and fresh and the scent of autumn was wafting in from the far north where the temperature had dropped to freezing last night. Inside the bar, a fire was lit. The room was comforting, decorated in soft leather chairs and brass lamps with green shades. Fred Rose was already seated with Zabotin when I arrived.

"She knows, doesn't she?" Rose looked unglued and didn't wait for the answer. "We did right. The Soviets won the war, no question. What about the cables sent from Homer? Gouzenko might have read them all," he said.

I took a deep breath as Rose dug into his apple pie and ice cream. He wasn't a drinking man.

"Did Gouzenko decrypt Homer's cables for you?" Rose pushed Zabotin. "If he read them we're on the hook for treason, for sharing nuclear secrets with a foreign power." Rose was sweating. He understood what this meant for all of us and particularly for him as a Member of Parliament. "Are Homer's cables now in Canadian hands?"

Zabotin looked at Rose as if he were the biggest fool on earth. "Perhaps I should never have let you in on the intelligence from Homer. What did you think could happen? That there weren't risks? I told you about Homer because you needed to know the facts, not the propaganda. After Hiroshima. I hoped you, as a Canadian Member of Parliament, would consider the implications of both sides having the bomb. Did you think about that?"

"Of course I did," Rose replied "If we, if the Soviets, don't have the bomb, the Americans will destroy us. Unless we have atomic weapons, we won't be able to defend ourselves."

Zabotin looked at me for a moment and then turned again to Rose. "Homer is describing a bigger bomb than the one the Americans dropped on Hiroshima. Fat Man, Homer calls it. The destruction at Nagasaki was more punishing than the first bomb. It vapourized a city crawling with civilians. Those innocent people received no advance notice." Zabotin raised his good hand to order more vodka, neat. He didn't mention Fuchs' drawings for Fat Man to Rose and how he'd kept them back from the Centre.

"The Director now wishes me to send a sample of plutonium from Chalk River. He believes that our Soviet scientists need it to make our own Fat Man, or maybe even a bigger bomb than the one dropped on Nagasaki," said Zabotin. "It should take some time for them to figure that out."

Rose flinched. "It's our fault if Soviet progress on the bomb is obstructed." Zabotin's words were falling on deaf ears.

"Before things stall, I'm going to send Vine to Chalk River. There's still time. Mackenzie King is dithering about what to do with Gouzenko and I believe even Truman doesn't quite understand how deeply we've penetrated Los Alamos." Zabotin was trying to scare Rose.

Rose wiped the sweat from his forehead.

"And yes, if you need to know," Zabotin continued, "I did have Gouzenko decode certain of Homer's cables for me before sending them to Moscow. Why wouldn't I? I'm here on the ground. I need to know what the Centre is expecting of me. Gouzenko's copies of the Homer cables are in the cache now in the RCMP's hands. They know everything I know."

Zabotin had planned everything, including how crucial it was to maximize the coveted atomic intelligence in Gouzenko's stolen documents—if the Western powers were to take notice. At the same time, he'd lied to me. My instincts were right. He had pretended that he had transmitted Homer's most important cables to Moscow without Gouzenko's assistance, and I believed him.

My situation was dire. I was in on the entire operation. The Soviets would eventually figure out that Zabotin was not being straight with them, and the Canadians would inform the Americans and the Brits that the rezident was engaged in the most dangerous level of espionage.

Long afterward Zabotin would tell me that the information in Homer's cables and the sample of plutonium we provided to the Director only shaved two years off the building of the first Soviet nuclear bomb, but those two years were crucial in Zabotin's mind. If they'd received Fuchs' drawings before Nagasaki they might have built their bomb earlier.

"Men need to get the slaughter out of their blood. The military on both sides must experience a long peace or the killing will never end." Zabotin took a deep breath, waiting for Rose's response.

Rose was perplexed. "We're on the right side, Nikolai. We need to demonstrate our power to the West right now or they'll destroy us. Isn't that what the war was about? To make a better world?"

"If there is a world left to make better," Zabotin replied.

Rose shook his head. This was not what he'd devoted his life fighting for.

"Don't worry Fred," Zabotin said. "I'll send Vine to Chalk River. He can carry a sample of plutonium for the Director…"

I cut him off. "No, not Vine."

"Who then? Fred is a public figure. Nunn May trusts Vine. We need to get that scientist out of Canada and back to Britain before the Americans figure out he was collaborating with the Soviets. Zabotin wouldn't budge."

I was quiet. I couldn't allow Zabotin to use Vine as a go-between. Not now. It would be safer if I collected the plutonium from Nunn May. No one would suspect a woman.

Zabotin snapped his fingers and asked for the waiter to bring me a martini. My hands were cold and clammy. "Drink, Freda," he ordered when the waiter placed the glass before me.

Rose was beginning to look ill. "She knows everything, doesn't she?" Rose asked as he readied himself to leave the bar. He was alarmed that Zabotin had let me in on so much.

When it was just the two of us, Zabotin clutched my hand. "If we are to be together, I must tell you everything. So you can prepare. Fuchs' drawings are in with Gouzenko's papers, too. At the last moment, I added them to his cache along with copies of Homer's decoded cables. I told Rose the truth. I'm not sure the cipher clerk knows exactly what he was carrying, but the West will realize how deep Soviet intelligence penetrated Los Alamos. They are being led to believe the Soviets have the actual drawings for a nuclear bomb. But at least I've delayed the creation of the first Soviet atomic weapon."

My head felt terribly heavy. It was weighing down my entire body. If I couldn't put a stop to this sensation, I would drop to the floor, never to rise again. Zabotin held the glass to my lips. "Drink. You need to be strong, if you are to survive. If we are to survive."

I didn't believe I would, survive with or without Zabotin. The odds were not in my favour He'd lied to me about holding back Fuchs' drawings and about Homer's cables. Gouzenko's documents were earth shattering. The détente between the Soviets and the West would come to a crashing end and all because of Zabotin.

"At first, the Director won't realize that I didn't send him Fuchs' drawings. It will take a little time for that information to filter back to Moscow. Yes, I slipped them into Svetlana's handbag at the last moment. The Centre doesn't know that Vine brought the drawings back from Los Alamos in June. Only you and I, and Vine know that. We're the only ones. And Fuchs, of course."

I was trembling as I clutched the glass.

"Now that the Director is asking me for a plutonium sample, we can comply, but he doesn't have the drawings. Not yet."

"Can't you stop? Haven't you done enough to endanger us?" I murmured. "Don't make things worse. Don't you think the plutonium sample will satisfy him for now?"

"Yes, I suspect you're correct. But I need a few months to map out our escape route."

"One side or the other will punish you, punish us," I said. "They'll figure out how you deceived them."

"Extracting plutonium for a nuclear bomb isn't a simple formula. Making it explode is even more complicated. It will take the Soviets a few years to figure it out. The uranium formula was easier to copy, but they'll want to work with the Fat Man diagrams and plutonium if they are to keep pace with the Americans. Why build an inferior bomb than the one the Yanks constructed?"

"If we ship the Director the plutonium, perhaps we can continue with our work. Spying on the debates in the House of Commons?"

"That was a cover for our serious work," Zabotin said. "Too bad you never understood that."

"Are you finished? For once tell me the truth."

"My intelligence is ruined," Zabotin conceded. "We aren't important anymore to the Centre. There's nothing left for me to give them. The Director will look elsewhere. To his American assets loyal to the Party. This Julius Rosenberg fellow in New York has contacts at Los Alamos. His brother-in-law, I believe. The mole, Homer, will be removed. Fuchs will be extradited to Germany. I'll be surprised if any of them makes it through alive." He folded his good hand over his bad one and sat completely still.

How he infuriated me.

"I don't want you to send Vine to Chalk River. He can't be the one to deliver the plutonium to Moscow. I won't let you do that to him," I whispered in Zabotin's ear.

But he only placed his hands on both my shoulders and in his most imperious voice, ordered me to sit up straight.

"What if Moscow eventually questions Vine and that leads back to us?" I demanded. My argument was that Vine was weak. He would betray us. I was determined to return to the Soviet Union to find out what had happened to my family and to see Masha. Better it be me who collected the plutonium from Chalk River and delivered it to the Director. I was reliable, and ultimately much stronger than Vine.

"I'll get you out of this. I give you my word. Vine is expendable." Zabotin rubbed his bad hand.

He was forcing me to choose between him and Vine, a choice I'd been dreading since coming to Ottawa. If I carried the plutonium to Moscow in Vine's place, the choice need never be made. Vine was the only person remaining from my beginnings, from before the war, from Nesvicz. He and Masha. I would not be the one to put him in harm's way, as I did my family when I abandoned them. It was on my head if they were dead and nothing could convince me otherwise.

"Don't look so glum," Zabotin said. "This is the moment I've been grooming you for since you arrived in Ottawa. Back there, in Nesvicz, I knew you were something else. Do you think I care what happens to Vine? It was you I chose to save. When I heard you were undercover for the Party, it was me who had you transferred to Ottawa, to be near me, to be at my side. And you've proved me right. You were made for his. There's something indestructible about you, Freda."

I didn't believe him. Most of the time, I was mired in guilt. I wasn't even certain I wished to survive, but that was none of Zabotin's business. "You were grooming me to betray the People's Republic, so you could share intelligence with the United States, to give up everything we've been fighting for?" Zabotin took me for a fool.

"No, I've been grooming you to act, to do the right thing when the moment came even if you are under Harry Vine's thumb."

I pushed my drink away. "You are delusional. War and retribution, that's all you know. That and deception. You lied to me about Homer's cables and about the drawings. You gave me your word you'd kept them away from Gouzenko. Now the entire world will know what we've been doing. You believe that single-handedly you can outsmart everyone, that you can stop a nuclear war and then return to living the privileged life of a diplomat. Nikolai Zabotin, the great war hero and now saviour of the world."

His face turned red. Zabotin didn't like it when I was honest with him. Without a word, he threw a twenty-dollar bill on the table and left me sitting there alone.

I sat still. A statue. The waiter asked me if I needed a glass of water and I declined. I was considering the men I'd seduced, young and old, from Klopot to Grierson, and how I wagered I was doing good work for the Party, for Communism, for international peace. Zabotin was fast disabusing me of that notion. I couldn't decipher why he'd bothered joining the Reds during the Revolution, other than wanting to be on the winning side.

But winning didn't appear to matter to Zabotin anymore. He was either taking the coward's way out, wishing to remain in Canada as an ordinary citizen after Gouzenko's defection, or he actually believed Stalin would use the bomb if the Soviet Union could replicate the American one. Why, then, hadn't he defected himself? Gouzenko was his proxy. Zabotin couldn't bring himself to be a defector, he just wished to remain in the shadows and try to live a normal life. Or perhaps he truly loved me and didn't wish to leave me behind to face the wrath of the Canadians and the Soviets.

* * *

Chernobyl journal
1988

Deep in the forest surrounding her dilapidated hut, I sought out Elka for our fourth meeting. The front wall of her home was crooked and crumbling. Air streamed in through the chinks in the wood. Buckets were placed under the corners of the sloping roof to collect the runoff. Beside the hut, mingled with the overgrown lilac bushes were tin cans and beer bottles that had been scattered by giant-sized rats searching for treats in Elka's rubbish.

Elka was collecting wood for the fire where she cooked her meals. I helped her carry the twigs and branches inside and she was thankful that I was saving her a trip. I could see that she was building shutters from scraps of wood that she'd collected from abandoned dachas in the Chernobyl forest. Clearly, she was planning to stay on.

Elka kept a horse, chickens and a goat. I had no idea where she found these farm animals, but she gladly showed me how she hooked up the horse to an old hay wagon. "That's how I travel, these days," she said. "I go into Pripyat whenever I wish and I find what I need to make myself comfortable out here."

"Good for you," I said.

"Everything I need is there for the taking." Elka was proud of her resourcefulness.

I was thinking that Zabotin and I could do the same. We hadn't hunted for furniture in Pripyat since settling in, just books and medicine. "I'd like a bathtub. We could heat water from our wood stove."

"What an idea. Come with me one day. I know where the best houses in Pripyat are. Where the mucky-mucks in the Party lived. No one moved anything. Remember?" she asked. "One minute they told us we were safe and by two days after the explosion, we had a few hours to evacuate."

I remembered. Zabotin had convinced us, Vine and me, Rose and Sybil, to leave town as soon as the reactor exploded.

"If we could use Comrade Zabotin's Lada, it would be quicker than taking the horse. With the horse, we must stay overnight in a ghost hotel. I prefer to sleep in my own bed here in the forest."

At first I couldn't figure out how Elka knew about the Lada since Zabotin kept it hidden under branches in the forest. Then I recalled that a few weeks ago, I'd caught her spying on us. She dashed away before I could approach her. I admired her pluck. I smiled at her.

"Don't laugh," she chided me. "You're accustomed to the best of everything. In Nesvicz you lived like a princess. Anastasia Romanoff, that's who you think you are! I've never had anything. In Israel I was sent to a Kibbutz to pick oranges. You try and see how you would endure that. Sweltering in the burning sun, twelve hours a day. No privacy at night."

"How do you know how I lived in Nesvicz?"

"I told you. Your brother Simcha was in the forest with us, the partisans, until 1942," she said.

"You knew him that well." I was skeptical, but desperate to know more.

"Well enough. He left a wife and two girls to come fight with us, but he was more like you than me. Soft. He couldn't take it. The partisans allowed him to go behind the Red Army lines, where he'd be safe, but he wanted to re-unite with his family. That's what he was like when I knew him. Our existence in the forest was too hard on him. I suppose he felt guilty for abandoning his wife and kids. They'd gone to Łódź in 1939 before the Nazis invaded. Simcha thought they would be safer there, in a big modern city. The Łódź Ghetto was liquidated eventually, most were transported to the Chelmno crematorium or marched to Auschwitz, as you know."

I was weeping by then. Elka was out of the practice of revealing so much.

"I'll tell you the rest the next time you come to visit," she said.

The next day, I walked over to Elka's hut again and lured her back to ours with the offer of freshly baked sweet buns.

"I suppose you can't wait to talk about your brother Simcha?" she asked, sitting on the sofa in our screened porch.

"Tell me."

Vine was hiding in the next room. He didn't want to face Elka, but he wished to listen in on what she had to report about my brother. He remembered Simcha from when he was a boy in Nesvicz. Vine was fond of him, recalling that Simcha was a bright child who asked the rabbi insightful questions during cheder. "He thought he could understand God's mind, by asking the rabbi questions like, why children must obey their parents when sometimes children were smarter," Vine reminisced. "I'm sorry about what happened to him," he said, putting his right hand over his heart.

"Does it hurt today, your heart?" I inquired.

"No more than usual." He looked so small, as if he'd shrunk to half the size he was in Ottawa. If Simcha had survived the Nazis, as Elka claimed, I wondered if he'd remember Vine.

Elka, who couldn't see Vine but kept gazing at the corner of the porch where he was hiding, crossed her legs. She was wearing mud-caked work boots though the forest was dry. "I've been fishing," she explained as I inspected her footwear. "You should try it. The fish are getting huge. You three could feast on one for days." She held out her arms to show me how long the fish were, more than two feet. "Big heads on them. It looks like they have ears. Be quiet as a mouse when you're fishing for them." She was trying to scare me.

"Vine prefers beef," I said calmly, but she countered by reminding me that red meat wasn't prescribed for heart patients.

Elka uncrossed her legs to put her boots up on the crates in front of the sofa. She was taking over.

"Get on with what you know about Simcha," I said.

"After he left the partisans, Simcha returned to Łódź to find his wife and two children. It was 1942, early in January. Word has it that he arrived on New Year's Day. There were more than two hundred thousand Jewish prisoners stuffed into four square kilometres in the ghetto. It was a hellish place, worse than Warsaw or Minsk where community leaders with good intentions tried to make life easier for the captives of the ghettos.

"That rich Jew, the leader chosen by the Nazis in Łódź, Mordechai Rumkowski, he was corrupt. He and his cronies kept the best food and medicine in the ghetto for themselves. He worked the other Jews to death; he starved them, children too. He forced them to work in makeshift factories. Freezing in the winter. Slave labour. When Simcha arrived, he was immediately detailed to the shit brigade."

I didn't want Elka to continue, so I put up my hand, but she didn't quit.

"He and others collected the shit in tanks to pull outside the ghetto walls where they poured it in empty fields. It was important work. So many people, in such a tiny space. You can imagine. The men pulled the tanks themselves, not horses."

"The deportations to the Chelmno Death Camp began days after Simcha arrived. His wife and girls had been strong. They'd survived for more than two years without him, but they weren't good for much by the time he found them. The girls were young and exhausted from labouring in Rumkowski's factory. They and their mother were among the first ones sent to Chelmno. Of course, they were exterminated.

"Simcha remained at Łódź. He worked for Rumkowski and the other devils who tortured the starving Jews. Unlike Warsaw or Minsk, there was no rebellion, no uprising in Łódź. Rumkowski made certain of that.

"Your brother, from what I've heard, collaborated with Rumkowski. He helped him. Just before the ghetto was liquidated and the remaining residents joined the death march to Auschwitz, Simcha disappeared. He must have run away when he was dumping shit in the field outside the ghetto. Maybe he was burying the dead. There were lots of jobs for those who were willing. You must take into account how thorough the Nazis were. There are no photographs, no films or audio recordings of the exterminations in the ovens. Someone had to destroy the evidence of what happened in the Łódź Ghetto. Maybe Simcha helped them."

"What are you saying? That he was a collaborator? What proof do you have that my brother destroyed evidence or anything else?"

Elka was enjoying her moment. "People talk, they remember things."

"That doesn't make it true." For a moment, I thought back to what I knew, about Fred Rose, about Gouzenko, about what Zabotin and I had done back in Ottawa more than forty years ago. "People remember things in different ways." It was impossible for me to accept Elka's verdict. I wanted to slap her. Next to beg forgiveness from her. I held my head in my hands.

"Ask him yourself. I told you, he's alive."

I looked up at Elka. "Do you mean to tell me that he is actually alive? That you aren't making this up to torment me?"

Elka wasn't surprised by my response. "You can find him if you try. Reunite the Linton family. Somehow the three Linton children made it. Masha has known all along where your brother is."

All I could think of was finding Simcha. I was ashamed of him, but he was my kin. At first, I hadn't believed Elka, but her story was detailed enough that I couldn't discount it, although she couldn't recount exactly what Simcha had done. She wasn't inventing simply to wound me or was she? What would she have done in my brother's place; what would anyone of us have done that we can be so sanctimonious?

In Pripyat, before the disaster, I'd met Jews who'd remarried after the war. Their first families, their wives and children, had perished in the war and they'd managed to re-marry, usually a landsman, a friend from their old community, the shtetl now devoid of Jews. It was impossible for them not to search for someone who remembered what life was once like. Surely, that was the connection between Vine and me. We could recall the colours of the lop-sided houses on the laneways of Nesvicz, the crooked windows that wouldn't open in summer or keep out the cold in winter; the doors which would not close properly. And the singing. The singing in our shul on the Sabbath, the melodic sound of the cantor raising his voice in honour of God.

"Those who collaborated with the ruling elite, some survived. Don't look so shocked," Elka chuckled. "There are always survivors." She enjoyed taunting me. "Look at you and your men friends. Survivors."

Simcha was the weakest among my parents' children. He was clever, but he preferred lies to the truth. It didn't matter how small the lies were or how big. My mother would ask him if he wore his hat and mittens on a cold winter morning and he'd assure her he did, although I knew he hadn't touched them. He lied about his grades from cheder, or when he fell into trouble with the rabbi. He never admitted to doing wrong. I wondered how he'd changed or if he and Masha and I were essentially the same people we'd been in Nesvicz. She was the obedient one and although I was quiet, I was the rebel, at least in my mind. Even before Vine had knocked on the door of my father's house, I'd wanted to experience life beyond the borders of little Nesvicz. Simcha was the naughty one, but that didn't make him a coward or a collaborator.

When Vine poked his head into the screened porch, Elka was eager to greet him. She stood up and introduced herself. Vine moved back. He'd overheard her tale about my brother and wanted to know what he'd done, how he'd survived, but Elka had moved on from Simcha to Vine. She said I should contact Jewish Social Services in Kiev, the same organization that'd rescued her when she was about to drown herself after the war. She empha-sized she didn't wish to become involved in Simcha's case or associated with his name in any manner.

"Before the accident, didn't you try to collect a *minyan* at the old syna-gogue in Chernobyl?" Elka asked Vine.

Vine was surprised that she knew about his efforts and that he'd moved there after I'd settled in Chernobyl. He was proud of returning to the faith and of trying to pick up where he'd left off when he first disappeared from Nesvicz. He felt he owed it to his parents and his meagre beginnings.

"It goes back hundreds of years, the Jewish community in Chernobyl," Vine said, earnest as ever. "I tried my best. Every Friday night and Saturday morning, but often we ran short of a *minyan*. I haven't been successful in my life. I made too many mistakes. I should have let Freda remain in Nesvicz instead of forcing her to travel with me across the ocean. She's resented me ever since. She's never forgiven me, and I've never forgiven her for making me want to be a hero. I forgot how to be a human being."

Finally Vine was uttering what we'd been afraid to say to each other. Our shared secrets belonged only to us, a noose around our necks, along with the other disasters we rarely admitted. Not one member of Vine's family survived the war. They were either murdered by the Nazis in the ravine behind our shtetl or died fighting in the Great Patriotic War. And because he didn't know the dates of their deaths, he'd say Kaddish, the prayer for the dead, on July 22nd, the day the Germans slaughtered the Jews of Nesvicz.

Elka revealed that she'd been to Sabbath prayers at the old Chernobyl *shul* once or twice, sitting above the men, high in the balcony, in the separate section for women. "It was dicey in Chernobyl after the war. Not many Jews were alive and those who survived, didn't care for religion," she said. "Makes sense, after what they'd been through. Mostly scientists came to Chernobyl, people of exacting reason and irreproachable ethics. They intended to build the perfect Communist state and to make up for how backward Russia was. The research into atomic matter appealed to them, and to me." Elka chuckled again and leaned back. "You and Freda and your friend, Comrade Zabotin. The three of you were employed by the Soviet state at Chernobyl for many years, weren't you? The reactors were considered a beacon of light, a source of pure Communist energy."

Vine retreated to sit at the kitchen table inside the cabin. "Creative Communism," he added, loud enough that we heard him.

I was ashamed for my brother and for myself. Although we were isolated in the forest, all I thought about was hiding Elka's revelations about Simcha. Immediately I understood why Masha never spoke about him before. I might have spread the word that Simcha was alive and that would look bad on her particularly in front of her comrades who'd fought courageously against the Nazis. It would shame her, diminish her in their eyes, so she pretended he was dead, even to me.

I offered Elka a sweet bun that I'd baked that morning. "It's just flour, sugar and lard, nothing fancy, but they're tasty," I said, passing the plate.

"Good for you," Elka said accepting the pastry. "Continue baking and cooking. That's the way to survive this life." She packed two more buns in her knapsack before departing.

Zabotin wasn't curious about what Elka had to say about my brother. He left for a swim in the river before she arrived.

As for Vine, his interest was piqued. "Do you believe her, that Simcha collaborated?" he asked. "Surely, Masha would know if Simcha did that and if he survived. She would have told you."

"Not necessarily. I can't believe Elka, but I can't ignore her. I want to see Simcha if he is alive. If he collaborated, is that worse than dying? It was so close to the end. The Germans were losing the war. He must have realized the Allies would liberate the camps and the ghettos."

"Maybe," Vine said. He wasn't trying to hurt me.

"Imagine," I wondered, "if we'd never left Nesvicz, if Zabotin hadn't been the commanding officer in your mother's kitchen? What would have happened to us?"

"You know as well as I do. We'd be dead."

"Or not. Masha prospered and Simcha…"

"I'm not so sure we would have stayed in Nesvicz. You like to take risks," Vine reminded me. "I can imagine you in Moscow or Leningrad. We wouldn't have avoided the war. No one did. Not even us."

"Look at us now. What's the difference?" I asked. "It's much worse here than it was in Nesvicz before the Revolution. The Soviet Union is crumbling outside our door."

"For most people, it's better. You and I were caught in the storm. The tornado, as you prefer to call it, on the night Gouzenko defected. We did our best. Now democracy is coming to Russia. These changes take time." For all his complaining, Vine remained the optimist.

"What if Russia had opened up without the wars? If democracy developed gradually, without bloodshed? I'd learned about Lenin arriving by train at the Finland Station during the winter of 1917. How he, so devoted to the proletariat, defeated lesser men, the ones not certain that years of violence was the answer to the czar's crimes."

"It's in God's hands," Vine said, which meant the question was closed. He no longer wished to discuss the difference between the Mensheviks and the Bolsheviks. Or how desperation turned to revolution when the Cossacks refused to cut down the St. Petersburg demonstrators on the Nevsky Prospect and themselves turned on the czar. Those arguments were over for him once he transformed back to his former pious self.

As for me, I was among the lost after hearing about Simcha. How could I make sense out of what happened to my family? Mama, the devout Jewish wife: perfect, obedient, disinterested in modern thinking. Papa belonged to the Enlightenment. He was the new Jew who saw a breaking sophistication in Jewish literature and art and in the language itself. I was neither, nor did I have Vine's affinity for religion or Zabotin's taste for outwitting the Communist ideologues. People like me floated above the earth, half way between heaven and hell. Neither the sky nor the earth would take us. I didn't want to be like Elka, but she was fast moulding a Freda who was like her.

My brother Simcha was another story. I tried to imagine what he'd seen, what he'd felt watching his wife and children perish, knowing he could not save them. Why did he bother saving himself I wondered. On some level the answer was easy. Life is sweeter than death. I relish my days in the Chernobyl forest. The reactor seems millions of miles away on summer days like today when the trees are a lush verdant green and the sparkling river flows slowly toward the sea.

I asked Vine if he thought Zabotin had known all along that Simcha was a collaborator and that he was alive.

"He never mentioned it?" Vine inquired.

"Never. But that doesn't mean a thing. Masha survived. It was the old Count and Countess who, in their own way, protected her. Of course, they were not innocent, either. They'd allowed the others in my family to perish. He would have known that, but never let on when I worked for him in Canada.

He did not tell me about Masha until Gouzenko defected. By then, he needed me about as much as I did him."

"Why not tell you before?"

"Zabotin believes the more he keeps from me, the more he can control
me. He believes he can protect me, keep me from harm's way, if I know less
than he does. I must believe that or…"

"Or you'd be left with me?" Vine quipped. "I suppose he allows me to
stay with you to keep you distracted."

For the second time since we'd moved to the forest, Vine sat beside me
on the old couch. He'd grown so frail. He placed his arm around my shoulder and we sat together until we heard the sound of Zabotin's old Lada ap-
proaching. Vine tiptoed back to his room and I pretended to be asleep when
he entered the hut. I was trying to work out why Vine and I came apart as
soon as we landed in Canada. It might seem ridiculous that an old woman
reflected on love, and how Vine had treated me in Toronto and how I'd re-
taliated. That was love of a sort.

How I came to find my feelings of devotion for Zabotin wasn't any more
straightforward. How could they be, after he plundered Nesvicz? His treatment of me in Ottawa was criminal. If he'd loved me from first sight, as he
claimed he did, why did he force me to seduce so many men? His faith in
Communism had already shrunk to nothing.

The memories resurfacing about my brother were as convoluted. I'd favoured Simcha as a child, much more so than Masha, who was the dour one
while Simcha was adorable. Yet he'd abandoned his wife and children only
to see them transported to the crematorium. He survived by joining forces
with the collaborators, dragging shit from the ghetto's cisterns to the fields.
Or worse. If there'd been no war, I could imagine Simcha as a lawyer, taking
over from Papa, running a lucrative business. Simcha would have become a
big shot, a macher, in Nesvicz, married to a beautiful pious bride, father to
well-behaved children who respected him. Is that really how it would have
turned out for my brother, a born liar? Or for Zabotin and me? If we'd
remained in Nesvicz, I'd be the Jewish girl from the shtetl, someone who
would never dare enter his home, except as a servant. He'd try to make me
his mistress, at best, and that's how I might have survived the war. Or would

he defy his family, the engrained wishes of the noble Count and Countess, fallen on hard times in the midst of revolution and war? Had the Bolsheviks ever made Russia such an egalitarian paradise that Zabotin and I could be together as we are in the contaminated Chernobyl forest?

I needed to understand how my brother survived, while so many others perished. How had he managed to live with himself? Maybe he'd gone mad with shame. For now, that was the best answer I could come up with.

PART THREE

Chapter Nineteen

February 1946
Ottawa

It was the dead of winter. Snowbanks reached the second floor balcony of my flat on Florence Street. I'd been waiting for months to be arrested, but it was so quiet in Ottawa in February, it was difficult to believe that anything out of the ordinary could happen, even to me.

The farmers' stalls at the Byward Market were closed for the season with only the little storefront shops remaining open. Smoke rose from the wood stove at the butcher's where I bought my supplies. Most nights, I roasted chicken, not bothering to change my menu from day to day. Chicken, a potato and a half can of peas. When I ran out of peas, I substituted boiled cabbage. The cold kept me indoors. My boss, Comrade Tabachnick, at the TASS office, didn't expect me to come in every day. Parliament wasn't sitting and news was scarce. That winter I'd learned how to stay warm, putting on layer after layer of clothing when I did venture outside. Wool socks in my boots over my silk hosiery made me feel clumsy, but on the coldest of days, I wore whatever would keep my feet from freezing. I stopped caring how I looked or who noticed me.

Zabotin carried on with his duties at the Soviet Embassy as if nothing had happened, except for his attitude toward Rose and Vine, who he declined to see. Fred Rose believed that the Canadian government would cover up the stolen cryptograms. He was in Montreal at his constituency office. Vine was hiding out in Toronto, moving from one comrade's sofa to the other, still on the run from the Mounties who he was certain would arrest him. It was only a matter of time, according to him.

After the farce on the day of the defection, the RCMP scurried Gouzenko away to a military base, Camp X, near Trenton, a small town nestled along Lake Ontario. The Americans hadn't forced the prime minister to expose the spy ring yet so Zabotin convinced me to sit tight. As usual, I'd obliged him. Obedient Freda. Desperate Freda. Romantic Freda. Perhaps Zabotin was looking out for my best interests.

Since mid-September, Zabotin maintained that the Soviets and the Americans would come to an agreement about what to do with the cipher clerk. The deal would be brokered by Preston Ellery. A blind eye would be turned to Zabotin's band of spies, and on him, the mastermind, who had engineered a new era of world peace. That's how he saw it playing out. He actually believed Ellery could quell the noise the defection was making in intelligence circles.

Grierson continued to run the Wartime Information Bureau. He expected to be interviewed by the Americans for the director's job at their new documentary film centre, but the months passed and no one called to invite him to Washington. He told me that Truman had scolded Mackenzie King, but he was loathe to publicize the secrets Gouzenko's defection had uncovered.

The FBI hadn't exposed Homer, although I knew the Gouzenko papers must have implicated him. Either the Venona encryption project had gotten far enough that they already knew who Homer was before the defection or they were waiting for the perfect moment to release the information. Zabotin's theory was that the Americans hadn't yet managed to unravel the Soviet wartime code and the cables from Washington to him were in their original code. Why they didn't ask Gouzenko to decode them was unfathomable. Perhaps they didn't trust him.

Neither the Soviets, nor the Americans, wanted another war with atomic bombs dropped on civilians, or at least, that's what Ellery stated at Christmas when he invited Grierson to dinner at his home in Rockcliffe Park, a swanky neighbourhood in Ottawa. At dinner, Ellery made an impromptu speech about how the great powers were devoted to creating a lasting peace even with nuclear weapons in their arsenals. Zabotin, who was invited to

Christmas dinner, said that he thought exactly the opposite. He believed that the longer the Soviets went without the bomb, the better the chances that a nuclear showdown wouldn't erupt. He told me after the dinner that the other guests thought he was drunk or having them on.

Back in Ottawa, Ellery hadn't been offered the job of Secretary-General at the UN. He claimed he needed to spend more time with Patsy who was forever ailing. On New Year's Eve, he hosted a party to celebrate a lasting peace. Patsy got drunk and passed out, but all of Ottawa's A-list attended and no one minded that Ellery's wife was carried off to her bedroom or that he hadn't gotten the top job in New York.

After midnight, Zabotin asked me to meet him at the Château Laurier. We toasted the New Year, 1946, after which he fell asleep. I ordered an English breakfast at dawn and left before Zabotin rose from bed. The more we tried to analyze what the Americans would do next, the more dispirited we became.

His wife, Lydia, returned to the Soviet Union. She tried to find their son, but he had disappeared, as did so many soldiers after the war. Neither she nor Zabotin ever saw him again.

In February, Vine phoned. I was meeting Zabotin at the Elgin Theatre that night, so I told him to call back tomorrow. He didn't argue with me, agreeing that another day wouldn't matter at this point, and hung up.

When I met him at the Elgin that night, Zabotin was wearing his officer's uniform, as were the other soldiers in the theatre. We walked down the aisle to our seat, and the Canadian soldiers nodded to Zabotin. He returned the honour. Gouzenko's disclosures hadn't made the news. Not yet. Only a handful of us knew about the damage he'd done to Soviet intelligence. That night we were viewing a documentary about the atomic destruction in Japan. This time it shone a light on Nagasaki. I clutched at Zabotin's bad hand. He squinted but did not pull away. An artist had drawn a pattern over a map of the city, with rings superimposed over the parallel lines of the roadways. The rings were marked with "total destruction," "severe structural damage," "moderate structural damage" and "light damage." Most of the city was covered by total destruction with only a few edges determined to be light damage.

We remained in our seats until the theatre emptied. Zabotin wished to walk along the canal although the temperature was below zero. In the park, there were footprints in the snow: a solitary walker, and the rounded paws of a small animal.

Under the winter moon we could see each other's faces. "We stopped that from happening again," he said. "What we saw on the screen."

"For now."

"Good enough," Zabotin shot back.

I wondered, then, if what we'd done had actually slowed down Soviet progress on the bomb. "If you provide the Director with Fuchs' drawing, before he detains you, this nightmare will end for you. You could stay on in Canada, as the rezident." I sighed. "The rest of us are in limbo. We still don't know what the Americans will convince Mackenzie King to do."

"The Americans are watching Fuchs by now," Zabotin replied. "He's no good to us at this stage. No one gave me better intel. Unless I send Vine to Chalk River for the sample of plutonium, the Soviets are no farther ahead than they were months ago when Gouzenko defected. They need both to make the bomb: the drawings and the plutonium."

"It's not about taking sides, is it?" I asked, not quite able to let go of years of servitude to the Party. We both had come to the conclusion over the last few months that Stalin might use the bomb if he had it and that the Americans would fire back. "It's better that only one side has it," I said, recalling the scenes from the newsreel.

"We've all turned into murderers at Hitler and Stalin's behest." Zabotin grabbed my hand and kissed it.

I was surprised that Zabotin made such an admission to me. The rampage at Nesvicz occurred years before Hitler. He understood I'd never recovered from that. Perhaps the war really began earlier, in invisible places like my little village, where men and women were forced to act under pointless orders from a higher power. I was beginning to imagine another kind of place where people followed their consciences and not an ideology, or religion, no matter how perfect it looked on paper.

Of course, I never imagined we would end up in Chernobyl forest, where there was nothing but free will and the odd wistful glance back at the fateful dreams of the past. Back then, I was only concerned with escaping the dreadful consequences Zabotin and I were fast heading toward.

"Stalin isn't going away," I said. "You couldn't possibly believe he could be overthrown. A coup."

"Don't sound so defeated. All regimes fall eventually. Hitler was defeated."

"Not by his own people."

"There are pockets of resistance even in Soviet Russia."

We walked under the moonlight until I couldn't stand the cold. My feet were numb. We were more like apparitions than real people. We were forcing ourselves to give up on everything we'd hoped Communism could be.

The snow was piled in mountains along the Rideau Canal embankment, so high I couldn't see above them. The maple trees were bare and the evergreens swayed with the weight of the heavy, white, glistening snow. It was so cold that I felt I was roaming through another world, a strange planet, where creatures combed the frozen wilderness searching for shelter. Under the bridge, two men in beaver parkas lit a campfire to try to stay alive. An abandoned kitten cried into the night, crazy with the cold; a wolf howled from across the park. The moon hid behind the looming silver clouds.

Not able to bear the temperature, we slipped into a café beside the canal. We drank from mugs of tea laced with rum, and Zabotin offered to get me out of Canada. "It's now or never, Freda," he said, delighted by his choice of words in English.

"Everything will change in the next few days and you must be prepared. Don't warn Vine," he said to me, shrewdly. "Close the door to your apartment and walk away. Leave it as it is. Take one small suitcase, nothing else. I'll arrange for your transport to Europe, you can hunt down your family in Russia or what's left of it. I told you Masha is there. Maybe you could bring her back with you one day, to settle here."

Even I didn't believe that would be possible. Not after Gouzenko.

"Here's a copy of Fuchs' drawings. Hold onto them. You may need them to save yourself," he said, holding up a small manila envelope, one that contained the fate of the world.

"Or to rescue you," I replied. "Are you intending to disappear with me?"

He shrugged his shoulders, the way only a true aristocrat could. "Not yet."

Zabotin held out the envelop to me, and I accepted it. I shouldn't expect anything else from him.

"How are you going to get the plutonium?" I asked him.

Zabotin took my hand. "It's either you or Vine that must take it to the Director. If you won't put him in harm's way, it must be you. Think about it before you give me your answer."

I would be returning to the East alone. Zabotin's terms were the most dangerous I could imagine, but if I could find my family, re-unite with Masha, it would be worth the risk. Zabotin was always the first one to know when things were about to go awry. He'd done what he could to warn me and I was beginning to trust him.

On Saturday Vine phoned again. He was in Ottawa and asked to meet me the next night. I couldn't refuse. By telephone he told me that Drew Pearson, the American journalist, would be breaking the Gouzenko story on the radio. Fred Rose, who was already holed up in his office in the centre block of Parliament, had informed him. Sybil was with Rose. Vine thought it appropriate that we listen together, but felt it was safer if we met in public, at The Party Palace, a late-night diner, the only eatery in Ottawa open past midnight.

If the life had not been so tantalizing, if I'd been offered any other choice in Canada, I might have disappeared earlier, before these troubles. I could have deserted Vine when we lived on Beaconsfield, and made my own way back to Nesvicz, to the place where I once belonged. Home. If I'd stayed with my family after the pogrom, I might have been able to read the signs early enough and escape long before the Nazis invaded. I might have saved them, before the catastrophe. I was the oldest child. It was my responsibility. If only I'd taken heed of Masha's letters and paid less attention to the propaganda fed to me by Party brass, or to my own wild ambition.

When Vine noticed me walking toward him, I was gliding briskly in my black patent, open-toed, three-inch heels along Elgin Street, slipping here and there on the mounds of ice that would remain rock solid until the end of April. I wanted to look pretty for him.

From across the street I waited for the light to turn. Vine was pacing in the cold outside The Party Palace's foyer, drawing on a cigarette.

"Stand you for a cup of coffee, beauty?" Vine offered in his thick Russian accent, the one he'd never managed to erase after decades of living in Canada. He reached out to cup my face in his hands as if we'd seen each other yesterday. But it had been months. I could sense, as I always could, that he'd been with another woman earlier in the day. I could smell her on him when I kissed his cheek, but I didn't push him away.

I kissed him again, this time square on the lips and whispered in his ear that I needed him, as I had since the first day we landed in Canada. I placed my gloved hand on his heart. "Where've you been, Harry?"

Inside the diner, the other Soviet, American and British agents were sipping coffee and smoking. I surmised that their handlers had alerted them to Drew Pearson's broadcast.

Solange, the blonde all-night waitress, who was bored by conversations about the freshly carved city of Berlin, wiped her hands on the backside of her blue-striped nylon uniform. In her apron was a book by John Dos Passos.

"Back booth for you two?" She didn't need to ask. She'd seen the look in our eyes many times before at The Party Palace. Those who were in a desperate hurry to go nowhere.

"If we run now, tonight, we could make it out of the country," Vine spoke rapidly and under his breath once we were facing each other in the booth. He'd removed his grey-felt fedora, unwound his striped silk tie and tore open the top button of his white-starched shirt. I can see him still today, how careful he was with his appearance in Canada. He always wore an expensive tie and a finely pressed shirt, so that people would respect him, or that's what he claimed. We both liked to dress up. Behind round steel-rimmed glasses, his heavy-lidded eyes were fearful.

"Where do you propose we run?" I asked. He hadn't planned that far ahead.

I gulped down the coffee. Vine grew quiet and I tapped on the Formica tabletop. My nails were manicured and the red polish shone under the overhead light. Cigarette burns scarred the ersatz gold-speckled surface of the diner's table. The glass pepper shaker was empty and the creamer was stained chartreuse with drips of congealed liquid.

Bing Crosby was crooning on the wireless perched on the top shelf above the glass jars of red peppers and grey pickled eggs.

Would you like to swing on a star
carry moonbeams home in a jar
and be better off than you are
or would you rather be a mule?

I was accustomed to frequenting swankier joints than this one, but tonight was a special occasion, an emergency. Zabotin would never take me to a diner. We only went to the best places. By then, he didn't care any longer who saw us together.

"Do you honestly believe that after everything we've done, they'll just let us disappear? Who are you kidding?" I snapped my fingers in Vine's face. "If one side doesn't come after us, the other will."

Vine believed he'd been the most loyal of comrades. Party leader Tim Buck had told him so. He had no idea why the Soviets would punish him for Gouzenko's defection, but I knew better. Zabotin wanted him out of the way. He wished to send Vine to Chalk River to collect the sample of plutonium and either the Soviets or the Canadians would catch him and accuse him of being on the wrong side. Zabotin would make certain of that, unless I went myself. No one would suspect a woman.

"We're outlaws in Canada now," said Vine. He understood that I wasn't taking to his idea. "I've been on the lam for a long time. I've survived," he said, trying to reassure me. "It's not that rough."

"You prefer that life. I do not," I told him.

The waitress poured more coffee into our empty cups. We were waiting, like the others in the diner, for Drew Pearson's broadcast about Gouzenko.

"Let's go home," Vine said. "I'll marry you if you return to the Soviet Union. Make an honest woman out of you."

I didn't laugh.

"Don't doubt me," he pleaded. "When we get back, we'll find our families, yours and mine, and we'll move into your house. It's big enough for all of us."

He was losing his mind. "What if they're dead?" I asked. "Murdered by the Nazis. Neither of us has heard from our families since 1939. It's been almost seven years. Zabotin says that there aren't many Jews left in our part of Russia, not near Minsk or Kiev."

Vine wouldn't hear of it. "The Red Army smashed through the Nazi line in Minsk, on its way to Kiev. They marched through the Pripyat marsh. It was tough going all the way, but they made it."

"Our people were probably dead by the time the Red Army reached Nesvicz." I had no intention of mentioning Masha.

"Don't talk like that," said Vine. "You believe Zabotin? He's trying to trick you. Not everyone died. Soldiers who fought in the Great Patriotic War are alive. Our brothers could be living in Nesvicz. Rebuilding."

I'd drawn the same scenario for Zabotin, but he'd never allowed me to believe that even my clever brother Simcha could have survived the Nazi bloodbath, let alone Mama, Papa. Only Masha managed to outwit the Germans. "Do you believe Stalin? That he saved the Jews?" I was whispering, afraid that the NKVD had its own agent in the diner.

"Of course I do," said Vine. "The Soviet Union won the war. The West will never forget how the Soviet people beat back the Nazis. Stalin never waivers. It's others that I'm worried about. Zabotin is caving in. Fred Rose agrees our rezident isn't as courageous or committed as he pretends to be. After tonight, he won't protect you." Vine was trying to win me over. My handbag carrying Fuchs' drawings was nestled under my arm.

"Where do you suggest we run tonight? Stowaway on a tanker to Europe? Who's going to do that? Not me." I recalled how Vine had come close to death when we crossed the Atlantic twenty-four years earlier. I'd been afraid that I would float up to the heavens, if he was not by my side to protect me. How childish I'd been back then.

Just before ten, Vine and I gripped hands under the table. The waitress, who knew more than she let on, turned up the volume on the radio. It was the CBC announcer in Ottawa reporting on Drew Pearson's revelations to the American public. A CBC newsman spoke in a tremulous voice. The patrons at the diner, most of them wearing felt fedoras to conceal their faces, turned toward the radio.

A discovery of an espionage plot in Canada which disclosed Soviet agents…

I was going to faint. Vine came round to my side of the table to hold my head in his hands. He told me to breathe slowly. The men in the fedoras watched us as the CBC announcer's words became incriminating.

The prime minister is expected to make a public announcement about the Soviet spies tomorrow morning.

"Drink a *bisl* water," Vine murmured. We were back to speaking Yiddish. He motioned for the waitress to bring a pitcher of water to our table.

Vine's hands were trembling. "We're on our own. I'm not sure who we can turn to for help. Zabotin is the only one who can get us out of the country before the Mounties come for us."

I reached inside my handbag to touch Fuchs' drawings. The papers were there, hidden between my compact and my lipstick.

Vine knew he could never trust the rezident but he was desperate. "Don't reach out to Zabotin," I warned him. "Whatever you do, don't make the trip to Chalk River. It's a trap. You'll be caught. Zabotin will finger you for revealing Fuchs' drawings to Soviet military intelligence. You'll be blamed for everything." I was still trying to save Vine, or to put myself in his place. Vine was right to question Zabotin, although I knew I had no other choice than to trust him. The danger would be all mine if I agreed to be the courier, and who deserved it more than me?

"I'm not hiding anything. I gave the drawings to Zabotin last June. He sent them to Moscow."

"That's what you think. Don't go to Chalk River. You'll be ambushed if you do."

For once, Vine took my word for it.

Chapter Twenty

Vine wanted to walk. He couldn't sit still. He believed the police were going to rush through the door of The Party Palace and drag him away. I wished I had worn my boots.

The colour of Vine's skin started to look the same as it did when he had fallen ill on the boat to Canada. Back then he'd worried he would die, but he was also nervous about me, about how I'd survive without him. Then I met the lawyer and he saved us. If only the old lawyer from Minsk would stick his head around the corner and walk with us along Elgin. He would know what to do, as he had so long ago on the ship that carried us across the Atlantic Ocean.

I placed my arm inside Vine's to steady myself. We went slowly until reaching the iron bridge I'd crossed with Zabotin the night before. It was coated with ice and I didn't think I could make it. Vine egged me on and I tried until I fell, skinning both my knees and ripping my silk stockings. That's when he lifted me in his arms and carried me across the bridge.

On the other side of the canal, he set me down atop a snowbank and we both laughed. "Can you imagine what Zabotin would say if he could see us now?" I picked myself up and brushed the snow from my coat and my hair.

"I will go instead of you, to Chalk River and then to Moscow," I said, as I played my last card to convince Vine. "Zabotin didn't send the atomic drawings to the Director. He held them back."

"You've known this for how long?"

"Since the night Gouzenko defected."

"Who has the drawings now?" he asked. Vine looked like he was going to push me down into the snow.

"Zabotin has them. And me, I have a copy in my handbag. Gouzenko never saw them. But Western intelligence has seen them. They know about Fuchs and about us."

"The intelligence that Drew Pearson talked about. What was in the Gouzenko papers?" he demanded.

"The same drawings that are in my purse. The rest: mainly your reports for Fred Rose, the debates in Parliament. You told me you made most of them up, no?" I knew the answer before I asked.

"Or took them straight from the newspapers, embellishing a little here, a little there," Vine confirmed.

"I never believed you about the reports. I thought you were trying to keep me in the dark, you and Fred Rose. It seemed to me that you had information that you didn't want me to know, that the Party didn't trust me with."

"No, nothing. There was nothing much in my reports to Moscow that couldn't be found in the dailies. It wasn't until Zabotin sent me to Los Alamos to meet with Fuchs that any of it mattered. Before that we were playing at being spies." If this posturing had bothered Vine, I wouldn't have known it. Pretending to be more important than you are. Politics thrives on showmanship.

"I'll go to Chalk River. Better me than you. No one will suspect a woman. Zabotin will set up the meet with Nunn May. I'll wear a disguise. A blonde wig. I've always wanted to be a blonde."

"You won't look good as a blonde," he said, warming to my plan. "I prefer your hair the way it is. Black."

"Even if I get caught."

Vine smirked. I wanted to believe that he'd never let me take things this far, that he would shield me. But he was prepared to let me go. In his place.

"When I get back to Ottawa, you can join me on route to Moscow," I promised. "I'll force Zabotin to agree to that. If he allows me to take this risk, he must save you too. You'll return to Nesvicz and I'll join you there after the drop in Moscow."

For another moment, I hoped that he would try to dissuade me, claim it was too dangerous and that he would carry the plutonium and drawings to the Director. Instead he agreed. We'd meet in Nesvicz after I delivered the package to the Kremlin.

I knew, then, that Vine could never love me, not the way Zabotin did. Perhaps he'd never truly loved me and that's why he pushed me aside in Toronto, and why the Party became his everything. After we returned to the Soviet Union, my debt to him would be paid. I would save his life, as he believed he had once saved mine, and we could be done with each other.

He asked me how Zabotin intended to protect himself and I told him that the rezident had orders from the Centre to wait out the arrest of the Canadian comrades. "He's to act like he knows nothing about us, what intelligence we were collecting for the Soviet Union before Gouzenko defected. Everyone in Ottawa loves our rezident. He was at Preston Ellery's for Christmas and New Year's. Possibly the Canadians will give him immunity and he can stay on in Canada."

Vine was surprised, but he didn't quibble with me. He liked the idea of him and I returning to the motherland while Zabotin turned himself over to the Canadian authorities. Zabotin would be the traitor.

By the time we reached the Soviet Embassy my feet were soaking wet, my heels covered in ice. A guard stood at the gate. Vine bent down to brush the ice from my shoes, which were ruined. "You'd better get yourself a pair of boots before going up to Chalk River. There's more snow there than here. You'll catch a cold."

"Remember the snow in Nesvicz, how it piled up outside the windows? We'd be snowed in for days. Mama taught Masha how to play the piano on long winter days," I said softly.

"My father would close the shoe store and read to us on those days." Vine didn't usually speak nostalgically of his family, not since the war.

"You'd best stand outside for now, beyond the gate. I don't want Zabotin to know you're with me," I cautioned.

I approached the guard who delivered me to the doorman. I was ushered inside the building, and up the stairs to the plush drawing room on the second floor of the embassy.

I removed my soiled shoes, but no one offered to take my coat. I stood limply for at least an hour before Zabotin appeared. When he returned, bounding up the stairs to meet me, he was in full regalia. "If I'd known you were here."

He wore his tall Russian fur hat, and I noticed the pistol in his holster when he removed his military great coat.

"You know, of course," I said moving toward him.

"Drew Pearson on the radio. Yes, I know. I drove immediately to Florence Street. You were gone, but Sybil and Zsusza, I tried to protect them." Zabotin took me in his arms. "Fred Rose has barricaded himself in his office on Parliament Hill. The Mounties have surrounded the centre block of the House of Commons. I tried to convince Sybil to return to the embassy with me, but she was frantic. She begged me to take her to Rose, and I did."

I thought about Sybil, her piano legs wrapped in hefty snow boots, a paisley wool babushka tied around her hair. "And Zsusza? Please don't tell me she joined Rose as well."

"Zsusza is far too smart for that. I'll get her back to Romania. The Party will take care of her there."

Zsusza's splendid garden would go untended. The rose bushes, the fountains for the chirping birds, the little porcelain animals with their shining emerald eyes. I imagined them swept away by neglect.

Zabotin was exhausted. "The Hill is swarming with RCMP," he said. "Police brigades are out collecting my people. They're looking for you and Vine. I've talked to the Minister of Justice. Our comrades will be sent to a warehouse at the edge of town. I can't do anything for them now. They aren't covered by diplomatic immunity. My hands are tied." Zabotin put his head in his hands. For the first time, I saw him lose control. He was shouting profanities. Then he hit the wall with his injured right hand.

I winced. Without being invited, I removed my coat and sat down on the velvet wing chair, beckoning him to sit across from me. I wanted to comfort Zabotin, but there was nothing to say. How could I pretend that our little band of comrades wouldn't suffer for his grand scheme?

When the butler appeared, Zabotin had him light a fire in the grill. The room was icy cold.

"Look, Freda, I know you listened to the radio broadcast with Vine to-night. You're still trying to rescue that rascal," he said, trying to regain his composure.

I was stunned that Zabotin couldn't shake his obsession with Vine, who really didn't matter to anyone but me.

"I promised you I would help when Gouzenko's defection went public." Zabotin knelt down to take my feet in his warming hands. "You're freezing."

"What do you want from me?" I asked.

"I want you to come to me first when you are in trouble. Can you do that?"

I said that I could. It was the beginning of trust, if only he could leave it at that.

"After sharing all my information with you, you still don't believe in me?" Zabotin asked.

No matter how dangerous the situation became, Zabotin and I always found ourselves in the same place, testing each other, seeking assurance, with me unable to admit openly that I could trust him. "At first you said Homer's cables weren't in the Gouzenko papers. Nor Fuchs' diagrams, you'd claimed. You lied, and included both. Exactly how am I to put my life in your hands?"

Zabotin wasn't annoyed. "I do what I believe is best. Now you must act according to your conscience. Our comrades will be rounded up by morning. They'll be held incommunicado, no legal representation, not even a phone call to alert their families. When justice and democracy are no longer conve-nient, it's remarkable how these Westerners dispense with it."

"How do you know about these arrests?"

"Preston Ellery informed Grierson, who now makes drops to the Party office. I've known for weeks, but not about the exact timing. The Canadians will have one of their famous Royal Commissions and pretend it's a court of law. Everyone on Gouzenko's list will be charged with treason."

I was about to say I would surrender, but I already understood that Zabo-tin wouldn't hear of it. "You had choices, Freda," said he. "Grierson tried to convince you to leave Ottawa. He'd marry you to get you into England, but you refused. Why?"

For a second, I wondered why I hadn't taken Grierson up on his offer. He was a decent man. "You know why," I replied, pulling away from Zabotin and moving toward the fire.

"You're tempting fate, my dear, leaving it this late. The RCMP is looking for you. You know too much! About me, about the entire operation. You even know about Los Alamos. The Mounties have been to your apartment. What is their motto? We 'always get our man.'"

It occurred to me that I could leave the embassy. Put on my coat and ruined shoes and ignore Zabotin and his fantastical scheme to outwit the Centre. No one could stop me from heading into the night and taking my chances with fate or joining my comrades who were under suspicion.

"Sit down," he implored. "Do you really believe I'd abandon you after all you've done and all you mean to me? I have a plan."

I returned to my seat. "Don't tell me, I know. First I am to travel up north to Chalk River to retrieve the sample of plutonium from Alan Nunn May. Then back to Ottawa. How will you get me out of the country? I haven't figured out how you intend to do that."

Zabotin was surprised by my foresight. "Exactly. Take the bus from the Ottawa station to Renfrew. Have you been up north? Chalk River is a village in the Ottawa Valley, quite picturesque in summer. I once considered building a dacha there," Zabotin liked to embellish. "I predict, the laboratory there will become a fully functioning nuclear reactor before long. They are already making heavy water for a prototype of their small nuclear reactor. The scientists call it the ZEEP. The Brits sent Nunn May to collaborate with the Chalk River scientists. He's helped a lot, and indeed, the ZEEP demonstrated that uranium and heavy water could be used to create nuclear fission. The Canadians can be proud of their accomplishments."

"Good for them," I deadpanned.

"By the way, I have your disguise ready, plus your suitcase," he told me. "We collected it from your flat earlier this evening, as soon as you left to meet Vine. I thought tonight might be the night Drew Pearson went public. Inside your case there's a new passport. Use it to leave the country and revert to your proper one when you arrive in the Soviet Union. I've included one for Vine, a false passport, just in case you make him part of this deal, as I suspect you will."

It sounded as if he wanted me to make Vine part of the deal or he was waiting to see if I would be as willing to abandon Vine, as I was my other comrades.

"Use our false identities to leave the country right now? Me and Vine?" I asked. Zabotin was keeping his word. If it worked, we'd be out of reach of the RCMP. Zabotin had planned everything, possibly even the timing of Pearson's revelations about Soviet spies in Canada. I could never believe that he didn't know in advance that tonight was the night we would be ruined.

"Yes, as I said, use the false passport after your visit to Chalk River, and revert to the true one when you reach the Soviet Union. The Director must have the plutonium sample. Nunn May has encased the plutonium in titanium, inside a silver locket to wear around your neck. He's guaranteed it to be safe. It won't harm you. Put the locket on as soon as you meet Nunn May."

"And the drawings?"

"Ahh. Another story. Should Nunn May carry Fuchs' drawings to our friends in London, or should you take them to the Director? Which would you prefer?"

I wasn't certain if Zabotin was trying to trap me. "I'll take everything if you let Vine come with me. Get us both out of the country together and I'll deliver the plutonium and the drawings," I replied.

"Very daring! Yes, what else could I expect from you, my bravest operative? So you'll do it?"

I nodded in accord, but I didn't know how we'd get out of Canada without the authorities discovering our escape. Surely the Canadians would lock down the borders, but Zabotin assured me there was still time, if I did exactly as he ordered. I'd been taking his orders and before him, Tim Buck's commands, for a long time. How could I refuse now when it meant saving my own skin?

After Chalk River, I was to travel with Vine by train to Halifax where a plane would be waiting to fly us across the Atlantic to London. Along the route, we'd be met by a Soviet agent.

"Entirely reliable, this fellow," assured Zabotin. The Soviet asset will ensure a blind eye is turned to Vine and you, and alert the Centre of your imminent arrival. You'll be safe. When you are inside the USSR, no one will hurt you," Zabotin promised.

Once the plutonium was delivered to the GRU, Zabotin suggested I settle in the Ukraine, with my sister, Masha. "She is fully briefed and she will protect you as soon as you arrive in the Soviet Union. She's eager to see you. Masha is a highly committed woman. Too serious, but loyal nonetheless." He clenched his jaw. "She knows how to follow orders and it's saved her from destruction. Not unlike yourself."

"Following orders, that's what I will be remembered for."

"Is that such a bad thing?" he asked.

"And you, what will you be remembered for? Saving the world?"

Zabotin took me in his arms. "This will be over soon," he said with confidence. "We'll meet on the other side."

Zabotin would be ready by then to share his atomic secrets with the Soviets and to try to save his own life and mine. He'd calculated the time it would take for Russian scientists to replicate the American formula and decided that it would be at least another three years before they could collect enough plutonium at a heavy water plant to build the bomb. As it turned out, his calculations were remarkably accurate.

Chapter Twenty-One

That night, as Zabotin predicted, thirty-nine Canadian comrades were arrested and taken to an RCMP holding tank on the outskirts of Ottawa. They weren't charged with espionage, but were held under the laws of the War Measures Act. The order, set down by the prime minister, directed the Minister of Justice, Louis St. Laurent, to use whatever means were necessary to investigate Gouzenko's evidence of traitorous activity. Under the War Measures Act, the Minister of Justice had unlimited powers over the arrest, detention and deportation of any Canadian citizen, who could be held for an indefinite period. Ottawa's ability to detain citizens was virtually unchecked and, as I surmised, the government held and prosecuted the comrades to the fullest extent of this law, charging eighteen for treason, including Fred Rose whose parliamentary office was stormed the next day. I'd made my bargain with Zabotin just before Rose and poor Sybil were taken into custody and put in prison.

Zabotin's and my fears turned to how the Soviets would punish us when the full implication of Gouzenko's defection hit them. They wanted the plutonium and would be amazed by Fuchs' drawings, but I wasn't certain it would be enough to satisfy them, not after what we'd done. The new conflict had turned into a race for atomic weapons, and Zabotin, with my knowledge, had kept back the key intelligence the Soviets needed in order to catch up with the Americans. For that reason, we were more afraid of Moscow than Ottawa.

Our only hope was that the rezident still had connections to officials in the Party and in the military. General Zhukov, who'd won the war for Stalin, was his chum from military college. They'd served together during the Revolution. Zabotin believed that Zhukov would do his best to defend him. Keep him out the Lubyanka and away from the gulags. I wasn't so sure.

Vine was outside, standing across from the embassy, in a vacant lot when Zabotin and I were alerted to the number of comrades' disappearing during the night. I asked Zabotin for permission to bring Vine in, fearing he would be picked up outside the embassy gates, but Zabotin hesitated.

"In here, with us?"

"He'll freeze to death if we leave him out there. He has nowhere else to go. If they find him, he'll be arrested. You've said so yourself." I was begging him, this one last time, to rescue Vine.

"Why must you?"

But I cut Zabotin off. "It's a matter of loyalty. Why can't you understand?"

"It's a matter of love. Or something worse. Obsession. Let him go."

I reminded Zabotin that we'd just made a deal. I wouldn't leave the country without Vine. I couldn't. Zabotin knew that before we'd even spoke. That's why he painted Vine into the picture. If he did this for me, I promised I would never forget his kindness.

Zabotin walked across the room. His collection of pipes was lined up neatly in their stand and he began to fill one with tobacco, tamping it down and then holding a match over the barrel. "I want you for myself, Freda. If you can't forget Vine, I need to know now."

It was a fair question. If I were honest with Zabotin, I'd tell him that Vine was my first love. Each of us has one; the person we dream about when we're coming into consciousness after a deep sleep. If Zabotin rescued me this time, I would let Vine go, my Adam from the garden.

There were other good reasons as well, but I didn't know them at the time. Once I returned to Europe, I met couples who'd married days after being released from the death camps. Most had lost a wife or husband to the crematoriums, and when they discovered a landsman, a survivor from their village, they married, trying to quickly resume a life that no longer existed except in their minds. Vine was that person for me. I knew we would never be together as man and woman; not now, not after what I was promising Zabotin and what he was offering to do for me.

I walked over to Zabotin and took the pipe from his hand. I sat on his lap, a childish gesture, and wrapped my arms around him, as if he were my papa. "I promise you, I'll let him go after we return to Russia. No more of this, I promise." In a moment of vanity, I wondered if he'd engineered the entire escapade, including Gouzenko's defection, to tear me away from Vine, but I didn't believe in myself that much, no woman does, if she's being honest.

I wanted to ask him if he'd divorce Lydia now that we were to be together and if he wanted children since I was young enough to bear them. The normal questions that a woman asks when she agrees to tie herself to one man for the rest of her life. And I believe Zabotin had questions for me, not just about Vine, but embarrassing questions like how many others I'd been with. Too many to count, but before now, it hadn't mattered. We were beginning our ascent to normalcy, to becoming lovers who had questions that lovers ask just for the sake of knowing and not for the good of one country over the other.

Zabotin believed in me. I understood that as we kissed in the enveloping warmth of the embassy parlour. Whenever he looked at me, he saw the pretty young girl I'd been in the kitchen of Vine's house in Nesvicz and he continued to dwell on my innocence and my strength, no matter how far I'd strayed from his ideal. I was his Eve.

That night we made love, quickly and with true passion. It was many years before we would be together again.

When Zabotin escorted me down the stairs to the grand foyer of the embassy, he called for a pair of sturdy woman's boots. The staff was awake, waiting for his orders, so it only took minutes to locate a pair of brown leather boots in my size, fur-lined with thick laces. The heels were rubber like the tires on the giant plows that cleaned Ottawa's streets after a snowfall. I was in my stocking feet, the silk stockings, shredded around the knees that were scraped raw from hurtling on the ice. "You'll be fine," he said. He sat me down, reclined on his haunches and pulled the boots over my feet. Then he tied the laces, making certain there was a double knot at the top. "I'll get you out of the country. I give you my word."

He sent me outside to collect Vine. I spotted him across the street and to my eyes,unaccustomed to the darkened night, he looked like he was suspended between heaven and earth, as if he was dancing on a string and I was holding him down, preventing him from floating up to the sky. I knew the feeling. It's the same one I had on the ship when I thought Vine would die and I would be left alone in a new world I knew nothing about.

Tears began cascading down his cheeks when he saw me coming toward him. His nose was raw from crying in the cold. "We could disappear, Freda, run far away. No one would look for us in the wilderness. There are islands off the coast of British Columbia. We'd build a cabin, live off the land, be farmers."

We both knew it wasn't possible. We were never meant to become farmers. Vine would never manage the isolation or the monotony of the work. Before long, he'd tire of me, drive into town in our worn-down pick-up truck, strike up a conversation with the good-looking woman behind the bar and convince her she needed to be with him for the night. By morning, he'd be searching for a cause to join, any cause that would take him outside of himself and away from me.

Vine was afraid; he'd always been afraid. Only once had he beaten down the fear: with the village doctor in Nesvicz, proving to Zabotin that he was worthy of admiration. That February night in Ottawa, his bare hands, sticking out from the sleeves of his coat, were turning white with frostbite. How could he have forgotten his gloves in such weather? Or had he thrown them away in the snow? We survivors, how we find the will to continue, is a miracle. Vine is the smartest one of us, but he is weak. In Chernobyl, we each make sense of the days left, living with the ghosts of old and new regimes, and the memories of grandiose self-deceptions, but Vine complains, about the dampness, about the heat, about the food. He's never been able to get over himself.

"Come in from the cold," I coaxed, holding his numb hands in mine and kissing them. "Let me do the talking." Finally we were even.

A tall young woman met us at the door. "Irina," I said.

"Zabotin's gone to bed," she said. "His orders are with me." Irina and I had worked together at TASS since the beginning of the war.

She separated Vine and me immediately. He was to go downstairs where a room was prepared for him. Irina led me up to the third floor. Persian runners lined the stairs and potted aspidistras sat on the stairwells. She led me to a small, but well-appointed bedroom. There was an adjoining private washroom. My case was sitting on the single bed, as well as a heavy woolen coat with a fox-fur collar and hood.

"You'll freeze in your own coat up at Chalk River." Irina told me to take off my boots and dress and put on a plain green smock. "Have you ever dyed your hair?" she asked, taking a large bottle of peroxide from the bathroom cupboard.

"I thought I would be wearing a wig," I said. I covered my head with my hand, but Irina asked me to be reasonable.

"It will grow out in no time," she assured me. "No one will recognize you as a blonde."

When it was over, she dried my hair with a towel and brushed it. I was to sleep for a few hours, then Irina and I would be taking the bus from the Ottawa station to Chalk River, after changing in Renfrew. She'd be with me all the way. Alan Nunn May would meet us with the sample of plutonium in the village café.

I lied down on the bed, and got under the covers. I was too exhausted to ask where Vine was or if I'd see Zabotin before leaving for Chalk River.

In the morning, Irina brought me breakfast on a wooden tray. A soft-boiled egg, two slices of toast, an orange and coffee. "What if I don't wish to go through with it, if I change my mind?" It was a stupid question. I hardly meant it.

Irina pursed her lips.

I didn't see Zabotin before we left the embassy. A blue Pontiac sedan delivered us to the station and we waited for an hour, among the mothers, children, and elderly women waiting to catch the bus to Renfrew. Our bus followed the milk run, stopping at every hamlet along the way. The road was plowed, but during the night the wind had blown snow across the two-lane highway. The driver stopped the bus in front of each mountain of snow and he and the male passengers donned their toques and gloves, grabbed the shovels stored in the luggage compartment and dug us out.

Irina and I didn't talk along the route. Most of the passengers ate sandwiches and drank tea from thermoses. Some of the men brought beer and beef jerky for the ride. In my purse, I checked to make sure that Fuchs' drawings were safe. I wanted to believe that Irina was with me as protection, not to police me, but I wasn't certain that Zabotin trusted me completely at that point. I knew Zabotin loved me, but love and trust are two different things.

The driver dropped us off on the main street of Renfrew. It was dark by the time we arrived and the shops had closed for the night. There were three parked cars and a few horse-drawn wagons, driven by lumberjacks in red and black-checkered jackets. They whistled when they noticed two blondes standing in front of the general store, waiting for the next bus to Chalk River. One man, who spoke English with a Quebec accent, invited us to join him and his buddies at the tavern. I was hungry and thirsty so I agreed, but Irina said no. "Don't be foolish," she chided me in Russian.

The temperature was dropping. It was already minus 23 Celsuis. To protect ourselves from frostbite, we wrapped scarves around our nose and mouth and stamped our feet as we waited for the bus to arrive. A yellow school bus was the only transportation between Renfrew and Chalk River. In a few years the laboratories at Chalk River would grow to employ hundreds. Canadian Pacific would lay tracks from Ottawa so the scientists and their families could travel in comfort. But back then, it was wilderness as far as the eye could see, just pine trees and the enormous grey and purple rock formations of the Northern shield, and the air so cold I inhaled it deep inside my lungs. The cold air helped me to choke back the tears. Although I was Russian, I had no idea how to survive out here.

The same dark blue Pontiac, driven by the same burly man from the morning escort from the embassy, picked us up from the bus stop in Chalk River. He was wearing a fur hat, the flaps drawn down over his ears, and I recognized him from my rendezvous with Vine at The Party Palace. He'd been at the diner drinking his coffee and listening to the announcement. He was Zabotin's plant.

He spoke directly to Irina. His orders were to escort us to a cabin in the bush, north of the nuclear laboratory. Plans had changed. Nunn May would be there, not at Chalk River's only café. We were to spend the night in the cabin after which he'd drive us to Montreal's Windsor Station. From there, I'd be boarding the train to Halifax. I asked if Vine would meet me in Montreal or Halifax, but the driver said he couldn't be expected to know and that it was better not to ask.

Irina turned her head, not talking, and stared out the rear window into the starless night. The warm air from the Pontiac's heater wasn't reaching the back seat where Irina and I reclined. As she began to blow on her hands to warm herself, the driver removed a flask from the glove compartment. He took a swig and handed it to Irina.

She sniffed the mouth of the flask. "Brandy. Try some, Freda. You before me," she said in a kindly tone. "You're going to need it."

The brandy tasted good. I took another sip and passed the flask back to her. When Irina pulled a tissue from her handbag to wipe her mouth before drinking, I saw the glint of a revolver. The car bumped along the uneven dirt road following the steep pine-covered hills leading to the cabin. It was a frozen landscape devoid of people. The only light shone from the Pontiac's headlights. One wrong move and we'd skid on the ice and down off the road into the black ravine below.

The laneway to the cabin wasn't wide enough for the Pontiac to pass through, nor was it plowed. We hiked the last kilometre to the front door. It was snowing hard, in steady wet lumps that stuck to our clothes and hair. The driver gathered two ropes from the trunk and tied one around my waist and the other around Irina's.

"You get lost in snow," he said.

I couldn't see six feet in front of me. Irina argued that she'd make it without being tied to a rope, but the driver insisted.

"Don't get any ideas," the driver shouted.

As we approached the cabin, I sighted a kerosene lantern flickering in the window. We followed the light to the tiny cabin. Inside, along the back wall, stood a wood stove with a caste-iron door that wouldn't shut. The cabin was filled with smoke. There was no electricity and no running water. The owner, a man named Jack Brown, offered to take our coats, but Irina and I declined. He laid out uncooked oats and maple syrup for dinner along with four brown half-rotten apples.

"I slaughtered the pig before Christmas so from February on it's been oats or canned beans, three times a day. You didn't happen to bring supplies with you? Jam or lard." The driver shook his head., handing Jack Brown his flask.

We were sitting at the table when a stranger arrived. He removed his coat, but kept his toque pulled down over his silver hair. His suit was navy with pin stripes. He wore leather gloves.

"I'm Alan Nunn May," he said, reaching out his hand to me. "I suppose you're Freda."

"I am, and this is Irina."

Nunn May shook her hand and the driver's. He didn't acknowledge our host, who was shovelling oats into his mouth. "I'm delighted to meet you. I'm certainly looking forward to our travels together," he said to me. "I was told you're a brunette."

"I used to be. Now I have a new identity," I replied.

Jack continued eating, uninterested in the conversation. "It's cabin fever," Nunn May explained as if the distracted fellow wasn't in the room. "Common up here. But extraordinary! Men living alone in the bush for the entire winter." His accent was the same as John Grierson's and it turned out they'd been at Cambridge together in the thirties.

Nunn May refused the paltry meal, preferring to keep his gloves on and sit perched near the wood stove. The room was overheating and the smoke was blinding. Everything was covered in a layer of black soot and we were all coughing.

"Unfortunate really, the isolation, the cold, the darkness in winter, drives these loners to the brink of madness and sometimes beyond," Nunn May continued, analyzing the situation.

"I'm certain you know how it feels, Doctor, all alone in the wilderness," suggested Irina. "Chalk River can't be much better than this place."

"Not much better," he conceded.

Irina was smarter than she behaved at the TASS office in Ottawa, where she giggled and ran errands as the girl Friday.

The outhouse was forty metres up the snow-covered hill behind the cabin, but the driver instructed us to "do business outside door." Irina and I were to sleep on a mattress on the wooden floor and to share a blanket for warmth. At night the fire would die out and it would begin to freeze inside the cabin. The driver brought in my case and Irina's as well, but we slept in our clothes under the down-filled bag. Nunn May sat in the chair throughout the night. Jack Brown and the driver shared the bed in the corner of the room. They fell asleep immediately and within minutes they were snoring in unison.

The driver apparently didn't think it was necessary to keep watch over me or Nunn May throughout the night. The temperature gauge outside the cabin read minus 28 Celsius. The night "cold and black as a witch's tit," was how Jack Brown described it.

Irina and I huddled together for warmth. "Zabotin promised me that I could accompany you by train from Montreal to Halifax. From there we'll board a flight to London and then on to Moscow," she whispered.

"It will be good to be home," I replied.

I was guarding my handbag with Fuchs' atomic drawings under my arm. I opened the bag to assure myself they were safe and offered Irina a peppermint. I suspected Nunn May had the plutonium for my locket, but he hadn't revealed it yet.

"Why on earth do you want to return to Russia?" she asked.

"Don't you?"

Nunn May began gibbering from chair, where he sat with his head

"No. Are you crazy? I want to stay here. My husband died in the war and so did my family. Starved to death during the siege of Leningrad—my mother and father and three sisters. There's nothing for me at home. Besides, I like it here. The freedom. How about you?"

"Perhaps one day I'll return to Canada." I spoke softly in Irina's ear. "My sister is alive. I'm going to find the other members of family, if it's the last thing I do. Zabotin will help me."

"Do you believe him?"

"Most days."

We snuggled closer. The fire was burning out in the wood stove. Only a few embers remained and the room was clearing of smoke.

"Why don't you run now?" Irina asked.

Her question startled me. "I stand no chance of making it out of here without being caught. You'd track me down and then I'd be in trouble."

Irina tied a wool scarf around her curls. The cabin grew colder every minute. "Don't be so certain. Two women, alone, we'd find someone to take us in. We could hide until the spring melt."

Irina was testing me. She would report back to Zabotin if I agreed.

"You have no idea how bad conditions are back home," she whispered. "You won't survive."

For a moment, I considered she was telling me the truth. I was her ticket to freedom if we managed to escape in the dead of night in the middle of this frozen wasteland. I reached into my purse for Fuchs' drawings. Nunn May could deliver the plutonium himself, but the sample was worthless without the diagrams. Undoubtedly Zabotin would be blamed for my disappearance and he'd abandon Vine. They would be imprisoned or worse, as soon as they returned to the Soviet Union.

"Is Nunn May flying with us to London?" I asked, making it clear that I was determined to finish this mission and return to the Soviet Union.

"Yes. You're travelling as man and wife. We're staying overnight in Montreal at the Princess Elizabeth Hotel. Not even the Mounties will suspect you, such a well-heeled couple,with Dr. May, speaking in his best Canadian accent. Then we go on to Halifax and across the pond to London."

Irina liked to imitate the English, but I was more concerned with Zabotin, who'd already altered our escape route. I'd understood that Vine would be accompanying me on the train to Halifax and then the flight to London. I still didn't know where he was.

"I've never stayed in a fine hotel. Have you?" Irina asked.

"Oh yes," I replied, leaving out the details.

"With Zabotin?"

She knew more than I suspected.

"At the Château Laurier. Many times."

"He admires you," Irina whispered. "Lucky girl." Irina acted as if she hadn't mentioned her intention to escape.

"Is that why you are here, to ensure my luck holds?"

"In a manner of speaking. It's more that Zabotin wants to ensure your safety. Harry Vine will meet us in Halifax. It's safer than in Montreal, where he's known to the RCMP. I'll be travelling with him, posing as his wife. Two fine-looking couples off to England."

"Two bourgeois couples, dressed in mink and cashmere," I joked, but Soviet Irina didn't respond.

I fell asleep a little more confident that Zabotin would keep his word and that Irina's escape plan was just a momentary lapse in judgment.

The sun didn't rise until after 8:30 a.m. Jack Brown lit the fire, and the room filled with smoke. Everyone was wearing the same clothes from the night before, although we were now entirely coated in a fine layer of soot. He carried in two pails of snow, which he melted on the stove. A bar of carbolic soap was floating in one bucket and we were invited to wash our face and hands in the icy water.

Coffee was brewed with the melted snow from the other bucket. "The lumberjack method," Brown remarked, throwing a handful of coarsely ground chicory into a pot of water.

Our driver went out to start the Pontiac and kept it running until we were ready to depart. "I make it warm for ladies," he said with uncharacteristic politeness.

Irina brushed my hair and pinned it up around my face like a halo. I looked like a Hollywood star, at least from the shoulders up. She fixed her hair in the same style, only hers was longer and not dry and frizzy as my dyed hair was. No matter that she'd slept on the floor in her clothes in a freezing cabin in the bush, she was a beautiful woman, young and vibrant.

Nunn May ate his oats and asked Brown if there was tea. Our host ignored him, and when Nunn May grimaced, the driver passed him his flask.

The scientist ignored the offer and walked over to where I sat waiting to leave. He reached into his suit pocket and handed me a tiny capsule of plutonium embedded in a titanium locket. I placed the locket over my head and snapped shut the clasp. On one side of the locket was a picture of Masha; on the other, plutonium. Irina made certain that the clasp was closed. She asked me if the drawings were in my handbag and I assured her that they were. No one bothered to bid goodbye to our host.

The snowstorm had stopped during the night, so we hiked to the car without being tied to ropes. The snow was up to my knees. In the Pontiac, Nunn May joined me in the backseat, while the driver and Irina rode up-front. Irina was animated. She confessed that she loved the great northern shield, the limestone, the pine trees and the wildlife. She felt sorry that I'd never have the opportunity to explore it. Four car lengths, out in the field, a red fox was keeping pace with us. We crept behind a farmer's Massey Ferguson tractor with a snowplow attached to the front. The back end of the tractor sprayed slush over our windshield, but our Russian driver said it was safer to follow the plow than try to make tracks after yesterday's heavy snowfall.

On the radio, we heard that Fred Rose was refusing to vacate his office on Parliament Hill. The Mounties encircled it, and two officers held guns to Fred and Sybil's heads. Everyone else had been evacuated from the building. Louis St. Laurent, the Minister of Justice, was standing outside Parliament beside a statue of Canada's first prime minister, Sir John A. Macdonald. The Justice Minister was quoted as saying he vowed "to punish Rose and others of his ilk for spying for a foreign power." No one from the Soviet Embassy was available for comment.

About half way to Montreal, we began careening down the rocky hilled road to the flatlands beside the St. Lawrence River. The driver was drinking from his flask. The road was covered in black ice and the three of us were holding onto the passenger straps above the windows. Irina was becoming increasingly fidgety. She opened and closed the latch on her handbag over and over. Finally she begged the driver to stop. She needed to pee, she said. At first, he refused, but when I joined in, he agreed. He pulled off the highway, onto a dirt road, leading to a farmhouse surrounded by a fence constructed entirely of rocks.

"I'll go into the farmhouse," she said, but the driver held her back.

"Plenty of space. Go behind the bushes," he ordered.

"Okay, okay!" she said, as she grew increasingly frantic. "Let me go."

The doors of the car would only open if the driver unlocked them.

"Could we stretch our legs?" Nunn May asked.

There were no lights burning in the farmhouse and the fields were bare with bunches of brown mullions peaking up above the mounds of melting snow. A scarecrow left over from the summer harvest was pressed against the frozen earth.

Irina, who was sitting beside the driver, told the scientist to be quiet. She turned to look at me, motioned to the door handle, but I shook my head. The second the driver extinguished the engine, Irina leaped from the car and began running across the field toward the rock fence. When she fell, she picked herself up and continued running. It was after four in the afternoon and a dusky gloom was settling over the grey landscape. She was serious about wanting to stay in Canada. Nunn May and I got out of the car to watch her escape. I wanted her to break free

The driver shouted at her in Russian, ordering her to stop, but she kept going, never looking back. From under his seat, he pulled a rifle, aimed and shot at Irina, piercing her shoulder. She tumbled forward, staggering to keep on. The next bullet pierced the back of her head and she fell forward in the snow. We could see the bright red blood streaming across the grey snow. I wanted to check if she was alive, to get her to a hospital, but the driver motioned us into the car with his rifle. Nunn May and I leaned against the doors, unsteady on our feet. "What have you done?" I screamed.

"Get in car," the driver ordered, pointing the end of the barrel in my face.

I stood my ground beside the car, not willing to abandon her. "Please," I begged the driver. "If she's alive."

Nunn May was stunned into silence.

The driver placed the rifle next to my temple. "Get in car," he ordered again.

Nunn May tugged at my arm and pushed me into the back seat of the Pontiac. Neither of us spoke. I grabbed for Nunn May's hand, but he pulled away. The Russian continued driving until we reached the outskirts of Montreal. "No one discover her 'til spring melt when won't be much left to find," said the driver. "The bears."

For years, I'd been pushing the danger out of my mind, trying to keep the fear at bay. Of course, I understood that I put my informants in harm's way, but I never believed I would be punished, or worse. I still wanted to be the invincible girl who rushed the waves in Lake Ontario, who swam until she couldn't catch her breath. If the driver could do away with Irina without a moment's thought, what about Nunn May or me, why not get rid of us now that the plutonium was in hand? Just tear the locket from around my neck and be done with us. And what about Vine? He was to meet me, to travel alongside Irina. How could I save him, if I couldn't protect myself?

"Where's Vine?" I asked. My voice shook. "Are we meeting him in Montreal? Do you expect him to travel on his own?"

The driver remained silent. He parked the car at a Texaco station, retrieved an over-sized Eaton's bag from the trunk and handed it to me, without speaking. Inside was a full-length mink coat with a matching pillbox hat. Nothing was forgotten, even a hatpin attached by a pink pearl to the veil.

I was instructed to remove the flat-soled winter boots Zabotin gave me at the embassy and replace them with fashionable ankle booties trimmed with fur that matched my mink. The driver took a diamond wedding ring from his pocket and put it on my finger. "You look nice, like married woman." He'd murdered Irina, not an hour earlier.

To Nunn May, the driver handed a camel-haired coat, matching fedora and polished brown brogues. We changed in the service station washrooms. In our coat pockets were new passports. As Irina predicted, Nunn May and I were travelling as a Canadian husband and wife to London. Dr. and Mrs. Craig Asselstine, from Toronto. The doctor was attending an infectious disease conference in London. Under no circumstances was I to remove the locket or the diamond ring, and Nunn May was to "talk with Canadian voice."

I asked the driver again when we would be meeting Harry Vine and this time, he admitted, we wouldn't. We weren't going to Halifax. "Plans change. You meet Vine in Moscow. No problem."

I sunk into my seat. No problem for him.

Nunn May remained silent beside me. This time he grabbed my hand in his clammy one, and I didn't pull away. At this point I didn't know if Zabotin was running me, or the GRU was directing him. In any case, there was no one to blame for this disastrous turn of events but myself.

Chapter Twenty-Two

At the hotel desk the driver asked the clerk for adjoining rooms. Nunn May and I in one room, posing as the doctor and his wife, and he in the other. He declined help from the porter with my small case and Nunn May's larger one, carrying both up the elevator himself.

The room was on the sixteenth floor, high enough to view the city of Montreal, the mountain and the St. Lawrence River. In truth, I had no idea where Vine was, if he was travelling alone to Halifax, as Irina believed, or if he would meet me in Moscow. It was possible that Zabotin had concocted this mission to trick me.

"Do you know what will happen in London? How will we make it through customs?" I asked Nunn May. "The Canadians must have alerted the Brits by now. They must realize we are missing."

"I haven't the faintest idea," he said, steadying his voice.

In the hotel room there was one double bed and two upholstered chairs. Nunn May reclined on the chair and offered me the bed. I hung my mink coat in the closet and removed my boots. When I looked at myself in the mirror, I could see the traces of soot from the night before smeared across my forehead and my chin. My hands were covered in the same black grime.

In the washroom, there was an array of expensive soaps, shampoos and thick towels. I undressed, throwing my filthy clothes in a pile on the floor. In the shower, I turned on the water as hot as it would go, until I felt it might scald my skin, but I didn't cry. If I did I would be done.

After changing, I suggested to Nunn May we head down to the dining room for a bite. It was Murray's, a small restaurant chain serving traditional English food. I knew it from previous assigments in Montreal.

"I don't believe that's possible. We're not to leave," he said, handing me the room service menu. "Are you actually hungry?" He was surprised that I could eat after what had happened to Irina. How could he know that I'd seen worse in Nesvicz?

"This could be our last good meal for some time. You'd best take full advantage," I advised.

We both ordered T-bone steaks rare, with Caesar salads, baked potatoes and lemon meringue pie. Nunn May suggested wine and I didn't object. When the bellhop arrived with the rolling table for our meal, he dropped coins in his hand and the boy grinned. The steak was perfectly done and the wine full-bodied and aromatic.

"My roots are already showing a tiny bit," I said, touching the locket around my neck. Both of us were dead tired but tried to keep up a conversation during dinner. "Why do you do it?" I asked. "You could be in England, safe and sound, working on atomic theory rather than sitting here with me, wondering if you'll be detained at Heathrow or if you'll even be alive tomorrow."

Nunn May stretched his long legs under the table. He was reclining on the chair. I used the bed as a bench.

"Look," he said. "Heisenberg was a hair's breath away from building the bomb in Germany. If he'd been successful, the Nazis would have won the war. Heisenberg failed because the Dane Niels Bohr refused to come over to the German side when Heisenberg invited him. He wouldn't budge even after the Wehrmacht offered him free rein in the laboratory with a gargantuan budget. You know, Bohr did the foundational work on atomic structure and quantum theory. Without him, the Manhattan Project wouldn't exist."

I cut into my steak. "I can't stop imagining Irina's face as she fell in the snow," I said. "We only saw her from behind."

"Try not to think about what happened," Nunn May advised. He relied on science to keep sane. He saw himself as an ethical man, a hero like Bohr.

During the war every man I met wanted to be a hero, particularly those who weren't on the battlefield. My choices were limited. If I contacted Zabotin to tell him about Irina, he'd only order me to continue. One life was expendable for this mission.

"I met him, you know, in London," Nunn May said. "In 1939, Bohr did the right thing, the only thing a civilized man could do."

"Do you believe that's what you're doing now?" I asked. "For Bohr it was a choice between FDR and Hitler. Your choice is Stalin."

"Truman is no FDR," Nunn May countered. "I'm surprised at you, Freda, if I may call you that. Zabotin assured me you've been on our side since the Party was founded in Canada."

"You could put it that way. Is that all Zabotin reported about me?"

"I'm a scientist, Freda," he replied, avoiding my question. "It's my responsibility to ensure that the atomic bomb is never used as a threat against the Soviet Union."

"Of course," I said. "And you trust Stalin not to exercise the bomb against his enemies?"

"Yes, I do. Entirely. I've come too far to change my mind. I was at Los Alamos before Chalk River, and at the Cambridge-based nuclear lab before that. Only the equilibrium between world powers will stop an all-out nuclear confrontation. Nuclear deterrence. The Manhattan Project has made it all too easy to destroy our planet."

"Stalin could use the bomb against the West," I countered.

"The Soviet Union must be able to defend itself. You appear to have forgotten the Americans have already used it."

I pushed my dinner plate away. There were scraps of bone sitting in congealed fat. Nunn May was like Grierson, naïve and trusting. He'd never lived in Russia. He didn't know what happens to people on the battlefield. He'd concocted an alibi, in his own mind, for Irina's death, no matter how spurious. Somewhere along the line, so many comrades convinced themselves that a single life was expendable. Brilliant as he was, Nunn May was no different. His dream of a world run by the proletariat was the ultimate goal. If someone as insignificant as Irina died, so be it.

After the wine bottle was empty, he pulled two chairs together, took down the extra pillow and blanket from the closet and settled in. "I'm married," he said by way of explanation. He was the only man I'd ever spent the night with in a hotel room who didn't intend to share the bed with me.

I could have told him then that Zabotin was playing both sides against the middle and that our mission was much more complicated that he'd been led to believe, but the driver was in the adjoining room and probably listening in. He wouldn't hesitate to shoot us if forced to and find another means of getting the plutonium and the atomic diagrams to Russia.

The room was warm, but I was shivering. Nunn May pulled a blanket over my shoulders and looked down at me sitting cross-legged on the bed.

"Look, I used to believe in the purity of science—science for science sake. Progress. Positivism. That's what I was trained to believe. But these eighteenth-century ideas have not stood the test of time. Not after two world wars and millions dead. Science must be based on ideology."

I pulled the blanket tightly around my neck and touched the titanium locket. My handbag with Fuchs' drawings was tucked beside me, concealed under the bedspread. I wanted to turn off the light and sleep, but Nunn May needed to defend himself.

"Everything is political, science more so than anything. The twentieth century will go down in history as the epic battle between ideologies. Fascism versus democracy. Capitalism versus Communism. Releasing energy by splitting atoms is political. We must endeavour to do right for the majority of people. Atomic power can liberate humankind, or destroy it."

I switched off the light. Nunn May's reasoning was a refrain I would hear over and over until the meltdown at Chernobyl, when no one made arguments like that anymore.

Chapter Twenty-Three

The next morning, Nunn May and I were deposited in BOAC's first class departure lounge from Montreal. Harry Vine was scheduled to be on the same aircraft, sitting in economy alongside our Russian driver, who'd accompany him to Moscow. Irina was forgotten. Again our plans had changed. I wouldn't be flying from London to Moscow. Only Vine was to meet with the Director. No one told me where I was going to end up.

"Vine on same plane. We all go down together," the driver teased.

I couldn't stop fidgeting during the long flight. Nunn May and I roamed around the makeshift airport in Gander Newfoundland where the BOAC plane refuelled. In the air, I was ordered not to walk back to the economy section so I hadn't caught sight of Vine yet, and I wasn't certain if he was actually onboard as we flew over the Atlantic.

What happened at Heathrow, occurred in an instant. Dr. and Mrs. Asselstine had no trouble passing through British customs. As soon as we stepped through immigration on the way to collect our baggage, a man approached Nunn May from behind and he was gone in an instant. I never saw the scientist again. I only discovered later that MI5 was there to snatch him up at the baggage counter. The RCMP had already sent Gouzenko's information, which implicated Nunn May in the plot to steal atomic secrets, to London intelligence. But the Soviets had also been tipped off about our arrival, and they acted with increased alacrity while the English took their time. Later I was to learn that a double agent warned the GRU about the danger their man was in and rescued him.

As I waited at the baggage claim, I spotted Vine and the driver collecting their cases before they disappeared. I was shaken after seeing Nunn May disappear in an instant, but knowing that Vine had at least made it out of Canada ahead of the RCMP put me a little more at ease. It was true that he'd been on the same plane as me and that he'd gotten out of Canada ahead of the RCMP. I assumed they were changing planes to Moscow where Vine would be well treated. I imagined him remade in his new life as a junior apparatchik in the Kremlin. If I wasn't found out, I'd settle in Moscow, too. We would be friends, perhaps living in the same building. As I stretched out my arm to grab my own suitcase from the conveyer belt, another man crept up behind me. "I'll get that, Mrs. Asselstine," he said, ensuring that I didn't attempt to catch up with Vine.

"The doctor is heading straight to the conference hotel, but I understand you'd prefer to see something of the English countryside," the Soviet operative said.

I had no idea where I was going.

"Come with me," he said, directing me with his arm.

In the taxi, we drove to Paddington Station. I was to take the passenger train to Plymouth and then board the ferry, across the Channel to Roscoff, where I'd be met by another friend. The man handed me a wallet of pound sterling notes and reminded me to get some sleep on the ferry. A private cabin was awaiting me. I wouldn't be joining Vine in Moscow, the man informed me.

Upon boarding the ferry, I descended to my cabin to lie down on the lower berth. I was too exhausted to remove my mink coat or leather boots. I must have fallen asleep, because I woke when I heard a key turning in the door's lock. This time it was a porter, arranging a dinner of bangers and mash on the counter beside me. "Eat your food now, Miss Linton," he said in his cockney accent. "Channel crossings can get rough. At Roscoff, you'll switch to the train to Paris and then on to Vienna. A friend will accompany you, so there's no need to worry. You won't be alone."

"Where's Vine?" I asked. "I was told we'd meet in Moscow. Where am I going?"

"Be patient, and be quiet," he whispered putting his finger to his lips. The porter warned me not to attempt to leave the cabin, slamming the door shut and locking it when he departed.

On the tray carrying my dinner was a letter addressed to me.

My darling Freda,

By now you are sailing across the Channel and you are safe. You know that I've honoured my promise to get you out of Canada. I have kept my word. Soon you will be in the Soviet Union. Your sister, Masha, will meet you in Kiev, and that is why her picture is in your locket. So you recognize her at first glance. No mistakes.

A comrade, a friend of the Soviet people, will accompany you when you disembark in France. He will protect you and ensure the locket gets into the hands of the right people.

Please don't worry about Vine, as you are want to do. He also has a copy of Fuchs' diagrams and he will deliver them to the Kremlin, not you. I never wished to expose you to danger, my dear, you must realize that by now.

Vine will plead with the Director that it was Gouzenko who exploded our operation in Ottawa and the worst that could be said about me is that I was too lax, too easy with the embassy staff, which, in and of itself is a breach of protocol, and one for which I will be punished. I am optimistic that my punishment will not be unduly harsh.

Vine will report that Gouzenko made one copy of the atomic diagrams, while I kept the original. He will say that I was intending to courier the information to Moscow, but only when the time was right. He will admit that I was excessively cautious and concerned that the Canadians were examining our diplomatic pouch and I didn't wish to risk it.

When I reach Moscow I will admit my lack of courage, that I should have taken all risks necessary to get the diagrams to the Director. But it was nothing calculated; only a mistake in judgment. An error.

In the meantime, Vine will be the hero. He will bring Fuchs' diagrams to the Centre. What he doesn't know is that it will take our Soviet scientists hundreds of hours in the lab—making heavy water—before they will be able to build the bomb.

Gouzenko's copy of the diagrams has been in the RCMP's possession for six months. London and Washington knows what we were up to in North America, spying on our allies in order to build a Soviet atomic weapon.

I believe, my darling, that we will wiggle out of this one together. The Brits will press for leniency since this mess is partly their fault. The comrade who will meet your ferry will explain in greater detail. He knows the entire story and intends to see the British Empire fall into ignominy.

Now I must tend to my duties here in Ottawa. You must believe in me and know that I love you deeply and forever and will never rest until we are together.

Your devoted servant,
NZ

I cursed the day Zabotin plundered Nesvicz, as I drifted into an uneasy sleep with his letter in my hand. By morning the ferry came into view of land and I heard the key turn the lock of my cabin. I rushed to the door and found it open. Zabotin did love me, I admitted that, but at what cost?

On shore, a man raced toward me. "Darling," he said, wrapping one arm around me and with the other hand, presenting me with a bouquet of white roses. He whispered in my ear, "Do not try to run. Do not scream." He kissed my hand. "You must be seen as sneaking away from boring Dr. Asselstine to be with me, your lover. Act like it."

The man hailed a taxi to carry us to the train station. We boarded the train to take us south to Paris and on to Vienna.

"Who are you?" I asked him.

"Not to worry," he said. "We have more than enough time to get to know each other. In the meantime, be quiet as a mouse. I'll discuss the changes to your mission when we are alone. My name is Kim Philby, and we are lovers. I met you in Canada when I was there last." He shoved a handful of letters into my hand. "Keep them close. Show these letters if anyone suspects us."

"Where's Vine?" I asked, defiantly.

"I'll explain everything," he assured me. "Let's wait until we're alone in our compartment. Try to be patient."

The first-class compartment was ornate, with pullout beds and a wash basin for the long trip to Vienna. There were more flowers and a bottle of champagne awaiting us.

"You look swell as a blonde, but I prefer you as a brunette."

"How do you know what I looked like?" This man was infuriating. "I need to know what's really going on and where we're going."

"Things change, Miss Linton. You already have been told that Vine will deliver the drawings to the Director in Moscow. You'll give me the plutonium. Simple and straightforward, no?"

"Nunn May, he was taken away as soon as we landed at Heathrow."

Philby looked at me quizzically. "You didn't suppose we'd allow him to be questioned by MI5, did you? Nunn May is safe with us. He really doesn't know much except that the scientists at Chalk River have built their own little reactor. I know about the ZEEP. He's already told us about that. It's not exactly news."

I removed my mink coat, but kept my hat on. "Who is us?" I asked.

"I'm on your side, my dear," he said, clutching my arm. "You must trust me or we'll both be in trouble. MI5 thought they'd get to Nunn May at Heathrow, but we're quicker than them. I had our boys positioned to pick him up. Zabotin let me know Nunn May was on the plane with you."

"Our boys?"

"Don't be dense. It's not impossible to figure it out. I work for the Soviets."

"And the British?"

"Yes, at the same time."

"How do I know who you're working for now?"

"I suppose you can't. But I'll get you back to Soviet territory safely. I'll deliver you to your sister Masha. Now, do you believe me?"

I asked him about Zabotin, if he was still in Canada, but Philby was coy. "Wouldn't you like to know?"

"Are the Soviets… are you protecting Grierson as well?" I inquired.

"Not entirely. Let me be frank," Philby said, clenching his teeth. "Prime Minister King is calling a Royal Commission to investigate our Canadian-based spies. It's handier than a court of law where justice must be upheld, and more brutal. Grierson will be called upon to testify. A few questions, mostly about you, my dear girl, and he'll be dismissed. Shortly afterward he'll be relieved of his position at the Wartime Information Bureau and a new Head will be hired for the National Film Board."

Grierson would defend me to the bitter end, no matter what the personal cost. I was confident of that much.

"Ellery will cover for Grierson to a certain extent." Philby stuttered for effect. "Or be exposed as a dupe of Soviet intelligence himself. Grierson must resign himself to a life of total obscurity. You might have joined him at his home back in Scotland, but I suspect you'll be happier in the Soviet Union."

Zabotin was working with this odious man. That much was clear, but I didn't know how much Philby knew, or if he knew that Zabotin was trying to outsmart the Centre.

"Your colleague, Homer, what is he to expect?" I wanted to show Philby that I knew a thing or two.

"Ah Homer… he will be re-assigned to Cairo. It's a damn pity. British intelligence needs men of Donald's caliber. He really is an extraordinary agent, a workhorse, but a bit soft on straddling both sides. I shouldn't worry about him."

"Trust me, I won't."

"But mostly you are concerned about your lover, right? Zabotin. Don't concern yourself. He has friends in Moscow. They'll take good care of him. There are always insiders who wield more power than anyone realizes. That's how undercover clubs operate. Rather cut throat. Cloak and dagger."

I wasn't certain if Philby was telling me that Zabotin would be executed or just ex-communicated.

"Don't look so grim," Philby said to me, taking a lock of my hair in his hand. "I'm rather senior myself. Not in the same way as Zabotin. I'm too valuable to MI6 to expire on the battlefield."

I brushed Philby's hand aside.

"Possibly you would find me more attractive if I was in uniform. Women prefer a man in uniform."

"No, I would not."

"Miss Linton. Please don't pretend that you haven't been around the dance floor numerous times. I know of your work for the GRU and I admire your fortitude, your longevity. Think of it this way: we're both attempting to stop World War III. If you've forgotten, we're on the same side. Even your hero Zabotin will regain his sanity once he returns to the fold. I can understand why he withheld Fuchs' diagrams from the Director. His allegiance is to Mother Russia and not to Communism. In that way we are slightly different, but our goal is the same: for the Russians to make the bomb. I would have preferred if he'd shared Fuchs' diagrams with the Centre earlier, before Hiroshima; but in the end, he did the right thing. And so we'll protect him. And you, of course, with your locket of plutonium."

"And then what will you do with me?"

Philby sat back on the upholstered seat. He unzipped his trousers and spread his legs. He expected me to kneel in front of him, and I did. We spent a great deal of the trip in that position.

Chapter Twenty-Four

In Vienna, Philby and I checked into a modest pension, far from the palatial glories of the Ringstrasse. It was a working man's bed and board, without any pretensions, but the sheets were clean. The linen was disinfected in carbolic soap, and the smell permeated the room. At the end of the hall was a toilet in one cabinet and a bathtub in the other.

I needed to sleep and Philby allowed me a few hours. When I woke there was schnitzel, potato dumplings and a bottle of wine. Philby was reading from Graham Greene.

He looked up at me and said, "If I hadn't become a spy, I would have been a novelist, but St. John, my father... well he was the exotic in the family, the rebel. He took a mistress, an Arabic girl and actually married her while my mother was alive. In our part of little England, that takes nerve. I'm really just a bureaucrat doing as I'm told."

"Are you married?" I asked.

"Oh, yes, to the same old girl for years now. My lady wife is fragile, under the weather much of the time, but she's a good sport. Puts up with me, as do the children. I shouldn't expect you'd be as long-suffering as my wife." He pointed to his side of the unmade bed.

Philby crawled in beside me. He undressed me as I turned by back to him. That's when he let me know how much the Director admired my work. "He holds you in the highest regard."

"As the Americans say, that and a nickel will get me a cup of coffee," I deadpanned.

"*Au contraire.* The Director is a very powerful man. For now, he has captured Stalin's ear." Philby wrapped his arms around my breasts as he penetrated me. "You must face the fact that you'll never be allowed to leave us again, you'll never return to the West." He was panting with excitement. "It would be much too dangerous." For a few moments he grew silent, until he expired.

Within minutes he began talking again. "If I were to let you go, the Americans would interrogate you, and we must never underestimate their brutality. Your knowledge about how the Soviets got their hands on the plutonium and the atomic diagrams… well," he said, stuttering. "It's something only a very few of us will ever understand."

I pulled away from his grasp and sat up to cover myself with a blanket.

"The job is never over, you know," Philby continued. "At Los Alamos, Oppenheimer's scientists are hard at work devising a more powerful bomb. Bringing the plutonium to me is courageous. I commend you, as will the Director. You should be thankful. You are allowed to survive, but not to tell the tale."

I grabbed at the locket around my neck.

"There, there. Hand it over," he ordered. "I wouldn't want you escaping tonight. I must meet friends for a few hours while you catch up on your beauty sleep."

I took the locket from my neck and placed it in his hand. Philby was finished with me. I'd served my purpose. I didn't know what would happen to Zabotin, but I feared he'd be punished, perhaps killed. Philby was furious with him, for withholding the diagrams.

"Aren't you curious about what's going to happen to you once you're back on Soviet soil? You're going to the Ukraine, to your sister. She'll ensure you behave."

I refused to cry.

"By the time I return late tonight, Vine will have delivered the atomic diagrams to the Director. Once you are with your sister, Vine can do what he wants. He may choose to reside with you, in case he gets lonely. The powers that be won't be hard on either of you. I don't expect Vine will betray you or Zabotin to the GRU. There's really nothing in it for him and I've reminded him that Zabotin is more useful to us alive rather than in an unmarked grave.

"Without you, poor old Vine would be isolated in the Soviet Union, lacking a friendly face to cheer him up. He does appear to require quite a lot of cheering up. For all his faith in Marxism, he does get worked up when the situation gets dicey. The man relies most heavily on you, Freda, but all the men in your life appear to. Extraordinary, really! Grierson is inconsolable apparently, sorry old bugger."

Philby dressed. He removed a one-time pad from his valise, the kind the Soviets used to transmit messages during the war. Then he left without bidding me goodbye.

I spent most of the night alone. Philby didn't return until the early hours of the morning. "Vine made the drop. He's free to go," he declared, a cheery ring to his voice. "Get dressed right now. We have a train to catch."

In the taxi to the station, I knew that Philby had no reason to keep me alive. He had the plutonium. "Where is Zabotin?" I tried not to sound desperate.

"He must stay in Ottawa until this Gouzenko affair blows over."

"That could take years." I was holding back the tears. "Give me back the locket."

Philby acted surprised. "You are smarter than that. Do you actually expect me to? Ah, Freda. For a clever woman you can behave like an idiot. You and Zabotin believing you could stand in the way of history. Don't muddy the waters for him. It could seal his fate."

I remained silent as we drove by the Schönbrunn Palace. I'd accepted by then I'd never see the inside of Vienna's stately buildings, untouched by the war.

"Read your Marx," Philby said with authority. "It's inevitable that the Soviet Union will prevail, that we'll have the bomb in no time. And you will be safe."

"How can you be so certain?"

"Silly woman. Zabotin, of course. If it weren't for him you wouldn't be on your way to Russia. You'd be in custody in Canada. Do you believe you are that significant to us? Zabotin has threatened to defect if we lay a hand on you and we can't have that. As I've explained, he's still useful to us and would be even more useful to the other side."

At the train station, Philby paid the driver and escorted me to the platform.

"Where is Zabotin now?" I repeated. If I knew Zabotin was safe, I could control my tears.

"If you must know about the fate of Zabotin," Philby said "he'll be in the USSR within six months, if he keeps his word. Then off to the gulag. He can't get away entirely after what he's done."

I wanted to break down, but Philby grabbed my wrist and ordered me to stop blubbering. We were starting to get glares from nearby passengers milling around the station.

"When he's served his sentence, he can join you. You can wait, can't you, for the man you love?"

I nodded my head.

"You do love him? I can see why, if indeed you do. I met Zabotin for the first time at Yalta. He was with the Soviet delegation, a chest of medals decorating his uniform, very debonair, very robust, except for his right hand, of course. His English was excellent. I enjoyed his company."

My tears began to flow once again.

"What a treasure you are," Philby said, as he patted me on the behind and handed me my train ticket and his handkerchief. "I can see why he gave up his wife for you. What is her name? Lydia, isn't it?"

"Yes, Lydia."

"We all have blood on our hands. Did you know Lydia well? Were you chums in Ottawa?"

I turned away. How dare he?

Philby offered me a cigarette, but I declined. "Brave, deluded Miss Linton. I must admit I admire your pluck. I'll vouch for you with the Director. I'll say that Zabotin made you do it, that he's the one to blame, keeping the atomic diagrams from us. The ones you've been hiding in your purse. They're not much use to you now that Vine has delivered the same plans to the Centre."

I avoided Philby's gaze while he pulled out a cigarette.

"If you wait for Zabotin, he should be out in, oh, I'd say ten years. If he survives the gulag, he still has friends in high places. All exemplary military organizations are traditional in the best English sense of the word, the Soviet military not excluded. For Generals, it's always a matter of patriotism over politics. That's how Stalin won the war."

There was a glimmer of a chance that Zabotin's life would be spared. I had to count on that, or I'd fall to pieces.

"We need translators now," said Philby. "You fit the bill rather well. Your sister will explain."

"My sister? How will she be involved?"

"Masha, the very one. How many years has it been since you've seen her? It is she who will be responsible for your safety and for your silence once you are back in the USSR."

"Is Masha in danger?" I asked Philby. I'd gone so far to try to reunite with my family and now I worried I was dragging my poor sister back into harm's way.

"Quite the contrary. You will advance her standing in the Party. One day when we construct a Soviet nuclear reactor, she'll be on board. Chernobyl is the perfect spot for one. With your information, and the plutonium, we'll be thinking about a suitable location to build a heavy water plant. Not unlike the one the Canadians are putting together at Chalk River. Thanks to you and Alan Nunn May, we have those blueprints in our safekeeping as well."

As we waited for the train to arrive, Philby assured me that I would fit in at the new laboratory at Chernobyl. "Lots of Jews at the lab. Your people are good at science. There's even one synagogue left standing in Chernobyl."

I put up my hand to stop his chatter, but he pushed it away. "Don't say it. I know. You're not in the slightest religious. All my Jewish friends claim so. But we know differently, don't we, Freda? Once a Hebrew, always a Hebrew. That's why Hitler was so intimidated by your people; each of you answering to a higher power. The chosen people, and all that rot."

In the short time I'd spent with Philby I grew to loathe him more than I thought was possible. Charm was a cover for his innate odiousness.

As the train pulled into the station, I spit at him and he wiped his face without blinking. I no longer cared who saw us. I boarded the train, travelling by route to Kiev through Budapest. My ticket was for first class until Hungary and then I was to change to third.

From the station in Budapest, I kept my head down in the overcrowded third-class car. I looked foolishly overdressed. The other passengers stared at me in disbelief. Most had boarded in Budapest, where I changed trains. They were women with little children, covered in coats that were no more than rags, and with the heels splaying from their boots, their belongings stored in potato sacks. Red Army soldiers played cards and made obscene gestures to me, inviting me to lift my skirt.

The passengers nibbled on stale bread wrapped in newspaper. They carried metal cups to the samovar simmering in the corner of the rail car. Not one person offered me a bite of bread or a cup of tea until we crossed into Soviet territory, where a government official welcomed Russian citizens back to the motherland and handed out packets of cured sausage, boiled eggs and cooked cabbage. I received rations like everyone else.

As we pulled into the railway station in Kiev, I saw that the station was in ruins. Nothing remained of the original structure. Flocks of refugees camped by the tracks, waiting for a train to take them home. There were few men among them. When the Red Army had re-captured Kiev from the Germans, the fighting was fierce. So many had perished at that very spot. I hadn't seen the war up close until this moment. Women and children without their men.

I stepped onto the platform and saw Masha standing there, waiting for me. She walked over and stuck out her cheek for me to kiss. She was dressed in a uniform and cap with a pin of Lenin on the brim. "Welcome to the USSR," she said in English, shaking my hand. It had been twenty-five years since we'd set eyes on each other. Masha had been twelve when I left Nesvicz.

We took the tram to her flat, me carrying my little case and wearing the mink coat and matching hat. I realized that Philby intended for me to be highly visible. He didn't need to arrange surveillance. No one who noticed me on the train from Budapest to Kiev, or on the city tram, would forget the woman wrapped in mink.

Chapter Twenty-Five

February 1946
Kiev

Masha's flat was one room with a tiny kitchen, on the third floor of a Ukrainian aristocrat's mansion. The house was divided into living quarters for Party officers and their families. The old count occupied the morning room on the second floor, where he positioned his rocking chair to face the window. When he saw Masha from the window, he stood to attention and saluted.

I was to discover that the house was noisy both day and night. Babies wailed and children ran up and down the grand staircase. Adolescents smoked in the hallways. Men sat outside on the second floor verandah, reminiscing about the courageous battles they'd waged against the Nazis during the Great Patriotic War. Some of them were missing a limb and on crutches. The most seriously maimed rested in wheelchairs.

"Nobody has any money, but we are satisfied," Masha declared, pride overflowing. "The ruble isn't worth what it once was. We haven't tasted coffee or enjoyed chocolate since 1941, but Stalin will fix it. Reconstruction takes time.

"How was your war?" she inquired when placing a glass of weak tea before me.

I hadn't removed my coat. The apartment would remain cold throughout the winter. I was to share a bed with my sister, who'd commandeered a feather pillow and woolen blanket for me. She offered me the side nearest to the stove.

"Consider yourself lucky," she said, handing me strips of yesterday's newspaper. "Take a towel and soap with you." One lavatory served the entire third and fourth floors. "We can wash in the kitchen basin," added Masha.

"Be prepared," Masha continued. "I leave for work every morning before dawn. We only have a few hours of electricity in the evening, so we must shut off the lights now." It was 8 p.m. "We're building a laboratory near Chernobyl, not far from here. In the spring, I'll move you out there. You and me, and your friend Vine. I remember him from Nesvicz. He's allowed to join us. Our apartment will be ready by May."

"You actually remember Vine?" I asked her.

"I couldn't pick him out of a crowd," she replied, "but I've seen faded pictures recently. You needn't fill me in. I know the whole story. Vine has done his duty by reporting to Moscow. Have you handed over the locket?"

"Of course," I said. Masha was more than a Party official, she was a member of the secret police. I understood, then, that I was to remain in the Soviet Union under her watch. "Am I under house arrest?" I sipped the hot tea.

Masha placed two bowls of watery cabbage soup on the table. "I wouldn't go that far," she replied. "Call it what you will, but before I can leave you alone, you must prove to me that you will be loyal to the motherland. You've betrayed us, you and your Colonel Zabotin."

"Is that what you believe, Masha?"

"Vine swears that you did it in the name of world peace," she replied. "However, I find that ludicrous. What would you know about peace, or about war? You've been in Canada throughout the entire tragedy. You did it to save your own skin."

Masha had been a serious child, responsible and more than willing to betray Simcha when he dissembled to Papa. I wondered who Masha had become or if it were in her nature to follow orders and bow to authority? Was it possible that a certain kind of person, one who is diligent and eager to please and follow orders, rose to high positons in the Soviet Union? She had become much more than my little sister, more than the girl I'd longed to rescue. Masha was a functionary of the state and it was not her that needed rescuing, but me.

"In the spring, you'll go to work as a translator at the laboratory. Academic articles on atomic theory reach us that are not written by Russians. You can translate. You can speed up the making of the bomb."

"I can't see how I can help with that," I told her.

Masha crossed her arms over chest. "You don't have a choice. You need to do your duty to your country. That doesn't end now that you're back here. No one knows you or realizes what you have done. You're lucky you're even alive. Don't play the innocent with me. It's surprising you're alive. I know your entire story. The West has a copy of the same atomic drawings Vine snuck out of Los Alamos. Now we have them too, but it was Zabotin who held them back from our Director. You helped him, now you help us."

Inside my handbag, folded next to my compact and lipstick, was a copy of the diagrams for Fat Man. I was now the only person, aside from military personnel, who kept a copy. Except for Zabotin, of course. I took the pin from my hair and removed the pillbox hat.

"If it were up to me, I would have you interrogated in the Lubyanka. But Moscow insisted, and so here you are, with me. After what you've done, how can I trust you?"

Masha sat across the wooden table from me, spooning soup into her mouth. The scar on her face was as red as a cherry. It hadn't faded after twenty-five years.

I might have tried to convince Masha that I'd devoted myself to the Party as no other woman in Canada had done. My actions were meant to stave off nuclear obliteration, and not to encourage it. But on our first day together, I'd do more harm than good to argue with her.

Even after the accident in Chernobyl she remained resentful and I understood why. Masha lost everything during the war, except her faith in Communism. She married a soldier in the Red Army and they shared the house in Nesvicz with Mama and Papa until her husband was called up for active duty. He died at the front during the first wave of battles against the Germans. "No trace," Masha said. By the time Count and Countess Zabotin took her on as the their maid at the dacha, they'd made it clear there was room only for one more. Mama and Papa and Masha's little girl remained at the old house, praying that the Nazis wouldn't bother with such an insignificant place as Nesvicz.

But they did. Every Jew counted. On the day after the Germans invaded Nesvicz, all three were taken to the ravine behind the synagogue and shot. All the Jews died on that day. Except for Masha, who was saved by the Zabotins.

Chapter Twenty-Six

1957 and 1986
Chernobyl

After Philby, I remained faithful to one man: Zabotin. I waited for him for eleven years to come to me. Masha remained true to her word. She protected me, found me work as a translator at the laboratory in Chernobyl and allowed Vine to live with me while I waited for my lover.

Vine attempted to exist in Nesvicz for a few months before joining Masha and me in the spring of 1946. He hoped to revive his father's shoe shop, but he was the only Jew, with the exception of one other, in the village. New inhabitants, who had taken over the village when the Jews were murdered, avoided Vine. It was as if he didn't exist. I asked him if they felt guilty about expropriating the homes and businesses of the Jews, but he said no one ever spoke about what happened during the war.

"I asked for my father's house to be returned to me," Vine recounted. "The deeds to the property were still in my family's name, but the new occupants were angry I'd returned from the dead. They refused to believe me and, of course, I had no papers proving I was my father's son."

The rest of Vine's family had died in the massacre at the ravine behind the synagogue, all except for Yitzhak, who perished with the Red Cavalry years earlier. Vine reported that the other Jew who resided in the village avoided him like the plague. If Vine caught sight of him, he'd race away. They never spoke. Not once. The mysterious man built a shack near the ravine and lived as a hermit, appearing only to replenish his supplies. He had money, rubles from the old regime, which he traded for goods on the black market.

When Fred Rose was released from the penitentiary in Kingston, Ontario, he and Sybil joined me in Chernobyl. Rose's Canadian citizenship was revoked and so was Sybil's. They came home to the East, where the Party made a big deal of their bravery on behalf of the Soviet Union. Rose was feted for months as a hero and then sent to Comrade Masha who found him work at the laboratory. He became a teacher of English to the young, eager scientists who had time on their hands in a lacklustre spot like Chernobyl. Sybil never managed to recover from her sojourn in the women's prison, so she stayed at home, cooking for the four of us, seldom leaving the apartment across the hall from Vine and me. Her ancient mother, who returned to Romania after the war, was still alive.

Zabotin was released from the gulag when he was cleared by Khrushchev. Along with thousands of Stalin's enemies of the people, he was accorded leniency by the new leader. He returned to me a different man. His front teeth were missing, having been knocked out by a particularly brutal guard, and more had fallen out from malnutrition. He was as weak as a baby bird, but his frailty made me love him all the more. He'd suffered in ways my mind could not comprehend. I covered his emaciated form with a bearskin rug and kept him in bed for months, feeding him soup, first through a straw, and then sips from a spoon.

During that time, our love grew deeper and I came to accept that we would never leave each other. I asked Zabotin why he'd lied to me about the contents of Gouzenko's documents, first telling me he would send the atomic diagrams to Moscow just before the defection, next saying he'd kept them for himself, along with the cables from Homer. By the time I was on my way to London, I knew the truth. The evidence, incriminating the Soviets of atomic espionage, was in the documents Gouzenko handed over to the RCMP. Zabotin provided the West with more than it needed to put an end to Soviet atomic espionage. At least for a short time. I still keep a copy of the diagrams stored in a suitcase under my bed. Philby delivered the plutonium to the Centre, after ensuring that I was under Masha's supervision.

Zabotin argued that the more confused I was in Ottawa, the better were my chances of survival. I chose to believe him, as we do; accept our lover's alibis without much investigation, or else each of us would be alone.

The KGB, which carried on from where the NKVD had left off, began sending illegals to North America once the furor from the Gouzenko affair, the Royal Commission and the trial of the Rosenbergs in the US died down. The USSR exploded its first atomic bomb in 1949. Espionage was the life-blood of the Soviet state until it finally fell, keeling over from its own weight, its corruption and inefficiency, but not until a few years after the Chernobyl disaster. It wasn't so much Communism, not the Marxist bible that Kim Philby was fond of quoting when we travelled from France to Vienna, but the way men and women acted it out. After the war, a grand performance of selfishness, stupidity and paranoia ruled Soviet Russia.

After his release from the gulag and under my care, Zabotin grew strong again. His robust colour returned, and he began to walk straight without a stoop to his shoulders and without a limp to his gait. Slowly he returned to his natural weight, and his demeanour was no longer that of a prisoner. We strolled together each evening along the streets of Chernobyl, and when we moved to Pripyat, the city built for the workers at the nuclear reactors, we hiked in the forest every weekend. Nature was our solace. We found peace among the magestic, ancient pines. The natural splendour of the forest gave us hope that humankind would survive the stockpiling of nuclear weapons, the race to military supremacy between world powers.

When we were transferred to Pripyat, Masha remained in Chernobyl, standing as the head of the city council and spying for the NKVD all the while. For weeks at a time, she would disappear and none of us knew where she'd gone. Perhaps to America to advise the illegals operating in Ottawa and Washington and New York. Espionage moved on from atomic to germ warfare.

The bosses at the reactor continued to find work for the four of us. Vine, Rose, Sybil and I were useful to them, each in our own way. I continued to translate, Rose taught English, Sybil cooked for the Party brass when officials from Romania were feted by the Soviets. Vine was the least useful of all, but they coddled him. After all, he was a hero; he'd rescued the atomic diagrams against all odds and brought them to the Director.

Remarkably, Zabotin was promoted to the position of Chairman of Human Resources at Reactor Number Four, the one that eventually caused the demise of Chernobyl and the Soviet nuclear program. His management skills were unmatched among the Soviet bureaucrats who were responsible for the mood and well-being of the reactor's staff.

The men and women from Pripyat adored him. Everyone wanted to be under Colonel Zabotin rather than the three other chairmen of health and welfare, who treated their workers with disdain and stole from them. As Zabotin had been at the embassy in Ottawa, he was at Chernobyl: generous and permissive, always ready to turn a blind eye to human errors and misdemeanours. Perhaps the workers at Reactor Number Four grew lazy under his watch, or worse, reckless, but as I recall, Zabotin did encourage his people to take chances and to ignore the warnings from the top brass at the plant. He expressed pleasure in their discoveries and encouraged the scientists to experiment with ways that nuclear energy could enrich the human race rather than destroy it. I do believe he handed them much too much rope.

When Reactor Number Four exploded and a plume of radioactive vapour shot into the heavens, causing the greatest nuclear accident in history, Zabotin was prepared. For at least five years beforehand, he had claimed the reactors could explode at any moment and we should be ready to run. About twelve months prior to the accident, he'd convinced me to keep a suitcase packed, as I had in Ottawa before Gouzenko defected. Zabotin warned me that, otherwise, I would be without the clothes I cherished or my precious locket that had once held a sample of plutonium. Philby had returned it to me by registered mail from England after he delivered its contents to the Director of the GRU.

I was sleeping at 1:23 in the morning when the accident happened. Zabotin was reclining in front of our bed in his reading chair. He hardly slept at night but took catnaps during the day in his office at Reactor Number Four. The sound of the reactor exploding woke me. Zabotin crawled into bed with me and held me as the twelve-hundred ton cover of the reactor blasted into the atmosphere. Then we waited.

Zabotin explained to me that the scientists were undertaking an experiment that night and had turned off the safety mechanisms on the reactor. It was a combination of human error and faulty equipment, the same poison recipe that was destroying the entire country. From our apartment, we could hear the sirens of the first firefighters. They couldn't extinguish the inferno of raging plutonium and uranium.

"What frightens me is that the bosses at the plant believe they can put out the fire with water. With water," Zabotin said softly, still holding me in his arms.

"And they can't?"

"It could be a chain reaction. Another explosion that will not only contaminate us, but half of Europe."

Just after 5 a.m., Zabotin received the phone call from the plant. Gorbachev had been alerted to the disaster, but the information relayed to him was scant and he wasn't prepared to make the decision to evacuate Pripyat. The director of the nuclear plant was terrified he'd be blamed for the disaster, so he sent for Zabotin, who had the talent to be diplomatic when speaking with political leaders.

"I won't leave you to fend for yourself." Zabotin assured me, pulling me from the bed. "Get dressed. You're coming with me."

At the nuclear station, firefighters without protective gear were shooting streams of water onto the base of the melting reactor. The air was on fire with radiated particles that danced around our heads. Not one of the firemen was wearing a mask or gloves. Two died that morning. During the next weeks hundreds more as the radiation contaminated the flesh of the men sent by our leaders to control the damage.

Zabotin and I were handed protective suits as we were ushered into a lead encased office, a small room insulated from the exploding reactor. The director assured us that there was no cause for worry and demanded that Zabotin try to convince Gorbachev of the same. The director believed he'd be able to handle the fallout and restore order to the plant.

Zabotin kept shaking his head as the director spoke of his plans to pour more water over the meltdown.

"Water doesn't extinguish nuclear explosions," Zabotin said boldly. "It doesn't work that way. Once the energy in the reactor is released..."

The director cut Zabotin off. He asked his assistant to reach Gorbachev.

When Gorbachev came on the line, Zabotin began screaming into the receiver. "Evacuate Pripyat! Please, I beg you, Comrade—don't wait. This explosion is a thousand times more powerful than the bombs the Americans dropped on Japan."

I'd only known Zabotin to lose control once before, and that was the night our comrades were imprisoned by the RCMP in Ottawa.

Gorbachev offered to send a committee of the Soviet Union's best nuclear scientists to Pripyat to investigate the effects of the explosion. He'd wait for their decision before ordering an evacuation. He'd confer with the local officials.

Outside the office was mayhem. It was war, the conflict that Soviet leaders had been preparing for since 1946 but which had never come to pass, not in the fashion they'd envisioned. For them it had to be the war between the US and the Soviet Union that would harm Russian citizens, not something they'd built themselves. The Chernobyl disaster was unique. Our leaders couldn't see the enemy because the enemy was them and their entire fossilized system. The 2,700 Soviet warheads, each one more powerful than one hundred Chernobyls combined—and all aimed at America—couldn't save the people of Pripyat or those in Kiev and Minsk who suffered from the radioactive fallout.

Zabotin put down the phone on Gorbachev and demanded that we be taken back to our apartment. He was ready with his Lada to rescue us. He woke Rose, Sybil and Vine and rushed them into the car. Even our cat, Matilda, came along. As we drove across the town, we watched children and their parents strolling to school, playing on swings and slides or teeter-totters. Not one of them was aware of what was happening ten kilometres away at the nuclear power station. A travelling circus had come to town the day before the explosion, and the Ferris wheel loomed above the town square, awaiting the curious children who longed to ride to the top.

Masha remained in Kiev. A few hours after the accident, she was whisked away to an underground bunker with the other Party officials in our district. Not one of them ended up suffering from exposure to radiation, unlike the ordinary residents or the miners and soldiers sent into the bowels of the reactor to contain the damage—the liquidators, as they were called. They perished in droves. Those still alive are slowly dying from radiation poisoning. To this day, I can't fathom why it took the authorities two days to decide to evacuate the citizens of Pripyat after the accident.

We went to ground at Zabotin's dacha, until he discerned that the five of us would be better off surviving in the Chernobyl forest. No one would bother with us there, he proclaimed. He didn't want to come up against the director at the ruined reactor, who could scapegoat him for the accident. After all, it was Zabotin who had hung up on the Supreme Leader. In the forest we could live without interference, without rules and without responsibility, except to each other. "What else could anyone wish for on this earth, but that?" he asked, looking up to the heavens. It would be our own private paradise.

"Back to the garden," is exactly how Zabotin described our return to Chernobyl, but it was also where I discovered that my brother Simcha was still alive, so perhaps Zabotin's optimism was overstated. At least for me, the return to Eden was not possible. Perhaps not possible for anyone.

***

Chernobyl journal
1988

Masha was coming to visit. We'd know her by the white hazmat suit she would be wearing and the Geiger counter in her hands. A few days ago, she'd left word with one of the guards at the ruined reactor, who'd bravely made his way with the news to our cabin in the radiated forest. He brought hazmat suits for Zabotin and me in case we contaminated Comrade Masha just by standing beside her. It was only two years after the accident, and more and more of the former residents of Pripyat were falling ill and dying.

Yet again, Elka happened to be visiting when the guard had arrived with the message. After he left, Elka had mused, "Masha. Yes… Masha Linton, I remember her. The one with the long red scar on her face. She must have been beautiful once. Who ruined her face?"

Elka was anxious to see my sister, who she remembered from early days at the Chernobyl laboratory. We were sitting together on the screen porch drinking tea and smoking Elka's hand-rolled cigarettes. Zabotin had recently built a fence to enclose our cabin, and now he was out scrounging for wild flowers to plant along the barrier.

"Your man always disappears when things get interesting," said Elka.

"Not always," I replied.

"When was the last time you saw your sister?" asked Elka. "She looks like you, I think. I also remember her from Kiev, where she was a bigshot in the Party. I'm surprised she didn't help out her brother, find him a position in the bureaucracy."

I'd asked Elka to stop mentioning Simcha, but she didn't care what I wanted or how much her stories about my brother destroyed me. I changed the subject to Masha, who was easier to discuss.

"She's still a bigshot in the Party," I said. "We met as soon as I returned from Canada, at the train station in Kiev, just after the war. I haven't seen her for two years, since the accident." I never knew why I supplied so many details to Elka.

Elka looked me straight in the eyes. "You probably haven't changed that much, since the accident. High cheekbones, large grey eyes. Your parents were good looking."

"They were," I agreed. Elka's obsession with beauty knew no bounds.

Elka pursed her lips. "My folks were plain, round-faced and broad-nosed with small eyes, and that's why I turned out the way I did. Ugly. I was an ugly child. Wild hair, buck teeth, spindly arms and legs."

"No child is ugly," I said, correcting her.

"I was," Elka insisted. "You never know what happens to people, but I believe my life would have been different if I'd been a beauty like you."

"You never know." I understood that Elka was not complimenting me and that something worse would now follow.

"It's men who make the difference," she declared. "What if Zabotin came across an unattractive woman like me rather than you? He probably would have killed me in Nesvicz."

I had no idea how she knew about the Red Cavalry's pogrom in Nesvicz.

Elka changed the subject. "Your sister, Masha, is tough. Toes the party line no matter what the consequences. I admire that about her. You know that she gave the order to evacuate, but not until two days after the explosion. I was already gone. I escaped to the forest as I soon as I heard the explosion in the morning."

I wanted to slap Elka. "That's not true," I told her. "It was the director of Reactor Number Four who was charged with the evacuation orders." I refused to confess to Elka about our early morning visit to the reactor and how Moscow stalled for time.

"That's what you think," Elka retorted. "Masha was senior to the director. She was the conduit between Gorbachev and the scientists he ordered to investigate the accident. But what do you know? Spoiled, that's what you are. Spoiled and naïve."

I cut Elka off. "I need to prepare now."

"Just a minute," she said, clutching at my hand. "Didn't Zabotin contact the Supreme Leader on the night of the accident, but Gorbachev didn't trust him, not after what your man did in Canada? You and Colonel Zabotin. It's probably your fault, and his, rather than Masha's that Pripyat wasn't evacuated sooner. Think of how many lives would have been saved. And the suffering."

I pulled my hand away from hers. There was plenty of blame to go around. "That's ridiculous, Elka. Zabotin was trying to get people out of the plant and away from Pripyat. No one told Gorbachev for hours after the accident, and when he found out he didn't order the evacuation until two days later. It had nothing to do with Zabotin or me."

"Nope, you're wrong," Elka insisted. "How could anyone with a brain rely on Zabotin? Not after Gouzenko. He always makes things worse."

When Elka left that day, I told her never to return. I wanted her out of the way when Masha arrived. And out of my life. I didn't want Elka questioning my sister.

Masha had survived the Revolution, the pogroms, the Nazis and the radiation sickness caused by the explosion at Chernobyl. If Countess Zabotin hadn't hidden her in the cold storage room when the Germans stormed their dacha, she'd be dead. A Red Army sergeant carried my sister out of the storage room long after the Zabotins were shot. The Nazis never managed to find her. She hid for eight months on her own, eating potatoes and cabbage and drinking rainwater or melted snow.

The Red Army had carried Masha with them when they entered Kiev.

She weighed seventy-eight pounds. The sergeant deposited her at the military camp hospital, where she was nursed back to health. In the first forty-eight hours after the explosion, what choice did Masha have but to obey the Supreme Leader? What choice did anyone have?

I supposed Simcha's story was worse than Masha's, but I hadn't managed to locate him. Communication with the outside world was limited from our forest. No one was invited in, and no one left the forest. Ordinary people thought we were radioactive and that we'd contaminate them. Like the three-eyed beasts that roamed our infected corner of the earth, we, too, were medical curiosities, monsters of the aftermath.

Although I'd sent word to Masha months ago telling her that a neighbouring squatter believed Simcha was alive, I never heard back from her. Not until the guard showed up with her message.

I'd seen her infrequently after Zabotin came to me in Chernobyl. She avoided us. To my mind, Masha had never forgiven me for deserting the family during the pogrom. She couldn't stop judging me. Once when I challenged her and then begged her to exonerate me, she simply shook her head and stated that I was cooking up stories to make myself appear more important than I was in the larger scheme of things.

She'd added then, "Only you know what you did; how you endangered the family by leaving us. You were the oldest. Now you want me to comfort you, to assure you it is forgivable that you deserted us and didn't respond to my letters when I wrote to you that we were starving." Masha bit her lip. "Your own flesh and blood."

How could I argue with her? I was guilty. But when I considered what I could have done for them from Canada, I never arrived at a suitable answer, one that would assuage her resentment and my guilt.

Like Elka, Masha would never shake off the disaster of her life. Few could who had survived the war and the bleak years of Soviet rule. I came to understand that it didn't matter which side you were on, the Communists or the refuseniks, the warmongers or the peaceniks, no one could be a normal person again, not after the war. You either followed orders, joined a cause or disappeared. I didn't mind becoming invisible; it wasn't exactly the coward's way out. Although it certainly wasn't brave or noble.

Whenever I pleaded with Masha to forgive me, she spoke about our house in Nesvicz after the Revolution. "It was divided into twelve apartments, a family to each room, with the lot of us sharing Mama's kitchen. Mama couldn't stand it, the overcrowding, the noise, the filth."

"I'm not your enemy because I wasn't there, suffering with you," I would say in my defence.

But Masha would hear none of my excuses. "Our parents couldn't adapt to Communism and the house rules, the constant surveillance. Papa was once caught stealing chocolate from the commissar's room. Our parents thought they were special, that they deserved better, and in that way they were not unlike Zabotin's parents. The count and countess believed they were unique, too. Aristocrats. But they were shot and killed by the Nazis just as our parents were. When you're dead, you are no longer special."

Masha and Elka were the same. They wore their terrible suffering like a badge of honour. They both loathed Zabotin, who was a symbol of old Czarist Russia and the ultimate traitor in their eyes. I saw it differently: Zabotin acted from good intentions. He didn't cave in to conformity. He'd saved innocent people in Ottawa and tried to again in Chernobyl, although he was less successful here than he'd been after the war. I was coming to believe that there were three kinds of people: those who acted, those who obeyed and those, like me, who made an effort to do both. My kind was the least effective. Maybe there was a fourth kind as well. A person who'd survived the ghetto or the camps who didn't act or obey but who forgave. I wanted to see my brother again and ask him who he had become.

When Masha arrived, the day after the guard told us she was coming, it was raining; a real downpour that trickled into our leaky cabin. Mud spilled onto the sloping floor, but Masha pretended not to look down her nose at how we lived. Two officers accompanied her. They rode in an all-terrain vehicle, outfitted in hazmat suits. The men looked frightened to be so close to us and the perimeter of the disaster, but not my sister. Nothing frightened Masha.

Zabotin returned to our cabin after Masha arrived. He was not kind to her. He refused to indulge her self-righteousness tinted with officiousness. "Take off that suit, Masha," he bellowed. "It's summer, hot and steamy. You'll suffocate inside that silly thing."

"I will not," Masha replied.

I could hardly see her face entrapped in the helmet.

"Look at us," Zabotin exclaimed. "Two years in the forest and we're healthier than ever. I'm a million times better here than I was in your gulag."

Masha retorted that it wasn't her gulag. "You got off lightly," she told him.

"Ahh... if it were up to you, you'd have me executed."

"No more talking, Zabotin," she commanded. "I've come to take you and Freda to Kiev. I've found a flat for the two of you, and I'll put you on a worker's pension and disability from the Chernobyl episode."

"Is that what you're calling it?" I gasped. "An episode?"

Zabotin shook his head in disbelief. "Leave us alone," he told Masha. "What business are we of yours? We're like the rats who survived the bubonic plague."

"Or the mice who survived the experiment," I added. Then, hearing a rustling beside the open window, I shouted, "You can come out now, Elka! I know you're hiding in the bushes. You wouldn't miss this family reunion for the world." I squeezed Zabotin's hand.

"Your sister is very brave," Zabotin said to Masha. "Braver than you. And you, too, Elka!" he shouted, opening the door for our neighbour to enter. "Now you can hear everything," he said, putting his hand to his ear and mocking her.

Masha was disappointed. I could tell because she sat down on our damp, tattered sofa with a deep, resentful sigh. She'd protected me from the secret police, from the Director of the GRU himself, and now, forty years later, she expected to be lauded and admired, maybe even loved. Once again, I was disappointing her, as only I could.

"I want to see Simcha," I demanded. "You must know where he is."

Masha agreed that she did, but said she hadn't visited our brother for decades. Not since the war ended. Not once since I'd returned to the Soviet Union.

My fear of Masha was subsiding. I'd grown strong of mind since I'd started living in the forest. "I want to see my brother," I shouted at her and stamped my feet.

"Fine," Masha replied. "I'll take you to him, Freda. Today. Get your things. You, who are so delighted with this world, overwhelmed with the goodness of humankind. You, who are in love with this traitor," she shouted, pointing at Zabotin. "You of all people should hear our brother. Then you will know what this world is about." My sister raised her arm to me.

As if on command, the guards reached for their revolvers, but Masha motioned them to put the guns away. Then she departed our cabin, her two officers trailing close behind.

No matter how frightened I was to see Simcha, to listen to his story, I knew it was worth the risk of discovering the truth. And so, on my sister's command, I grabbed my suitcase, the one under my bed that was always ready to go, and briskly walked the forest path to where Masha was waiting for me.

When I reached her, I said, "Elka claims it was you who gave the command to evacuate Pripyat. Why didn't you do it right away, in the early morning hours before the radiation worsened?" I demanded. "Why wait for Moscow?"

"It will take all night and half of tomorrow to get to Nesvicz," Masha stated, ignoring my question and still speaking through her helmet. "Get in the vehicle," she ordered. "And try to be quiet." The Geiger counter in her hand was chirping much louder than the chattering birds that circled above our heads. "Nesvicz is where your brother lives, so we'd best not lose more time."

Chapter Twenty-Seven

1988
Nesvicz

I t had been thirty-nine years since I'd seen my little brother, Simcha, but it was easy to recognize him, even though he'd aged profoundly. White hair, once red, sprang in every direction from his head. His beard, streaked with bits of food and stained by tea and whisky, tumbled to his chest. He recognized me immediately, too. We'd been the best of childhood friends. I'd favoured him over Masha, protected him from Papa's belt. Those are things that no brother or sister can forget.

I must admit to feeling sorry for Masha, as the three of us stood inside the old shoemaker's house, where Simcha scraped by. There was no time to waste with regrets. Masha had informed me that I had only a few hours with Simcha and then it was straight back to Chernobyl, no diversions along the way.

Simcha offered us sweetened tea and cookies baked by the neighbour lady. He invited Masha's two guards into the front room to offer them the same. When I glanced about Vine's old house, it looked like a dollhouse.

"Are you a shoemaker?" I inquired.

"No, I gave that up years ago," Simcha replied. "Vine tried before me, right after the war. I knew it was him, but I kept my distance. I was ashamed."

Masha cleared her throat. "As you should be."

"Now I teach music to the local children," he said. There was an upright piano in the corner of the room.

"You what?" Masha was disturbed by this revelation. "You. Teach music. You can't even read the notes!"

"That's where you're wrong," Simcha corrected her, covering his eyes with his hands. "I learned, after I forgave myself for what happened." His fingers were long and surprisingly elegant. "Sit down, sit down. All of you. I'll make the tea. Freda, you bring out the cookies. And Masha, you must play for us. Please," he coaxed, arranging the piano bench for her. "Once you begin, you will remember."

Surprisingly, Masha sat down and put her hands to the keys. Simcha pulled out a triangle from a cupboard crammed with sheets of music.

Masha began to play the same Chopin étude she'd chosen for her recital on the day of the pogrom. I remembered every note although I had not heard this melody since her recital so long ago.

Once the samovar was prepared, Simcha raised high the triangle. As his wand tinkled one side of it, the sound brought more to mind than the delicacy of Chopin's *Études* or Simcha's perfect touch. My vision in Ottawa of the little musical band, dressed in black, crossing the river that flows through Nesvicz, and how I'd described it to Sybil when I first learned that Gouzenko had stolen cryptograms from the Russian Embassy in Ottawa, came rushing back to me. There was the elderly rabbi, with his long white beard, leading the musical troupe through the blowing snow. The kosher butcher who carried his cello over his shoulder, and the plump baker banging his tambourine with gusto. Only the skeleton that had once walked beside the rabbi had disappeared. The red-haired young triangle player at the rear of the troupe was Simcha, I now knew. He'd lagged behind, but he'd made it.

"I'm happy you survived," I spoke with resolve to Simcha, putting my arms around him. Masha continued to play.

Tears streamed down Simcha's face. "I made a choice. When the guards came to take away my wife and little girls, I might have tried to stop them. The girls had only cloth shoes and spring jackets for transport to the crematorium, no hats or gloves. They would freeze within hours. My children hadn't grown since I'd seen them last, and my wife was emaciated. She gave most of her food to our girls."

Masha stopped playing and ordered Simcha to be quiet, telling him,

"I don't want to know. I'm ashamed."

But Simcha ignored her. "I knew they would perish during the transport," he said softly

I sat very close to Simcha, my hand in his stronger one, as he continued to speak.

"Yes, I might have thrown myself in the way of the guards, tried with my bare hands to beat them back. They would have shot me, and my family would face their demise, with or without me. It's almost impossible to grasp, but nothing I could do would have saved them." Simcha covered his eyes again as if were reliving the moment in the Łódź Ghetto when his wife and children were torn from his grasp. "For a moment I stood tall between my wife and the guards, clutching them, but they threw me across the room. I was healthy and strong from fighting with the partisans in the forest. I could haul the shit wagons for miles into the empty fields outside Łódź. The guards were instructed to keep me alive—I was useful. As for most who survived, I served a practical purpose. So few had the strength I did, and someone had to unload the shit."

Simcha was grinning, more a grimace than a smile, as he recited his confession.

"After the war, I returned to Nesvicz. Every Jew was dead—not one survived the Nazis. When Vine came back from Canada, he made an attempt to start up again in his father's shoe shop, but the villagers shunned him. They were afraid, as was I, to face him, a Jew, after what we'd witnessed and after what we'd done."

"You should be ashamed..." Masha piped in, but her words were drowned out by a group of children bursting into the house.

"These are my students," said Simcha proudly, introducing each one by name. There were ten.

"Enough for a minyan," Simcha joked.

The children crowded around Simcha, pulling at his beard and groping in his pocket for the candy they appeared certain they would find.

Simcha asked the children to sit and to listen. "I am ashamed of what I saw and what I did," he said to all in the room. "But I have forgiven myself, as you should, Masha, and you too, Freda. We've each done unspeakable things, deserted our families, worshipped false ideologies, admired the wrong people and wounded those who truly love us."

The children became as quiet as little mice.

"When the world goes mad, to survive is not a crime," said Simcha defiantly.

I moved to sit next to Masha and she allowed me to take her in my arms. Her body was as hard as a young soldier's, but her heart was the most fragile of the three Linton survivors. Simcha rose to kiss her sweetly on the top of her head. Masha covered the scar on her face with her hand. She would need to be treated with delicate kindness as she recovered from the long nightmare that began the day the Red Army cavalry ransacked our little village of Nesvicz.

Today the restoration begins.

Afterword

My father, whose Yiddish name was Aaron, was born in Nesvicz, Belarus, and his stories about the Red Cavalry galloping into that village during the Russian Revolution have reverberated with me throughout my entire life. After arriving in Canada, Aaron joined the Communist Party, where he worked as a labour organizer in the Montreal garment factories until revelations about Stalin's reign of terror filtered into Canada.

My father never recovered from the disappointment of learning how Stalin and the secret police treated the Jewish population in the Soviet Union. He left the Party in 1947. Many of my relatives remained stalwart members until their deaths. The demise of Fred Rose was a much-debated topic of conversation at family gatherings, and the one which planted the seed for this novel.

Members of our family who remained in Nesvicz after the revolutionary war were murdered by the Nazis in July 1942 when the liquidation of the Nesvicz ghetto began. During the 1920s, my father's older sister, Dvora, moved to Moscow after he and most of the family immigrated to Canada. Dvora endured physical hardship, starvation and religious persecution. Her husband was executed during Stalin's reign of terror, and her children and grandchildren, who were living in Kiev at the time of the Chernobyl nuclear disaster, were exposed to the radioactive fallout from the reactor.

At times when writing this book, I've allowed oral testimony and storytelling to take precedence over historical record. My intention has always been to be true to the fictional narrative of this particular story.

In my book, John Grierson is portrayed as an operative for Soviet military intelligence, and I do believe he was under the influence of the Soviets during World War II. Igor Gouzenko's cache of documents, stolen from the Russian Embassy in Ottawa, implicated Grierson, and that is why he left Canada after testifying at the Kellock–Taschereau Commission (officially the Royal Commission to Investigate the Facts Relating to and the Circumstances Surrounding the Communication, by Public Officials and Other Persons in Positions of Trust, of Secret and Confidential Information to Agents of a Foreign Power). Grierson was, of course, the founder of the National Film Board of Canada.

More information about the illusive Freda Linton can be culled from FBI and MI6 files. I recall my father describing her as a great beauty and the bravest of women.

Acknowledgments

Sandy von Kaldenberg, my husband, is the reason why I continue to write. Together we pulled through many drafts of this novel. My daughter Hannah's enthusiasm inspired me. She insisted that Freda, Zabotin and Vine's story come to life. I am indebted to a tight-knit circle of remarkable writers and original thinkers: Rob Delaney, Maheen Zaidi, John Choi, Sandra Rossier and Terry Leeder. Each helped guide me through the process of writing this novel. I would also like to thank Howard Aster and Matthew Goody at Mosaic Press for their unflinching support and encouragement. Not only are they my publishers, they have become friends. Lindsay Humphreys, who copyedited this novel, is a marvel.

I am grateful to the Ontario Arts Council for their support.